RAINBOWS OVER PUDDLEDUCK FARM

DELLA GALTON

Boldwood

First published in Great Britain in 2023 by Boldwood Books Ltd.

Copyright © Della Galton, 2023

Cover Design by Alice Moore Design

Cover Photography: Shutterstock

A CIP catalogue record for this book is available from the British Library.

Paperback ISBN 978-1-80280-906-0

Large Print ISBN 978-1-80280-905-3

Hardback ISBN 978-1-80280-904-6

Ebook ISBN 978-1-80280-907-7

Kindle ISBN 978-1-80280-908-4

Audio CD ISBN 978-1-80280-899-5

MP3 CD ISBN 978-1-80280-900-8

Digital audio download ISBN 978-1-80280-901-5

Boldwood Books Ltd
23 Bowerdean Street
London SW6 3TN
www.boldwoodbooks.com

For Ian Burton, with love

1

_____

Kneeling in the middle of a muddy field up to her elbow inside a ewe struggling to lamb was not how Phoebe Dashwood had planned to spend this February Sunday morning. She was hot and panting, although she knew she couldn't compete with the mother who'd delivered two lambs already and was too exhausted to push out her third, which Phoebe had just discovered was stuck.

Up until that moment, the morning had been going very well. Phoebe and her boss, Seth Harding – ex-jockey and experienced country vet – had been called out to Elm Tree Farm an hour ago because of another lambing issue, which Seth had swiftly resolved. He was the expert when it came to farm animals. Phoebe had spent most of her career in a pristine surgery, seeing dogs, cats and kids' pets, but she was on the brink of opening a practice of her own and wanted to expand her repertoire. Shadowing Seth was the perfect opportunity.

They'd been about to leave when the shepherd, Tom Dean, had shouted across: 'I've got another one here that needs some help.'

'Over to you,' Seth had told Phoebe and she'd nodded, eager to put what she'd learned into practice. Watching was all very well, but there was no substitute for getting your hands dirty.

Elm Tree Farm had a small flock, twenty or so sheep, most of them got on perfectly well with lambing and Tom, who worked with his father, didn't usually have many problems. It was bad luck that his dad was away this weekend on a family emergency and Tom wasn't quite as experienced as the older shepherd.

Not that he could have foreseen this, Phoebe thought, as she felt around blindly inside the sheep. However experienced you were, you could only deal with one problem at a time and they seemed to have had several simultaneously today.

'I can only feel one leg,' she told Seth. 'I think the other one's bent back. That's why she's struggling.'

'You've got this,' Seth's voice was reassuring. At fifty-five, he was twenty years Phoebe's senior and hugely experienced, and he was always calm. He hunkered down beside her. 'Push the lamb back in, give yourself some more space. Then feel for the hoof.'

Phoebe followed his instructions and tried desperately to grab the other leg, hampered by the sheep's next contraction. For a second, she'd had it, but then it slipped away again out of her grasp.

'One more go,' she gasped more to herself than Seth. She was painfully aware that every second counted. She could not afford to mess this up.

She tried again. She could feel the small hoof. She tightened her grip, flicked the leg back into its proper position and, to her great relief, this time the timing was right. The sheep pushed, Phoebe pulled and the lamb emerged in a whoosh and landed on the grass.

Both Tom and Seth cheered as Phoebe cleared the lamb's

nose so it could breathe and hauled it round to join its two siblings.

'Thank God,' Phoebe laughed delightedly as the lamb shook his head and the mother grunted and nosed him.

It was moments like these that made it all worthwhile. Moments when you knew for sure that you'd helped – that without you there could have been a very different ending.

Phoebe had never planned to be a country vet, but working for Seth had changed her views. There was something immensely satisfying about going out to farms. She might now be filthy and tired and covered in all sorts of unmentionable gunk, and she knew she stank to high heaven, but kneeling here watching the utter miracle of life, you just couldn't beat it.

The ewe, still lying down, was licking the newest arrival, and all three of her offspring were shaking their heads, bleating and looking about, slightly bemused at their first view of the world. Three white lambs and their mother. It was an amazing picture. Even the sun chose that moment to peek out from behind the grey February clouds.

Phoebe stood up carefully. Both of her feet had gone numb from inactivity inside her wellies and she now had pins and needles, but she was grinning from ear to ear as she stamped them away.

Tom and Seth were smiling too.

'Come in and get cleaned up,' Tom said. 'And thank you so much. You've been great.'

They followed him into the farmhouse utility room and cleaned up in the old Belfast sink, after which Tom insisted on making them coffee, which he brought through in two huge white steaming mugs. Phoebe was grateful for his thoughtfulness and Seth was delighted – he existed on strong coffee – but Phoebe was also conscious of the time. The drama had pushed everything else from her head, but they'd been at the farm a lot longer than they'd planned.

She drained her mug and clunked it back on the wooden worktop. 'We should get going,' she told Seth. 'It's the twins' christening today. I'm their godmother.'

'Oh hell, I'm sorry. I'd forgotten all about that. We'd better get you back then. What time are you at the church?'

'In just under an hour.' Phoebe wrinkled her nose. 'And I definitely need a shower first.'

* * *

Five minutes later, they were rattling across the New Forest in Seth's old boneshaker of a 4x4 back to Woodcutter's Cottage where Phoebe lived, as fast as Seth dared without breaking the speed limits.

Phoebe broke the speed limit for getting ready, though. Thank goodness she'd had the foresight to leave her christening outfit, a blue turtleneck maxi dress, ironed and ready on a hanger. She was showered, changed and out of the house again in just under fifteen minutes. It was still going to be touch-and-go, she thought, glancing at the dashboard clock on her Lexus, especially as she was picking up her grandmother, Maggie Crowther, en route.

To her huge relief, the old lady was ready and waiting by the five-bar gate at Puddleduck Farm. She wore a primrose-yellow hat and lemon jacket – a world away from her usual attire of old boiler suit and wellies – and she tutted impatiently as Phoebe hurtled into the turning circle in front of the farm and leaped out to open the passenger door.

'You're cutting it fine, darling. What happened?' Maggie fumbled to clip in her seat belt as Phoebe got back into the driver's seat.

'I went on a lambing call with Seth.' Phoebe shot out of the gate again, the Lexus spitting gravel. 'It took longer than we'd expected. But, wow, it was amazing. I delivered a stuck lamb. My first one.'

'That's very special.' The old lady sounded wistful. 'There's nothing quite like helping to bring a new life into the world.'

This was something her grandmother knew all about. Puddleduck Farm had once been a dairy farm. Now it was an animal sanctuary – still run by Maggie, who'd recently employed a full-time manager so she could semi-retire, but Maggie was still very much in the business of saving lives.

Before either of them could say anything else, Phoebe's mobile rang and she saw her brother's name flick up on the car's info screen. She pressed answer on her steering wheel and Frazier's anxious voice came over the speaker.

'Where are you? Alexa's getting worried. The service is starting in five.'

'We're five minutes away,' Phoebe said at the same moment as Maggie yelled, 'We're trying to park.'

Frazier sighed. 'I'll stall them. Seriously, hurry up. But don't crash.'

Phoebe disconnected. 'Why did you say we were trying to park?'

'No point in all of us getting stressed to high heaven. We'll be there when we're there. Focus on driving.'

She probably had a point, Phoebe thought, feeling her heart thumping madly as she negotiated the country lanes.

Luckily, it really was only five minutes before they were pulling up outside St James', the tiny twelfth-century church where the christening was taking place.

Phoebe had an impression of grey stone and a scattering of sunshine-yellow daffodils as they hurried through the lychgate towards the ancient stone building. It was a beautiful spot. A neat cinder path wound between higgledy-piggledy headstones and she could hear jackdaws chak-chaking across the cooing of pigeons. It was deserted. Everyone must already be inside. Then Phoebe saw Frazier in his best suit, standing in the church doorway. He beckoned frantically.

'Sorry, sorry,' Phoebe gasped.

'You're fine. Alexa told the vicar you had an emergency call.'

Alexa was a sweetheart. Phoebe met her sister-in-law's eyes as she hurried up the aisle, Maggie following in her wake. Alexa had been planning the twins' christening for weeks. Anything to do with babies, Phoebe had discovered, particularly when there were two of them, needed military precision. Alexa, who was one of the most laid-back people Phoebe knew, had created a spreadsheet to plan today. Phoebe bet there hadn't been a column for delayed godmothers, but Alexa was lovely enough to just nod and smile as Phoebe and Maggie sneaked into the pew at the front. No sooner were they settled than the vicar began to speak.

* * *

The service went without a hitch. Even Flo, who wasn't known for being a quiet baby, only yelled briefly when she was splashed with holy water. Her brother, Bertie, dressed in a matching cream outfit to his sister, but with a tiny B sewn onto the front, just smiled serenely.

Phoebe managed not to fluff her lines and very soon they were all pouring outside again into the lunchtime air. Cameras and phones clicked, people chattered and caught up and had cuddles with the twins.

The post-service celebrations were taking place in the Red Lion, opposite the church, but no one was in a hurry to go across.

The churchyard was a sunny spot and, right now, Phoebe was chatting to her parents, James and Louella Dashwood, who were having a proud grandparent moment. They were cuddling a twin each while Frazier and Alexa took the opportunity to chat with their guests.

Phoebe apologised again for holding everyone up and told her parents about the lambing.

'I'm guessing you won't do too many farm calls, once you've launched Puddleduck Vets,' Louella said, in between cooing over Bertie. 'Aren't you planning to treat mainly small animals then?'

Phoebe glanced at Maggie, who was more up to date on her plans than her parents were, and nodded hesitantly. 'I'd planned to, but lately I've been coming round to the idea of doing both. Seth's planning to retire in the next year or so...'

'And when he does, there'll need to be another large animal vet in the New Forest,' Louella said, nodding.

'Yes, that's right. We've talked about it a lot. In fact, Seth's persuaded me to make it my USP. No animal too small or too large. So I've capitalised on that and made it the logo.'

'That's not a bad idea,' James said. 'Cover all bases. I would.'

Phoebe's father, James Dashwood, was a solicitor with his own family law firm and covering all bases was second nature to him.

'A vet in the heart of the New Forest is never going to be short of clients,' Maggie put in. She looked out of her comfort zone in that yellow skirt suit, Phoebe thought, catching her eye. They were both more at home in scruffs. Maggie straightened her hat and winked and Phoebe knew she had read her mind.

Alexa drifted across, having caught the tail end of the conversation. 'What am I missing? Are you talking about your launch day?' Her voice was bright. 'That's only a couple of weeks away, isn't it?'

'I know. I must be mad.' Phoebe pulled a face. 'Setting up on my own so quickly. I still feel like there's masses to learn.'

'Nonsense,' Maggie said. 'Looking after animals is in your blood. You've been around them since you were a little girl.' That was true. Phoebe had spent many of her childhood weekends and evenings 'helping' her grandmother at Puddleduck Farm.

'I'm guessing that being a vet is like being a parent,' Louella added, nodding. 'There will always be masses to learn.'

'Hear hear,' Frazier said, joining them and taking his wife's hand. 'And you've been working for other people for twelve years, Pheebs. You're hardly a novice, are you?'

'I know.' Phoebe looked around at her family gratefully. 'Thank you. I could never have dreamed of owning my own practice so soon if it wasn't for you all.'

That was true on several levels. They were a close-knit family and they supported each other unconditionally, but they had supported her on a practical level too. Phoebe had spent the last eight months overseeing the conversion of a barn on Maggie's farm into her shiny new venture, Puddleduck Vets. She'd got a business loan, but her parents and Maggie had helped her to finance it. It had meant taking some of what Phoebe would one day inherit from Puddleduck Farm. But it wasn't just about Phoebe launching her own business. It was about all of them helping Maggie to stay on at Puddleduck Farm where she'd lived all her life, surrounded by the animals she loved. The old lady was fiercely independent and refused to ask for help, but if Phoebe was there working every day, she could keep a surreptitious eye on her. Paying rent for the barn also gave Maggie another income stream.

Louella's voice broke into Phoebe's thoughts. 'I must pop to the ladies. Would you like to hold your new goddaughter?'

'I'd love to.' Phoebe held out her arms and took Flo, who was delighted and cooed up at her. 'I almost feel maternal,' Phoebe said, taking a deep breath of her niece's gorgeous baby smell. For a moment, the contrast of this morning's frantic scramble on her knees in a muddy field beside a sheep and now this time in a peaceful churchyard, holding her beloved niece, struck her forcibly. She was so flaming lucky. Having such an amazing supportive family and doing the job she'd spent all her life dreaming she'd do. The clouds had all but gone now, the sky was a blue backdrop to the picturesque church and the midday sunshine felt unseasonably warm. What a difference a few hours could make. Phoebe's heart swelled with gratitude. Just as baby Flo decided to sick up her last feed down her new godmother's shoulder.

2

On the day of the grand opening of Puddleduck Vets, Phoebe, who'd been too excited to get much sleep, got up very early. She tugged on old jeans and grabbed her launch outfit: caramel cords and polished boots – they were flatties, at five foot ten she didn't need any extra height – and an emerald-green scrub top with Puddleduck Vets emblazoned on it in white. Emerald and white was her colour scheme.

She picked up her clipboard with its lists – she'd taken Alexa's advice and created a spreadsheet to help – and headed over to Puddleduck Farm.

It was barely seven thirty when she parked at the front of the farmhouse, let herself through the side gate and walked around the back.

She'd hoped the warm weather they'd had for the christening would hold, but her hopes had been dashed two days ago when they'd had the biggest storm of the year, which had brought with it a monsoon of rain and wind that had wreaked havoc on the south of England.

It had been stormy last night too. The evidence was all around her. The daffodils dotting the path that skirted Puddleduck Farm weren't just flattened, they looked as though they'd need major resuscitation to ever rise again, the primroses were stem-deep in water and the ground was sodden.

Phoebe stopped just before she reached the barn door, which housed the purpose-built shiny new reception, two consulting rooms and an operating theatre, and sighed. The lovely spring launch she'd envisaged with guests milling about outside was already looking very different from her perfect vision. In her fantasy, there had been a pristine white duck – Jemima or one of her contemporaries – waddling about. Not to mention, a well-behaved dog or two, also groomed and shiny-coated, claws clipped, collars polished, wearing emerald and white ribbons which would match the emerald and white balloons which she planned to tie to various points shortly. There wasn't much chance of any animal being pristine in this weather!

Phoebe bypassed the barn and hurried past a kennel of barking dogs and on towards the donkey field. Instead of the three cute donkeys she'd groomed yesterday, she could only see two. Of these, Roxy, who was usually light grey, was covered in mud. She'd clearly been rolling. Neddie had mud clods in his nostrils – Lord knows what he'd been doing – and Diablo was missing altogether.

Phoebe swore under her breath. Where was he? The fence still appeared to be in one piece, despite the battering it must have taken during the night. Quickening her pace, she checked the perimeter and discovered a broken post at the far end which was leaning slightly and allowing the wire to gape. Diablo, who was a master escapee and could have given Houdini a run for his money, had clearly taken full advantage and legged it. At least Roxy and Neddie hadn't followed him. Those two knew which side their bread was buttered on, besides which they'd obviously been having far too much fun doing a spot of early-morning mud rolling.

Phoebe bent to shove the broken post back into the ground, which was too soggy to hold it, so the whole thing just listed sideways again. One of the emerald and white nail extensions, which she'd been talked into, against her better judgement, by her best friend, Tori, flicked off and landed in the field.

Phoebe swore again. She knew they'd been a mistake. She wasn't a nail extension kind of girl. She scooped it up, just in case a donkey decided to eat it, and shoved it in the back pocket of her jeans, which now had a splodge of mud on one knee.

'You don't sound very happy,' came a voice from behind her, and she turned to see Maggie – where had she sprung from? 'For a girl who's about to start living the dream.'

'Diablo's gone walkabout.' Phoebe met her grandmother's clear hazel eyes. 'And the other two are covered in mud. And the fence post is broken.' She bent it back to demonstrate.

Maggie didn't look very concerned about any of this. 'I've just turfed Diablo out of my kitchen. I came up to see if the other two were still here. When did you get here? I didn't hear your car?'

'Ten minutes ago. I thought I'd just whizz down and check everything before I came into the house. Things are going wrong already,' Phoebe sighed.

'No they're not. The fence post can be fixed. Is it just the one? The neddies can be brushed and a bit of mud never hurt anyone. You're too stressed, my darling.'

'I'm sorry. I just wanted today to be perfect. I groomed those little beggars yesterday. Now look at the state of them.'

Neddie and Roxy had followed her along the fence line and now Neddie nodded his head up and down as if in agreement, then snorted so a clod of earth flew out of his nose and hit Phoebe in the cheek.

'Ouch!' She swiped at the mud, smearing it across her face and transferring much of it to her fingers. 'And I've lost one of these flaming nails! Look!'

'Good! Whoever heard of a vet with false nails anyway?' Maggie snorted and when Phoebe caught her eye, she saw she was shaking with laughter which she was clearly trying to suppress. Her shoulders heaved as she struggled not to explode.

It was contagious. Phoebe started laughing too and for a few moments neither of them could stop. Maggie was now bent double with it, slapping her jean-clad knees. Phoebe was struggling to breathe and there were tears pouring down her cheeks. Or that could have been raindrops. In the last few moments, the sky had darkened to an ominous moody purple and a few heavy drops had begun to plop onto the ground.

'We'd better get back.' Maggie finally had enough breath to speak. 'Do you fancy grabbing a fence panel from the kennels. There's a couple there. I'd better fetch Diablo.'

'Where is he?'

'I've shut him in the feed room. He likes it in there. He lives in hope of getting the lid off the pony nut bin, but unless he's learned how to pick locks, he's got no chance.'

'I wouldn't put anything past that donkey,' Phoebe muttered, as they hurried back towards the yard beneath what was fast turning into a cloudburst.

* * *

An hour later, the donkey field was shored up with the fence panel and some cable ties, at least temporarily. A disgruntled Diablo had been returned to the fold, and Maggie and Phoebe were back in the farmhouse kitchen, drinking coffee.

Phoebe had dried her hair, with Maggie's ancient dryer, and

resorted to plaiting it, which was how she usually wore it. She'd been hoping for it to be nicely curled and waved around her shoulders, as it had been when she'd set off, but the rain had put paid to that.

'According to my weather app, the rain will stop around three,' Phoebe said. 'I guess it doesn't matter too much. At least we'll be inside.'

Maggie glanced out of the window. 'It'll stop by eleven and the sun will be out by midday. Not much later than that. You mark my words.'

Phoebe suspected she'd be right. Maggie had spent her entire life out in all weathers, which made her an excellent weather forecaster. Far better than most apps anyway.

'Now, what can I do to help? Where's your list?'

Guided by her sister-in-law, Phoebe had made up a huge, multi-paged spreadsheet with dates, times, tick boxes and scrawled notes. And she had to admit it had been very useful.

Today they were on the final list:

10.00 Set out glasses and drinks on long tables.
10.15 Blow up balloons and put out. Don't forget ones at entrance.
10.45 Put out gift bags.
11.00 Check any animals in attendance are still looking pristine.

(She should definitely have waited to do that one.)

11.10 Check own appearance is pristine.

(Hmmm. Probably that one too.)

11.20 Canapés put out (covered).
11.15 Media coverage arrives.

Media coverage was her best friend, Tori, who was owner/editor of *New Forest Views*, the free local magazine.

11.45 Guests begin to arrive in reception area.

12.00 Guests gather in reception.

12.30 Celebrity makes welcome speech and cuts ribbon.

12.45 Cake is cut. Canapés unwrapped.

12.50 Guests given grand tour of facilities.

12.50 to 1.30? New customers registration and gift bag presentation.

Each item had a tick box alongside it. The first six items were now all ticked. Next on the list was 'media coverage arrives', but there was loads of time. It was only just gone ten.

Maggie scanned through the final page. 'What time are your helpers arriving?'

'To be honest, I don't need much help. Tori's coming at eleven fifteen to take some set-up shots. She hates being late for anything. Mum and Dad said they'd be here close to lift-off. Frazier and Alexa are bringing the twins at the last minute. Seth's coming quite early, though.'

Maggie nodded. 'Nice chap that Seth.'

'He is.' Phoebe knew she owed Seth a huge debt of gratitude. Not only had he forgiven her for leaving Marchwood when she'd worked for him for barely a year, but he'd also been an incredibly supportive mentor. He'd even agreed to be the 'vet celebrity' who would cut the tape at the grand opening of Puddleduck Vets.

But for Seth, Phoebe may also have had to name her practice The Puddleduck Vet. Because he was her backup vet too. Phoebe would be the only full-time vet. She'd also employed an experienced veterinary nurse, Jennifer Anniston, not the famous one – they just shared the same name. Jennifer, or Jenna as she preferred to be known, was also an ex-employee of Seth's. She had left Marchwood to take maternity leave thirteen years ago – her children were now thirteen and eleven – and she was keen to get back to work. She was a no-nonsense, down-to-earth, but very warm woman and Phoebe had liked her as soon as they'd met. Jenna would assist with minor procedures, dispense medicine and help to cover reception. Maggie had also volunteered to cover reception part-time while they got going and Phoebe, after much consideration, had agreed this might work. Although she would be open full time, she did not expect to be very busy at first, but Marchwood would be helping with the twenty-four-hour call-out service that vets were required to provide.

In return for Seth's help, Phoebe would continue to be on the evening and weekend call-out rota for Marchwood. If she needed any help with the equine side – this was Seth's speciality – she would call him. She would also send clients she couldn't cope with his way. And he would do the same.

'I'm not going to rush into replacing you,' he'd said. 'To be perfectly honest, Phoebe, you'd be a pretty hard act to follow. My plan is to ease down gently into retirement.'

'I'm so proud of you, darling.' Maggie's voice interrupted her thoughts and Phoebe glanced up. Maggie was topping up their coffee and their eyes met over the jug.

'I wouldn't be here without you,' Phoebe said softly.

'Yes you would. When you came back from London after all that business with Hugh, I was so worried, but you just picked yourself up, dusted yourself down and carried on.'

'I didn't have much choice...' Phoebe began. She hadn't thought about her ex-boyfriend lately. Hugh had also been a vet and they'd worked together at a posh London practice and lived together for six years in his father's Greenwich apartment.

Maggie put up a hand. 'No, hear me out. When Hugh did the dirty, you didn't just lose your partner you lost your home and your job. Most people in that situation would have crumpled. But you didn't. You made a brand-new life for yourself. That takes courage, my darling.'

Maggie wasn't in the habit of being sentimental or dishing out compliments and Phoebe felt a huge lump in her throat.

'I had a very good role model in the art of picking yourself up and getting on with things, though, didn't I?'

Maggie acknowledged this with her eyes and for a moment they both sipped coffee in easy silence in the Aga-warmed farmhouse kitchen.

Phoebe bent to stroke Tiny, the Irish Wolfhound, who was stretched out on the flagstone floor. He was never far from Maggie's side, and Buster, Maggie's elderly Labrador, was snoring in his sleep in his basket beneath the table.

It was Maggie who broke the silence. 'Is Sam coming? I mean, what with it being a Saturday and the Post Office's busiest day?'

Aside from Tori, Sam Hendrie was Phoebe's oldest friend. They had grown up together, the four of them – Phoebe, Frazier, Tori and Sam. They had played as kids at Puddleduck Farm and had gone to the same school. They'd always been in each other's lives. Sam's mother, Jan, who owned Hendrie's Village Store and Post Office where Sam worked, was Phoebe's mother's best friend. Phoebe's life had been entwined with Sam's for as long as she could remember.

'Yes, of course he is. He's my oldest friend.' She gave her grandmother a curious look, pretty sure that she was fishing.

'I just thought he might be working,' Maggie added idly. 'So is he still just a friend?' She widened her eyes which, instead of making her look ultra-casual as she had clearly intended, just made her look even more like she was fishing.

'Yes, Sam's still just a friend. A very good friend, obviously.' Phoebe could feel herself blushing. Maggie had always been able to read her like a book. She hadn't told her grandmother that Sam wanted more from their relationship than he once had, but the old lady wasn't unaware. Far from it.

'That's a pity. Sam's always been a very steady sort of young man, I'd say. Wouldn't you agree?'

'Yes, he is,' Phoebe said, thinking that 'steady' was the perfect word for Sam. He was as reliable as the dawn and he was kind and also undeniably attractive if you went for the dark-haired, blue-eyed look. It wasn't that Phoebe didn't acknowledge he was attractive, it was just that she'd known him all her life. He was too familiar. Too... She hesitated.

'Is he too nice?' Maggie prodded.

Phoebe shook her head. 'I have no plans to go out with anyone. Sam included.' She smiled to soften her words and then added, 'Not yet, anyway. I want to focus on Puddleduck Vets.'

'That makes perfect sense, darling. As long as you're happy. And you remember that there are other things in life as well as work.'

'Like my lovely family. I won't forget.'

Maggie shook her head in mock defeat. 'I assume you've asked the neighbours, for diplomacy's sake?'

They only had one neighbour, who also happened to be their landlord. Rufus Holt and his father Lord Alfred Holt, lived at Beechbrook House, which was the big house on the estate next door.

Maggie owned Puddleduck Farm and the land in the immediate vicinity, which included the outbuildings and the dog kennel area, but she rented the grazing they used from the Holts. Phoebe hadn't met Lord Alfred himself, but she'd had some dealings with Rufus and his eight-year-old son, Archie, last year. If she'd had to sum up the nature of their encounters she'd have used the word difficult.

Rufus Holt had an edge of danger about him that had been apparent from the second she'd laid eyes on him. He was charismatic too, although Phoebe was certain he didn't mean to be. On the few occasions they'd met, he'd shown no sign of wanting to impress. On the contrary.

But there was definitely something about Rufus Holt that speeded up her heart. She felt drawn to him. In the same way, she suspected, that moths were drawn to an unpredictable flame.

She blinked, aware that Maggie was still waiting for her to answer.

'I've invited Rufus and Archie and Lord Holt,' she said, aware of Maggie's perceptive gaze. 'They're pretty reclusive though, aren't they? So I doubt very much that they'll come.'

3

Tori arrived at Puddleduck Farm just after eleven. 'Sorry I'm early, but I couldn't wait any longer.' She stood on the doorstep kitted out in a waterproof coat, with her camera strung around her neck. 'You look the part. I love the personalised scrubs. There's a balloon in the hedge up the road. Was that originally on the gate?'

'Yes it was. Oh dear. Do you think I should replace it?' Phoebe saw that two were still bobbing on the five-bar gate.

'I wouldn't worry too much. The others are tied on tight. I just checked.'

'Thank you. And thank you so much for coming.'

'I wouldn't miss this for the world. My best friend, starting her own business. Wow. Go, girl.'

The sound of a car engine slowing distracted them and they both looked back at the gate to see Sam's Subaru pulling in.

'Looks like your biggest fan couldn't wait to get here either.' Tori shot Phoebe a knowing look. 'His mother must have given him the morning off. I thought Saturday was the Post Office's busiest day.'

'She did,' Phoebe said, deciding not to rise to Tori's teasing. 'She's coming over at lunchtime too. Bless her.'

'Hi, Sam,' they called in unison as he climbed out of his car, a bunch of flowers in one hand. He was wearing a wax jacket, but Phoebe glimpsed smart trousers beneath it. She rarely saw Sam outside of the Post Office in anything but jodhpurs. He spent most of his spare time at the stables where he kept his horse. Sam gave riding lessons to kids – he was a qualified and brilliant instructor.

'He's dressed for the occasion,' Tori hissed. 'And flowers too... Nice touch. Is he still mooning over you?'

'He's fine with us just being friends.' Phoebe blushed. 'I expect he came straight from work.'

'I thought you said he had the morning off,' was Tori's parting shot as Phoebe went to greet Sam.

He held out the flowers.

'That's so nice of you, Sam. Thank you.' She leaned over them and pecked his cheek. She could smell his citrus aftershave beneath their sweet scents.

'I'm really proud of you.' His voice was gruff as his blue eyes met hers.

Phoebe had seen a lot of him lately, so maybe it wasn't surprising Maggie had quizzed her. Sam's father, who was a kitchen fitter, had done the refurbishment of the vet unit. It was natural that Sam had been in and out, dropping off wood and various other bits and pieces, but he'd never once outstayed his welcome. He certainly wasn't mooning over her, despite Tori's teasing.

Since he'd laid his cards on the table last year and told her his feelings had grown beyond friendship – and Phoebe had told him gently that hers hadn't – he'd never once referred to the conversation again. Neither of them had. Sometimes Phoebe thought that he'd moved on. Although he hadn't dated anyone since, as far as she knew. Mind you, neither had she.

Blinking away her thoughts she led him and Tori around the side of Puddleduck Farm towards the unit.

'Tori's here early to get some shots for the magazine,' she told Sam. 'What's your excuse?'

'Ma said you'd under-ordered on the canapés. And I didn't want to miss out.' He clicked his tongue. 'You know me, Pheebs.'

'I would have saved you some.'

'I thought it best not to take the chance.' His blue eyes sparkled. Phoebe was never entirely sure how much he was joking. Despite the fact they'd known each other most of their lives, Sam had always been better at reading her than she was at reading him.

* * *

A few minutes later, the trio stood outside the door of what had once been a hay barn but was now a fully fitted out veterinary practice. Sam had seen it more recently than Tori had – she'd not seen the final touches, but now Phoebe flung back the door with a 'ta-dah'. And the gasps of her two closest friends were very gratifying.

The space looked amazing. Even if she did say so herself. As she stood between them, she tried to view it with impartial eyes. The main door opened into an oblong room with two waiting areas on the right-hand side, separated by a low, long wooden bookcase, which was currently lined with glasses, bottles of wine and fizzy water, plates and the canapés Sam had mentioned.

'The waiting room this end is for dogs,' she told them, indicating the picture of a cartoon Rottweiler on the wall just to the right. 'The one at the far end is for cats and other small animals.

It's less stressful for the patients, and their owners, to keep the waiting rooms divided.'

'Less fights too,' Tori said. 'I mean between the patients. Not the owners.'

'I've not seen many fights, thankfully,' Phoebe said, 'although I did once hear about a punch-up in a waiting room after two dogs had been in a fight.'

Sam whistled through his teeth. 'Probably fighting over who was going to pay the bill. Vets are pricey.'

Phoebe shot him a glance. 'I aim to keep my costs very competitive. Anyway, back to my tour. On the left, as you can see, we have the reception. Which is where my lovely, young smiley receptionist will sit, once I've employed her.'

They all looked at the banner over the reception which said, 'Puddleduck Vets – No animal too large or too small.' White writing on an emerald background. Below it was the wooden desk, which held a phone, a computer and a printer. An office chair was tucked behind and there was a door that led out the back to the operating theatre and the second consulting room. The main consulting room was via a doorway straight off the cat reception area. Phoebe had designed a space with two consulting rooms in preparation for the second vet she would one day employ. In the meantime, Jenna would use it for routine procedures under Phoebe's guidance. On the wall was a framed picture of Phoebe's qualification.

'Very swish,' Sam said. 'Why haven't you employed your receptionist yet? You can't manage without one, surely?'

'Jenna is going to cover reception, as well as do nursing duties, but...' Phoebe swallowed. 'Maggie's going to help out for the first few weeks. I've tried talking her out of it, but she won't be swayed. You know how stubborn she is. According to her, answering the phone and taking appointments will be a piece of cake compared to running a dairy farm – or an animal shelter come to that. She reckons she has all the necessary experience. And she does have extensive knowledge of animal husbandry.'

Phoebe knew she sounded a lot more confident than she felt. She already had several reservations. Maggie certainly knew her animals, no one would have questioned that. What she wasn't so well known for was her tact and diplomacy – her attitude being that the world would have been better with more animals in it and considerably fewer humans. Phoebe wasn't convinced she'd be able to resist offering opinions and advice dispensed in her unique abrasive manner, which, while it might be accurate and would definitely be in the animal's interest, would probably be unwanted.

Maggie was also hopeless at answering phones. Or at least she had a history of being hopeless at answering her own phone. She thought phones were overrated. And as for the computer side of things, Phoebe knew her grandmother would struggle. But Phoebe hadn't wanted to say no outright, not when Maggie was so keen to get involved. Phoebe would be able to keep a close eye on her if she was in reception too.

'We're going to see how it goes,' Phoebe added in her best diplomatic voice as both Sam and Tori threw her questioning looks. They'd known her grandmother nearly as long as she had – the three of them having grown up within a stone's throw of each other in the New Forest. 'If it gets too busy, Maggie might decide it's too much and at least it will stop her from having such a hands-on approach with the shelter. She's supposed to have toned things down since she had that mini stroke.'

That had been a difficult time and had happened barely nine months ago.

'I bet she hasn't, has she?' Tori said.

'Not much. Although she does complain she has nothing to do since she employed Natasha as manager.'

Natasha, who was passionate about animals, had worked as a volunteer for Maggie since she was a teenager. Now in her early twenties, she'd been delighted to get a full-time job at Puddleduck Farm.

They moved past reception. On the far wall was a big pinboard which featured animals for rehoming. These were all Puddleduck animals and included dogs, cats, Diablo the donkey, chickens, ducks, and more recently a tortoise called Terrence that someone had brought in a box where it had been hibernating when its owner had died. On the other walls there were posters about the life cycle of fleas and ticks and products to deter them and why it was a good idea to vaccinate your pet.

On the shelves of the dividing bookcase were items for sale: dog biscuits, claw clippers, household flea spray, carpet deodoriser, along with various leaflets on how to deal with things like taking your puppy or kitten home and the benefits of neutering.

A line of comfy green chairs with wipe-clean backs and seats were pushed back against the wall of both waiting areas. The flooring was a grey pebbledash heavy-duty vinyl that, according to the manufacturers, was ecologically sound, easy to clean and should last about fifty years. Seth had recommended that. 'It's what we've got at Marchwood. There are cheaper versions, but this one's also good to kneel on. You've probably noticed.' He'd grinned as he'd said that. 'We do tend to spend a lot of time on our knees, don't we, and when you get to my age, a comfortable floor to kneel on is very important.'

Two more emerald balloons bobbed from the reception desk with the words, Puddleduck Vets emblazoned on them in white.

'It looks amazing,' Tori said as they wandered around,

peeking into the consultation rooms and behind reception. She was already clicking away on her camera. 'Correct me if I'm wrong, but wasn't this once a dilapidated old hay barn?'

'It was. It's brilliant, isn't it?' Phoebe called across to Sam, who was looking longingly at the canapés. 'Your dad did an amazing job. He's a genius.'

'It does look fab,' Sam agreed.

Phoebe was beaming. She felt as though warmth was spreading from her heart around her whole body.

'Just wait until you see my operating theatre. Not that I expect to be doing much surgery until we're more established. But it'll be ready and waiting.'

* * *

A few minutes later, the trio emerged into the February sunshine. It had stopped raining. Maggie had been right. Her timing was spot on.

'Now, is there anything you need us to do before the hordes arrive,' Sam asked as they stood between black puddles that glittered in the sunshine.

Before Phoebe could answer, there was a shout and they all turned, just in time to see two small brown dogs hurtling across the yard, with a long ginger streak of a cat in hot pursuit. Natasha was close behind, also running. 'Can someone grab them.'

Tori's mouth dropped open. 'Is that cat actually chasing those two dogs?'

'That's Saddam,' Phoebe said, racing to help. She scooped up the closest dog at the same time as Sam, in a quick-thinking manoeuvre, whipped off his coat and hurled it over the ginger tomcat.

It worked. Saddam stopped dead long enough for Sam to

crouch down and grab him, wriggling within the coat, which served as a robust trap and stopped the furious feline from doing any damage.

Natasha reached them, panting, her hair dishevelled. She had two dog leads in her hand. 'Thanks. I'll swing for that cat. Be careful,' she called to Sam, who was now holding coat and cat in his arms. 'He's got claws like razors and he knows how to use them.'

They could all hear the sound of outraged yowling as Saddam tried to force his way free.

'He's half feral,' Natasha told Tori, who was still openmouthed. 'He's taken to lying in wait for the dogs when I do their walks and terrorising them. I've got to speak to Maggie about it,' she added to Phoebe. 'They're terrified of him. Especially the little ones.'

She was right about that, Phoebe thought. The fluffy one in her arms had stopped panting and was enjoying a snuggle, but the other little dog, still on the ground, was looking around her nervously.

Natasha picked her up and cuddled her. 'You may as well let Saddam go,' she told Sam. 'Hopefully, he's had his fun for now. I must remember to lock him in the barn before I start letting the dogs out. I completely forgot today. What with all the excitement.' She smiled at Phoebe. 'Happy launch day.'

Sam let go of his coat and a triumphant Saddam burst out of it and shot away across the yard, leaping across the puddles in several bounds, his ginger tail stiff with indignation.

'I've seen everything now,' Tori said. 'I should have videoed that. It would go viral on Twitter.'

Natasha grimaced. 'I'm looking into getting a cat behaviourist to come and see him.'

'Is that really a thing?' Sam looked amazed.

'Yes. Apparently so.'

'The sooner, the better by the look of it,' Phoebe said, as Natasha clipped leads to both dogs and took them back to the walking field.

Tori and Sam both turned back to Phoebe and, on impulse, she grabbed their hands. 'Never a dull moment at Puddleduck Farm. Oh my God, I can't believe this is really happening. Thank you so much for being here to share it with me.'

'Where else would we be?' Tori said.

Sam was distracted by something beyond Tori's head. 'Check that out.'

Both women followed his gaze to see a huge rainbow arching across the sky. It was dazzling, and every colour from soft indigo through to blazing red was clearly defined along its radiant curve. As they watched, another one began to form below it. One end was over Puddleduck Farmhouse and the other disappeared over the horizon.

'Wow,' Tori breathed. 'A double rainbow. You don't see them very often.'

'If that's not a good omen for your new venture, I don't know what is,' Sam added with a grin.

4

Despite the good omen of the double rainbow and despite her pleasure that so many people had turned out to support her new business, Phoebe felt increasingly nervous as the moment of the ribbon cutting drew closer. By midday, a small crowd was milling about outside the new unit.

Both her parents were there, dressed up for the occasion. Her mum was wearing an emerald blouse to go with the colour scheme. She was also wearing lipstick, which she reserved for special occasions. Her dad was wearing a green tie. He lived in a suit and tie, but Phoebe knew it was one of his best silk ones. Her brother was wearing the same suit he'd worn to the christening and Alexa was in a flowing, multicoloured skirt. She'd dressed the twins in dinky green rompers and jackets. Currently, both Bertie and Flo were also wearing angelic smiles, as they were the centre of attention.

Sam's parents, Jan and Ian Hendrie, had come, as promised. They were chatting with her parents. There were also Phoebe's colleagues from Seth's, along with several of her clients from Seth's. Phoebe felt a bit guilty about that.

Jenna was there with her husband and kids. Like Phoebe, she was dressed in an emerald scrub top and she'd been chatting to people ever since she'd arrived.

'I can't believe we're almost open for business,' she'd said earlier. 'It's so exciting to be working again.' She had smiled her lovely open smile. 'I also can't believe I've stayed away from the profession so long. The years just fly past.'

Jenna was forty-five but looked a decade younger. Phoebe was delighted she'd agreed to work at Puddleduck Vets and that Seth hadn't snapped her up as soon as she'd got back on the job market. She really did owe Seth a lot.

Natasha had brought a few of her animal-loving friends. They all looked to be in their mid-twenties and were clearly having a ball, laughing and joking together. A couple had got dogs with them. Phoebe hoped Saddam was safely back in the barn. Some people Phoebe didn't recognise, but who were carrying flyers about the opening, mingled with the crowd.

Tori was moving about taking candid shots of people and animals. Sam was chatting to Maggie, who looked very pleased with the way events were unfolding. Earlier, she had pointed at the sky which was now mostly blue and mouthed, 'I told you so,' at Phoebe. She could never resist having the last word. Her dogs shadowed her.

Tiny and Buster were an unlikely pairing. The huge wolfhound and the fourteen-year-old black, arthritic Labrador. Buster was doing very well on his latest medication. He was stiff, Phoebe noticed, but he certainly didn't look as though he was in pain.

The ducks had been shut away to keep them out of harm's way from strange dogs and the geese had been shut away to keep people out of harm's way from their beaks. Especially Bruce

Goose, who liked nothing more than to launch himself at the legs of unwary strangers.

The cats were keeping out of the way too. Or at least Phoebe hadn't seen any. There were too many strangers around for the cats, most of whom lived free range in a barn. Maggie got them spayed or neutered if they weren't done when they arrived, but she didn't believe in locking cats away. They had a high rehome rate for cats too. Not that Saddam had much chance of being rehomed. Phoebe wasn't holding out much hope for a cat behaviourist.

Seth tapped Phoebe on the shoulder, jolting her from her thoughts. 'Shall we cut that ribbon then, lass?'

'Please. I'll grab my scissors.'

'I brought my own.' He produced a pair of stainless-steel surgical ones from his top pocket and the two of them headed to the door of the unit where Phoebe had fixed the green ribbon.

Seth cleared his throat, but he didn't need to. The crowd hushed as they reached the door.

'We are gathered here today,' Seth began in his most sombre voice, 'to say goodbye to my lovely member of staff, Phoebe Dashwood.' He gave an exaggerated wink. 'I jest. Of course, I jest. We are here to celebrate the opening of Puddleduck Vets and to wish Phoebe all the very best of luck for her new venture. Not that she will need luck.' He paused for dramatic effect. 'As many of you know already, Phoebe is a superb vet. Her reputation goes before her. She is very much loved by her patients and their owners alike. I will be very sad to see her go – especially as she is setting up in competition to me.' Seth shot her a sidelong glance and she saw the warmth in his eyes. 'Seriously, Phoebe, I could not be more pleased for you. I know – we all know – that Phoebe will make a great success of this place and I was honoured and delighted when she asked me to come along and open Puddleduck Vets. So, without further ado.' He brandished the scissors with a flourish and posed so that Tori, who was standing close by, could get a good shot of him cutting the ribbon for *New Forest Views*. 'I hereby declare Puddleduck Vets open for business.' He snipped the ribbon. 'Phoebe and Jenna will be very happy to answer any questions you might have and give you a tour and a canapé – I hear they are very good. And I do believe there is wine too.'

There was a burst of applause from the small crowd.

Maggie, who was standing closest, had very sparkly eyes. If Phoebe hadn't known her better, she would have sworn she was blinking back tears.

Then, as the crowd surged forward, Phoebe spotted a tall, dark-haired figure at the back, holding a child's hand. She was instantly on hyper-alert. It looked very much like Rufus Holt and his son, Archie. But before she could get a proper look, a woman with a red beret moved forward to ask her a question.

* * *

For the next hour or so, Phoebe registered clients on her new computer system while Jenna fielded questions and they both handed out goodie bags containing a sample of dog (or cat) food, a grooming brush, some poop bags or catnip, a leaflet on Puddleduck Vets, a leaflet on pet insurance and a twenty per cent discount voucher on a new patient consultation. They were helped by Sam and Tori and from time to time Phoebe was aware of Maggie holding court about one or another of the animals in the shelter. With luck, they might rehome a few today.

She focused on the queue, feeling a growing excitement that so many people had registered their pets. Then, just as she finished with what she thought was her last customer, she realised someone else was at the desk. She looked up into a pair of very dark eyes and saw she'd been right. Rufus Holt, their enigmatic neighbour, had come to the opening day, after all, and now he was standing in front of her, with Archie by his side.

'You've made a really good job of this place,' Rufus said. 'It looks great. Wasn't it a barn?'

'Yes, but it's all official – we were granted change of use...' For a moment, she took his comments as criticism, but she realised when he looked surprised that they weren't.

'I don't doubt it,' he added quickly. 'I didn't mean...'

'Hello, Phoebe,' Archie interrupted. 'We brought you some flowers.'

Rufus was distracted. 'Archie, how many times. You do not address adults by their Christian names without checking. It's Miss Dashwood to you.' Rufus hesitated. 'Or, er, Mrs Dashwood. Or maybe it's Ms?'

He sounded flustered – and not at all as though he were fishing for her marital status, which Phoebe would have expected of some men. She thought, not for the first time, that Rufus, despite his privileged position, was quite shy and clearly not comfortable being around women – or perhaps it was people in general. Sam, who'd once met Rufus when he'd taken Archie for a riding lesson, had said he thought the man had some kind of social phobia thing going on.

Tori, who was within hearing range of their conversation, materialised beside him. 'It's Miss Dashwood,' she supplied help-fully while her eyes sent a thousand messages of 'get in there' to Phoebe.

'Hello, Archie. Phoebe is fine,' Phoebe said, taking the flowers from the small boy. 'How lovely. Thank you.' She glanced back at Rufus, who was still looking awkward and added out of devilment, 'Thank you, Mr Holt. It's great to see you here. Would you like to register an animal with the practice?'

'It's Rufus,' he said. He wasn't in a suit, but he did look smart. She wasn't as up on designer stuff as Tori was, but then Rufus was one of those men who'd have looked good in a sack. The fact he rarely smiled just added to the dark and moody thing he had going on. 'And yes please, I would.'

That was a bolt from the blue. She met his eyes, surprised. He was the last person on earth she'd have expected to own a pet. She wasn't sure why exactly. Maybe it was his reaction to Maggie's donkeys when they'd escaped onto his terrace last year. He'd called them 'creatures!' and hadn't been happy about letting Archie go anywhere near them when Phoebe had invited the child to come for visits, although he had softened eventually. He even sponsored a donkey now.

'What kind of animal would you like to register?' She put on her most professional voice.

'It's a guinea pig,' Rufus said.

A small pet for Archie was better than no pet, Phoebe thought as she found the page on the system and made the entry. 'And the guinea pig's name is?'

Rufus glanced at his son. 'Would you take it from here, Archie?'

Archie's eyes were lit with enthusiasm. 'Her name is Elasti-girl,' he said in his clear young voice, as he took a step towards the reception desk. 'From *The Incredibles*.'

'I see, and how old is Elastigirl? Do you know?' Phoebe found herself smiling.

'She is two months and four days.' Archie leaned over the reception desk. His little face was earnest. 'She's a tricolour Abyssinian.'

'She sounds very pretty,' Phoebe said, and thought not for the first time how intensely serious he was for a nine-year-old. There was something about him that plucked every heartstring she had. He was somehow a vulnerable boy at the same time as being a miniature adult. A serious little man child and every bit of her ached to pick him up and put him on her lap for a cuddle. She wondered if Rufus ever did that. He didn't look like the cuddling type. 'Would you like a leaflet to show you how to look after her?'

'I have a book. It's called *The Complete History of the Guinea Pig*.' Archie's dark eyes, as intense as his father's, held hers. 'Will that do the job?'

'That's a very good start,' Phoebe said encouragingly. 'But it's not quite the same as a leaflet on how to feed and care for her. I'll find you one.'

'OK.' He put his elbows on the desk and leaned forward. 'We've got a big hutch and Dad's made her a massive run. Do you want to come over and see it? She can, can't she, Dad? To check it's OK for Elastigirl to play in.'

'I'm sure it's perfect,' Phoebe said, catching Rufus's eye, who looked startled at the direction this conversation was taking.

'Phoebe is very busy, Archie. She doesn't have time to look at runs.'

'Oh please, Dad.' Archie jumped up and down. 'I want Phoebe to see Elastigirl.'

Phoebe smiled at him. 'Well, I think you should bring Elastigirl to see me here. And I can give her a proper check-over. How would that be?'

Archie looked for a second as though he might argue. He scrunched up his face. 'I suppose that would be OK. Can we do that, Dad?'

'Of course we can.' Now, Rufus smiled. His eyes were warmer than Phoebe had ever seen them. The warmth was for Archie. He adored his son. That was plain to see.

Phoebe fetched a leaflet on guinea pig care and handed it to Archie and again she was aware of Rufus's gaze on her, although it was impossible to tell what he was thinking.

Archie folded the leaflet carefully and put it in his pocket. 'Thank you very much.'

'You're very welcome, sweetheart.'

'See you soon.'

Phoebe had a feeling Archie wouldn't let his dad forget that promise.

* * *

From across the other side of the room, Sam had just witnessed the exchange and he felt an odd feeling curl up from the pit of his stomach. He could only see Rufus and Archie's backs, but he could see Phoebe's face clearly and she'd looked very jovial. He wondered what they were talking about.

Maybe Rufus was buying Archie a pony and was asking about registering it as a patient. Archie had become a fine little rider. It was about time he had his own horse. Most of the nobs bought their kids ponies. Sam was surprised Rufus hadn't already done it. Although Emilia, Archie's Swiss German nanny, who always accompanied him to his lessons, had once let slip that Rufus didn't like horses.

Sam was fond of Archie. Some kids gave up riding after a few lessons when they realised that ponies weren't machines that would do exactly as you wanted but had quirks and personalities of their own. Others went the other way and got fanatical about riding, wanting their own ponies to take to shows. If their parents felt the same way and were rich enough, they often got them.

Archie wasn't either of these extremes. He had a huge empathy and affinity with horses that was rare in a child so young. He was respectful and gentle, but he was also totally unafraid and firm. The school horses all loved him. They flicked their ears forward, blew on his hands and gently accepted carrots. Molly, the pony he usually rode, whinnied and banged the stable door with her foreleg when she saw him come into the yard. Not many horses reacted like that to a child. It was a sign of real affection.

Archie was a horse whisperer in the making – and it was something that Sam recognised on a deep level because he identified with it himself. Like Archie, he'd had it since he was a child too. His friends had teased him back then because of the amount of time he'd spent at the stables. Some of them had accused him of being part horse. An only child, Sam had found it easier to be around horses than people. He understood them better.

Except for Phoebe. She and Tori, and to a lesser extent, Frazier, had been Sam's closest friends in childhood. The times he'd spent with them right here on Puddleduck Farm – back when it was frequented by bovines – had been some of the happiest of his life.

Maybe it was the same for Archie, he mused, because he was an only child too.

Sam blinked a few times. Where was his head today? He felt all over the place. Conflicted and unsettled. He was thrilled that Phoebe's project was finally complete and Puddleduck Vets was up and running. But he was disappointed that now they wouldn't have such regular contact. When the unit had been mid-refurbishment, it had given him a good excuse to come over often and see his father and, by default, Phoebe.

Have a word with yourself, Sam, he berated. *Your lives aren't parallel, they're moving in different directions.*

Phoebe had made it perfectly clear that she wanted them to be friends – and just friends. He needed to move on.

He dragged his gaze away from reception. Rufus had been waylaid by a couple he presumably knew and was chatting. Some other people had recognised him too and were hovering, waiting to speak to him.

But Archie had just spotted Sam and was heading purposefully across.

'Hey, Sam. What are you doing here? Molly isn't sick, is she?'

'Hello, Archie.' They fist bumped. 'No, don't worry. Molly's fine. I'm here because Phoebe and I are old friends.'

'Oh,' Archie said, reassured. 'I've got a new guinea pig. We're going to bring her in for a check-over.'

'That's a good idea.' Sam focused his attention on one of his favourite pupils. 'So tell me all about her. What's her name?'

* * *

At reception, Phoebe glanced up. Rufus had just left the desk, but she'd felt for a moment as though someone had been watching her – that spooky sixth sense that alerts people to another's interest. No one was even looking in her direction. She must have imagined it. It was probably the effect of Rufus's proximity. Being near him definitely unsettled her.

At the other end of the room, she saw Sam and Archie deep in conversation. Archie clearly didn't take after his reclusive father, who she saw was trying to field off members of the public. No doubt asking about available tenancies or land as the Holts seemed to own most of it round here.

'So, what did the lord of the manor want?' Tori glided across. 'That all looked very cosy.'

'I thought you were listening?' Phoebe raised her eyebrows as she met her friend's inquisitive gaze. 'Judging by your earlier comments.' She smiled. 'He wanted to register his son's guinea pig as a patient. That's all.'

'I thought he was using that as an excuse to ask you to dinner.'

Tori was clearly in full matchmaking mode today.

'Dinner? No. Why on earth would he?'

'Because there's something between you, isn't there? My spider sense tells me there is.'

'Your spider sense is telling you porkies.'

'You must admit he's hot, though,' Tori lowered her voice, even though there was no chance of Rufus overhearing.

Phoebe avoided her eyes and straightened some pens on the desk. 'If you like that sort of thing. Trust me. There are no circumstances in which I could see myself having dinner with that man.'

5

Rufus had been instructed to go to the Puddleduck Vets launch event by his father.

'It doesn't hurt to give a show of support to the neighbours – particularly when they're tenants, Rufus.'

Puddleduck Farm had belonged to Maggie Crowther's family for over a century, but these days the Holts owned most of the surrounding farmland. Maggie had sold it to them when the place had ceased trading as a dairy farm fourteen years ago. A few months later when her husband had died, she'd rented it back again to house her growing collection of animals.

'If you're so bothered about diplomatic relations, why don't you go to the launch and do the show of support thing,' Rufus had asked his father.

'If I go, it turns from neighbourly support into something more political. It'll be in the paper. *Lord Alfred Holt gives backing to new vet practice.*'

'And that's not a good idea because...?'

'Because I might get asked to give similar backing to other local businesses. Stop asking stupid questions, Rufus. Besides,

Archie wants to go and register his guinea pig and it's useful to have a vet next door.'

Rufus capitulated. He hated letting Archie down.

Making small talk with strangers was his idea of hell. But the real reason he hadn't wanted to go had nothing to do with his dislike of social occasions. It was all about horses. The possibility of seeing a horse, or even a donkey, at Puddleduck Farm had filled him with dread. Neither his father nor Archie knew just how hard it was for him to be anywhere near a horse. He'd been seeing a therapist for nine months now and it was helping, but his PTSD was still alive and kicking. Rufus and the therapist had managed to deal with some of the triggers that set it off, but there was a long way to go yet. Everything equine was still anathema to him, and Rufus suspected it always would be. Watching your wife have a horrendous riding accident and then later die before your very eyes was a trauma that had been burned on his brain. Rowena had died three and a half years ago, but there was a part of Rufus that knew he would never get over it.

In a last desperate attempt to get out of going to the launch, Rufus had asked Emilia, Archie's nanny, if she'd take Archie to register his new pet, but she had shaken her head so her blonde ponytail swung violently, and told him she had that day off. 'It is my best friend's wedding. I told you this. It was arranged weeks ago.'

'Of course it was.'

Emilia had a gleam in her eye. 'But this is good thing to do with Archie. You can have – how you say – Daddy day bond time.'

'Father-son bonding time,' Rufus corrected her English.

'Father-son bonding time. It will be good, *ja*. Also you can put on record with vet the mini pig.'

It amused Rufus that she called Archie's new pet a mini pig –

it seemed a more fitting name for the creature – so he hadn't corrected that.

Archie had been thrilled Rufus was taking him.

'Can we see the donkeys while we're there, Dad?'

'I don't think they'll be around,' Rufus had said, praying he was right.

Rufus had left it as late as he possibly could – just in case there was an equine mascot – and had arrived only just in time to witness the cutting of the ribbon. But he'd gone – that was the main thing – and Archie had been thrilled that they were taking Elastigirl back for a new patient check. Emilia could definitely take him to do that.

It was now the Saturday after the launch and Rufus was sitting in his office at Beechbrook House going through some tenancies. But Phoebe kept interrupting his thoughts. It was surprising how often that had happened this past week, Rufus acknowledged, feeling slightly unnerved.

She was a contradiction. She was both feisty and gentle, emotionally open but also sunnily professional. There had been a moment when she'd been speaking to Archie that she had seemed almost maternal. Watching them, Rufus had felt deeply touched. It had taken him back to the days when he and Rowena and Archie had been a perfect little trio. The days when they had gone walking in the summer sunshine, had picnics in the silver birch woods, driven out to countryside shows, miles from the forest where no one knew who they were, and visited pubs with log fires in winter. The days when they'd had Sunday lunches with his father before they'd all finally moved into Beechbrook House because it was easier than travelling in each day to work on the estate. The days when Rufus had thought they all had forever.

His heart clenched violently in his ribcage and for a second he had to catch his breath. Rowena and Phoebe were worlds apart. They had nothing in common at all. Rowena had been the love of his life, his soulmate, the mother of his child. She had been his raison d'être, his everything.

Phoebe didn't even look like her. Rowena had been an English rose with classic bone structure, beautiful eyes and a bright sharp mind. She had a degree in law, although she hadn't used it. She hadn't needed or wanted to. Phoebe had ordinary brown hair, light brown eyes and darker eyebrows, and a nose that turned up ever so slightly. You could tell she was related to Maggie Crowther – although she didn't have the old lady's abrasive manner.

His train of thought was broken when Archie chose that moment to charge into the room. 'Dad, are you busy?'

'Yes,' Rufus said, although staring into space thinking about the past couldn't really be described as busy. 'Or at least I should be busy. What are you after, buddy?'

Archie waved something at him and Rufus realised it was the leaflet Phoebe had given him about guinea pigs. 'It says that guinea pigs are social animals that shouldn't be kept on their own.' Archie's lip quirked as he met his father's gaze, but Rufus didn't need to be a mind reader to know what was coming next. 'We need to get Elastigirl a companion guinea pig.'

'Is that right?'

'I've checked and the hutch is big enough and the dimensions of the run are fine for more than one guinea pig. I'd say we could have four in the space.'

'I see.' Rufus shook his head, inwardly berating Phoebe and her inciting leaflet.

'So can we get another one?'

'I suppose we can.' He could think of no reason to disagree despite the fact that he knew Archie would soon have a menagerie given half a chance.

Archie clapped his hands. 'Emilia said we could get a boy and call him Bob.'

And the next thing they'd know Bob and Elastigirl would be having little guinea pigs that would be called Violet, Dash and Jack-Jack.

'No, I don't think that's a very good idea,' Rufus called after Archie's retreating back. But his son had already skipped out of the room, presumably to go and tell Emilia it was all agreed.

Rufus gave a rueful sigh. On the other hand, maybe a garden full of guinea pigs would distract Archie from his pony obsession.

* * *

At Puddleduck Vets, Phoebe was blissfully unaware that she was the focus of Rufus's attention. Today was a red-letter day. She was seeing her first patient.

Jenna had taken a few bookings during the last couple of days. Most of them were for the following week. Several clients had taken her up on her new patient health check service, which included a free claw clipping, where needed.

But today's appointment was urgent. Maggie had taken the call when Jenna was at lunch.

'It's a sick rabbit,' Maggie had told her. 'Doesn't sound like it can wait.'

'There's no chance it could be myxomatosis, is there? That's so contagious, I might go out to see it instead.'

'It didn't sound like mixy,' Maggie had confirmed. 'It's a young lop-eared buck. It's a house rabbit and hasn't been near any wild rabbits. The woman said it was off its food and very quiet.'

'What was the name? You haven't put it on the notes.'

'Milo.'

'I meant the woman's name.'

'Oh. Lilian Anderson.'

Lilian, who turned out to be a very tall, slender woman in her fifties with curly brown hair, wearing an animal-print coat with a faux-fur collar, had just arrived in the surgery, carrying the patient in a small animal transporter.

Phoebe felt a thrill of pride as she showed her very first client into the immaculate consulting room. She could see the snowy white fur of the rabbit through the transporter as Lilian put it gently on the examining table.

'So how old is Milo?'

'He's eighteen months old. We have him and his brother, Maximilian. We got two for company.'

'Maybe you could just run me through his symptoms.'

'He's not eating properly and his eyes are a bit weepy. As I was telling your receptionist, it's not like him. He's usually such a foodie and he's been quiet the last couple of days. I wonder if he has an infection. Some kind of problem with his teeth maybe. Can rabbits get toothache?'

'They certainly can, but let's have a little look, shall we? Would you like to get Milo out for me?'

The lop-eared rabbit did look very sorry for himself and Phoebe felt her heart sink as she saw Milo's flat face and bent ears. Breeding animals with flat faces had become a thing lately and although they might look cute, flat-faced rabbits were susceptible to teeth problems because their teeth grew continuously throughout their lives and needed to line up exactly to wear down evenly. In flat-faced rabbits this couldn't happen because the bottom jaw was longer than the top one, which meant the teeth overgrew, causing all sorts of problems. The rabbit on the examining table was a classic example.

Phoebe gently checked his mouth, which confirmed what

she'd already suspected. No wonder poor Milo wasn't eating. He had an abscess caused by his own malformed teeth.

She explained all this to Lilian Anderson and her face became more and more stricken.

'Oh my God. I had no idea that could happen. Are you saying that this is all due to some kind of genetic thing? Is there anything I can do?'

'Milo will always have the same trouble, but fortunately you can manage the consequences. I'm just going to check his ears.'

'What do his ears have to do with it? Can they be affected too?'

'Yes, I'm afraid so. The bent shape isn't natural either and it can cause problems.'

Phoebe hadn't seen such a bad case of ear wax for a long time. No wonder Milo looked sorry for himself. He must have earache as well as toothache.

She informed Lilian of this, too. 'Don't worry. It's all sortable. I'll give Milo something to make him more comfortable and we'll get him on antibiotics. The good news is that his teeth can be filed back. This needs to be done about every six months – because, as I've explained, it can't happen naturally. It would also need to be done under general anaesthetic.'

'I see,' Lilian murmured. 'And how much will this cost?'

Phoebe told her and she frowned.

'That's quite a lot. I'm assuming I'd also have to get Max done – would he have the same problems?'

'It's possible. Have you noticed any issues with Max?'

'He's been shaking his head a bit lately. My other half mentioned it.'

'Head shaking in many animals can be something they do when their ears are painful. It is a warning sign.'

'Poor Milo.' Lilian had tears in her eyes. 'I'd no idea he was in pain.'

'Try not to worry. I've given him a painkiller and the antibiotics will soon kick in. Do you have pet insurance?' Phoebe asked the million-dollar question without much hope. Even if Lilian did have insurance, the companies often excluded dentistry work.

'No. We never thought to do it with rabbits. We honestly didn't think we'd have a need for it. It's not as though they go anywhere to get into mischief and they have the best care possible.'

'I'm sure they do,' Phoebe said gently. Compassion for Lilian was growing in her. 'And please let me reassure you again that Milo's problems are not the result of anything you've done. You don't have to make a decision about his ongoing treatment straight away,' Phoebe added, stroking Milo's soft ears and feeling him quiver beneath her touch. 'But you will need to do something for Milo soon.'

This was one of the hardest parts of her job. Waiting to see what course of action a client would take. Most people wanted the best for their pets, but that didn't mean they could afford to pay for it.

There was a small silence and Lilian took a step forwards and stroked Milo's soft fur, her eyes were downcast. A tear rolled down her face and dripped onto one of Milo's ears and she swallowed hard. Then she squared her shoulders and Phoebe knew she had made a decision. She held her breath as Lilian cleared her throat.

'I'd like to book him in for the dental work. And Max,' she said. 'We'll do this first one and then see how things go.' She met Phoebe's gaze and her clear grey eyes were determined. 'I don't know if I can afford his treatment indefinitely, we'll just have to see. I'll need to have a word with my partner. Does that sound OK?'

'That sounds like a very good start.' Phoebe breathed a sigh of relief.

6

A few days later, Milo had been booked in for his first treatment and his brother, Maximillian, for his initial consultation. Phoebe and Maggie were in reception discussing the situation and Jenna had gone to lunch. Maggie was sitting in the office chair, twirling it round like a child on a roundabout, and Phoebe was standing at the booking computer.

'What I didn't do, of course,' Phoebe said, as she scrolled down the screen, 'was ask Lilian the obvious question.'

'Lucky you've got me then, isn't it?'

'You don't even know what question I'm talking about.' Phoebe turned from the screen and Maggie twirled again until she was facing her once more.

'Of course I do. The question you should have asked is, "Which dodgy excuse for a bunny breeder sold you a rabbit that was destined to be so deformed it would never be able to lead a natural life and would die a lingering death without human intervention?"'

Phoebe met her grandmother's eyes and saw the sadness

there. 'I wouldn't have put it quite like that, but basically yes.' She sighed. 'What did she say?'

'I can't remember. You know what my memory's like these days. But I wrote it down.'

'Can you remember where you wrote it down?' Phoebe teased.

'Yep. It's right here.' Maggie flicked through a raft of pink and yellow Post-it notes stuck all over the desk. 'Hang on a minute, it's here somewhere. I've filed it.'

'Filed it on a Post-it note – wouldn't it be easier to use the card system?'

They kept a paper index card system for customers' addresses, which Maggie insisted was quicker and much more efficient than the all-singing, all-dancing computer system Phoebe had installed. Phoebe knew Jenna transferred Maggie's handwritten notes onto the computer whenever she got the opportunity.

'Here it is,' Maggie said, producing the red plastic box, with a flourish. She put it on the desk.

'Is it under A for Anderson or L for Lilian?' Phoebe began to flick through the cards. 'Or M for Milo?' She wouldn't have put it past her grandmother to use a filing system based on the animal's names – she could probably remember all those.

To her surprise, she discovered the card under A for Anderson. On the top, Maggie had written in neat capitals:

LILIAN ANDERSON – SKINNY BINT WITH PERM. ALL FUR COAT AND NO KNICKERS. KEEPS DODGY RABBITS WITH RIDICULOUS NAMES.

Phoebe shot her grandmother a look of horror. 'You can't put things like this on the index cards.'

'You said I could write notes to help me remember who was who.'

'Yes, I know, but I meant polite notes.'

'What's the use of polite notes? They're not going to help. Whereas that note brings her immediately to mind.' She clicked her fingers. 'I can see her clear as day with that memory jogger.'

So could Phoebe.

'OK, but maybe tone it down a bit.' She turned the card over and discovered there was nothing else on it. Not even a phone number. 'So where are the details of the breeder? I thought you said you'd made a note.'

'I did. But that's on a different card. No sense in putting it under A is there. Not when it's about bunnies. Try looking under B.' Phoebe shook her head; she wasn't sure there was any sense to Maggie's system at all.

There weren't many Bs – Maggie clearly hadn't had time to add that many entries to her card index system, but the second card Phoebe looked at said, 'Bad Bunny Breeder'. This one had a mobile number. An indecipherable name was scrawled beneath it. Clearly Maggie had been in too much of a hurry for neat capitals on that occasion.

'Bad Bunny Breeder,' Phoebe repeated. 'What does this word here say? Is this the breeder's name?'

Maggie peered at the card and screwed up her eyes. 'I think it says Bates,' she said after a few seconds' deliberation. 'Sorry. I'm not a hundred per cent sure now. It was the same day someone brought in that box of kittens whose mother had died.'

'Ah.' Phoebe softened. The kittens were now in Maggie's utility room at the farmhouse. She'd spent a few days and nights feeding them with pipettes every few hours until they were old enough to be weaned. Phoebe touched her grandmother's arm. 'You haven't really got time for this. You've got enough on your plate. Is Saddam still terrorising the dogs? Natasha said something about looking for a cat behaviourist. Did she find one?'

'I think she's spoken to a couple.' Maggie shook her head. 'I'm not sure how much good it will do. But it's worth a try.'

'He'd do well on a farm,' Phoebe said. 'Somewhere they've got a mouse infestation.'

'Or a giant rat problem,' Maggie added crisply. 'He'd be in his element then. As for me helping out here, I said I would.' Her chin jutted stubbornly. 'And I will.'

'And I really appreciate it.' Phoebe shoved the card index box back across the desk. 'You will make sure this is kept under lock and key, won't you?'

'All right, don't go on. What do you take me for?' Maggie's voice had returned to its usual brusqueness and Phoebe decided not to answer.

* * *

The next time Phoebe saw Tori, she filled her in on what had happened. It was three weeks after the launch and Tori had popped round to Woodcutters Cottage, which she owned but rented to Phoebe, to show her friend the pictures she'd taken of the grand opening and the feature she'd written for the magazine.

They were now sitting on Phoebe's sofa in the cosy lounge, with the log burner kicking out heat and a bottle of red on the low table in front of them. The air was fragrant with woodsmoke and wine.

'They broke the mould when they made Maggie,' Tori said, laughing as Phoebe finished telling her about her grandmother's unusual filing system. 'She really is a one-off, isn't she? How's she getting on beside that? Is it working out as you expected?'

'It's early days, but I guess we'll see. Jenna does most of the cover, so, fortunately, Maggie is only doing a few hours here and there. She can be a little, er, unorthodox with some of the customers.' Phoebe poured another glass of wine and offered the bottle to her friend.

Tori put her hand over her glass. 'Better not, I'm driving. How do you mean, unorthodox?'

'Well, last week one of my clients phoned to ask for advice about breeding her new show cocker spaniel and Maggie told her it was inadvisable because there were enough dogs in rescue already without making the problem worse. She started quoting the prices for spaying.'

'She didn't?' Tori chuckled. 'Oh my goodness. What did cocker spaniel woman say?'

'Quite a lot when she finally got through to me. She wasn't best pleased. She wanted to know if I had a "no breeder" policy at Puddleduck Vets, and if so, should she be unregistering her dog.'

'No way! Blimey, what did you say?'

'She calmed down after about five minutes. She eventually saw the funny side when I explained that Maggie has been involved in animal rescue for years and unfortunately sees some of the consequences of breeders who aren't so responsible.'

'Mmmm,' Tori said. 'Do you think it's going to work out? Or do you think she'll end up scaring away half your customers?'

'I don't know.' Phoebe took another sip of wine and her voice sobered as she told Tori about the lop-eared rabbit.

'Poor little mite. Is there anything you can do? Can you report the breeder? Did you get any details?'

'Some details, but they weren't specific enough. My client saw the advert online – she went to a private house in Burley to get her rabbits, but she couldn't remember the address. It was a while ago. Besides, I don't know how much good it would do. It's not illegal to breed lop-eared rabbits. And we don't get that many in. Although that doesn't mean there isn't a problem. Owners just may not realise.' Phoebe blinked, hating the thought of this but knowing she couldn't change it. 'Anyway, enough about me. How are things with you? How's your love life?'

Tori shifted on the sofa. 'So-so,' she said, her voice non-committal. So non-committal that Phoebe was instantly on high alert.

They'd always been chalk and cheese in their approach to dating. Phoebe's only serious boyfriend had been Hugh, but Tori was a serial first dater. She loved the chase, she loved getting to know people, but very quickly lost interest. Last summer, she'd confessed to Phoebe that she'd been on eleven first dates in eight months, but she hadn't talked much about dating lately and Phoebe knew she'd split up with her last boyfriend a few months earlier.

'What does so-so mean?' Phoebe asked.

A log shifted in the wood burner and a shower of sparks flew up against the glass. Still Tori didn't elaborate. This was unusual for her – she was normally very keen to fill Phoebe in about her dating exploits.

Phoebe tried another tack. 'How's New Forest Diners going?' New Forest Diners was the centre of Tori's social life. It was a dinner club where participants had meals at various places in the New Forest. Sometimes they were in hotels or pubs and some-times they were hosted by individuals in private houses.

'All right.' Tori's eyes flashed with a look that Phoebe knew well. 'I have met someone actually.' She gave a secretive little smile.

'I knew it. Come on, who is it? Why haven't you told me about him?'

'It's all very new and I'm still processing it.'

That didn't usually stop her.

'O-kaay.' Phoebe drew the word out. 'Processing it in what way? Don't get me wrong, I don't want to pry. Shall I shut up?'

'No, don't be daft. OK, so we didn't meet through New Forest
Diners. Although we did in a way – as in New Forest Diners was
key.' She broke off. 'I'm not making any sense, am I?'

'Not really,' Phoebe said, curious.

'I actually met him when I was on my way to an event. My car
broke down in the forest and he stopped to see if I needed a hand.
Very knight in shining armour.'

'Wow, tell me more. When was this?'

'A couple of weeks ago.' She paused. 'He's not my usual type,'
she added, staring into the wood burner, lost in the flickering
flames, her eyes dreamy.

'In what way?'

'I usually go for academics, don't I? Smoothies with clever
jobs. And this guy's different. I don't mean he's not educated. He
had a better education than I did by the sound of it, but he took a
different path. I think he had a misspent youth – he's definitely a
bit "bad boy" – but the bottom line was that he preferred practical
subjects. And he's more outdoorsy.'

'Like Sam, you mean?'

'Yes, like Sam in some ways, but more street-savvy than Sam,
if that's not doing Sam a disservice.' She met Phoebe's eyes. 'And
definitely more of a non-conformist.'

Phoebe felt a surge of protectiveness towards Sam, even
though he'd be the first to confess that he wasn't academic or a
rule-breaker. He was kind, thoughtful, respectful, gentle, and definitely not the type to treat 'em mean and keep 'em keen. Sam had
only had one really serious relationship too. Which had ended
when he'd realised her parents were never going to accept him
because he didn't move in the same monied circles they did and
he didn't want her to have to choose between them. Sam would
make some lucky girl very happy one day. Phoebe hoped that
next time he'd find the right girl for him.

'What does this bad boy do for a living? And, more importantly, what does he look like?' Phoebe giggled and clapped her hand over her mouth. 'Sorry, that sounded shallow. I've had too much wine. It doesn't matter what he does or what he looks like if you click.'

'Yes it does,' Tori said. 'OK, so he's tall, thick dark hair. Bit of designer stubble. Bit moody on first impressions, but totally different when you get to know him. He's got one of those light-up smiles. Pretty intense-looking until he laughs and then he just looks completely different.'

Phoebe felt a tingle of foreboding. This description sounded suspiciously like Rufus Holt. But surely she wasn't talking about Rufus. He was definitely bad boy, and she wouldn't have been surprised if he'd had a misspent youth. But if it was Rufus surely Tori would have just come out with it and told her. Or maybe she wouldn't – the last time the three of them had been in the same room, Tori had accused Phoebe of having a moment with him. Hell, what if that was the reason Tori had been so reticent to talk about the identity of her new fellow?

Oblivious to her friend's churning thoughts, Tori went on, 'He has a very hands-on job. Not office-based at all...' She broke off. 'Hang on, you've met him.' Her eyes sparkled.

Suddenly, Phoebe could feel her face burning. She could hardly breathe. Tori had no idea she had such ambiguous feelings towards Rufus. That she was torn between disliking him and finding him hotter than hot. She'd denied it on more than one occasion. 'You're seeing Rufus Holt?' she blurted. 'Oh my God, that's amazing. Get you.' She was so sure she was right she didn't register for a moment the slow growing amazement on Tori's face.

'No. I am *not* seeing Rufus Holt. Blimey – as if I'd be seeing a lord of the manor! You know what a socialist I am. Although you are pretty close, as it happens. Geographically anyway. I'm seeing one of his employees. Harrison McCarthy, he works for him on the estate. He's his groundsman.'

'Oh. Wow. Harrison... Wow. Really. That's brilliant.' The relief that rushed through Phoebe was so huge, she was blindsided.

Tori obviously registered it too. She caught Phoebe's gaze and her own eyes narrowed. 'You were really worried then, weren't you? Don't deny it. You fancy Rufus, don't you?'

'Not really,' Phoebe said, cursing the wine for making her fuzzy-headed enough not to deny it outright. 'I find him unnerving. That's all.'

'But attractive too?' Tori pressed.

'Disturbing's more a word I'd use.'

'But there's chemistry, right? I thought there was when I saw you together at the launch.'

'Please can we just drop the Rufus thing. Tell me about Harrison.'

Tori smiled and sighed dreamily. 'He's just lovely. Definitely the strong silent type. Doesn't suffer fools gladly, but underneath it, he's quite sensitive. I thought you'd met him? Have you not?'

'No. I think Maggie may have done.'

'He's also incredibly fit. He has the kind of body you'd have to spend years in the gym for – but he detests gyms. We've got that in common. He plays the guitar. He's got the most amazing hands.' She closed her eyes. If she'd been a cat, she would have purred, Phoebe thought. 'On our first date, we went to see an Irish band in Southampton. No one famous, but they were really good. He drove so I could drink. On our second, he cooked me a meal at his house and then he serenaded me on the guitar. He's really good. And he's kind, Pheebs. Really genuine.'

'I'm so pleased for you.'

'Thanks.' Tori drained the last of her wine. 'I will stop pestering you about Rufus.' She winked. 'At least I will stop pestering you until you're stone-cold sober. And then I will show no mercy.'

Phoebe knew she was off the hook, albeit only temporarily. Which, she decided, was probably long enough for her to think up several reasons why it would be a very bad idea for her to have feelings for Rufus, who she hadn't seen since the launch. She'd been relieved when it had been Emilia, not Rufus, who'd brought in Elastigirl and also another guinea pig Archie had acquired, for their new patient checks. Archie was a sweetie. Every time she saw him, she wanted to give him a hug. But she did not want to get involved with his father. Having Rufus as a client was one thing, but mixing business with pleasure never worked.

Phoebe's thoughts flicked back to Hugh. When he'd had a fling with their mutual boss, Phoebe had lost her partner, her home and her job in one fell swoop. She wouldn't be making that mistake again.

7

Sam was having similar thoughts about the wisdom of mixing business with pleasure. He was getting ready to go out on a date with Jo Saville, who he'd met at Brook Riding School. He'd been teaching her daughter, ten-year-old Abi, to ride for the past five months and he and Jo had always got on well. He'd known there was no Mr Saville because Jo had alluded to it before, but it had been a surprise to learn she was single. Then, the last time Abi had come for a lesson, Sam and Jo had discovered they were both fans of real ale.

'We should go for one sometime,' Jo had suggested. 'I know a great pub where they do three different types...' She'd broken off suddenly and glanced at his ring finger. 'I mean, I'm assuming you're not married or anything...?'

'You're assuming right,' Sam had acknowledged, flashing her a quick smile because she was flushing prettily and he didn't want her to feel too awkward.

Before he could say anything else, she went on quickly, 'Or would us going for a real ale be considered terribly inappropriate as you're Abi's instructor?'

'I don't think me being her riding instructor would make us going on a date inappropriate, no.'

'A date, huh?' she'd echoed and it had been his turn to blush.

It had been impossible to retract the idea of it being a date without embarrassment, so Sam had shrugged and let it ride. Why the hell not anyway? he'd asked himself. Jo was attractive and she was nice. What was the worst that could happen?

The worst that could happen, he thought now, as, freshly showered and shaved, he put on a clean shirt, was that the evening would be a disaster and he would lose Jo's future custom for the riding school.

That was unlikely. Abi could always see a different instructor. Even so, it could be awkward.

Sam shook his head. This was crazy. Going out with Jo for a drink would do him good. He hadn't had any fun for ages. It was about time he reinvented his social life. And it would help him move on from the fact that he and Phoebe were not – and probably never were going to be – an item.

Half an hour later, Sam opened the door of The Brace of Pheasants – it turned out that Jo's favourite real ale pub had been his local anyway – and decided that coming out had been a very good move.

Jo was sitting on a stool at the bar in profile to him and she looked stunning. Sam had only ever seen her in a wax jacket and jeans, but tonight she was wearing a blue dress that moulded to her curvy figure and a short navy jacket. Her blonde hair was loose around her shoulders and she was wearing make-up – but not too much.

She didn't see him until he was almost at the bar and then she turned in his direction and smiled.

'You look amazing,' he said, as they stood in those first awkward moments, and he wondered whether to peck her cheek.

Jo made the decision for him. She jumped off her stool and kissed his cheek. 'You scrub up pretty well yourself, Sam.'

The awkwardness melted away and for the next couple of hours it didn't return. They chatted as easily as though they were old friends and at the end of the evening, Jo said, 'I've had worse first dates, how about you?'

'Same.'

'Shall we try for a second one then?'

'I'd like that,' Sam said. And it was a surprise to him that he meant it.

* * *

The next day when Sam was out riding his horse, Ninja, along a track in the New Forest, fragments of the previous evening kept replaying themselves in his head. Jo's smile. The way her blonde hair curled around her face. The way she threw her head back when she laughed – she laughed a lot. The way she talked about Abi, whose father, it transpired, had been off the scene since she was a toddler.

'He couldn't cope with the whole family thing,' Jo had said on one of the few occasions they weren't laughing. 'He upped sticks and moved to Cornwall. Last thing I heard, he was teaching surfing.'

'He doesn't stay in touch then?'

'He does not. And he stopped paying maintenance when Abi was four.' Her clear blue-eyed gaze had met his. 'I'm a single parent to all intents and purposes.' She had lifted her chin determinedly. 'We manage fine, though. I work part-time at Tesco and we have English language students lodging with us a lot of the time. That's a big help towards paying the bills. My parents are brilliant too, Mum pays for Abi's riding lessons.'

Sam had wondered about that. Pony riding lessons were expensive.

He'd thought that maybe he could offer Abi the occasional ride on Ninja. She wasn't quite experienced enough yet to ride his flighty 16.2 hh thoroughbred cross, but it was something he could suggest one day in the future maybe. If things worked out.

As if he could read Sam's mind, Ninja snorted and tossed his head and Sam laughed at himself as he leaned forward to pat his horse's soft bay neck. 'You're right, mate. We've only been on one date. I'm getting way ahead of myself.'

He gathered the horse's reins and Ninja, responding, bunched up a little and trotted on the spot. Never mind women. This was what it was all about, Sam thought, sitting deep in his saddle, aware only of the rhythm of his horse and the birdsong that filled the air and the earthy scents of the countryside, a mix of heather and dampness and fresh air. For the next few minutes, there was only him and his horse. Nothing else existed.

* * *

A few miles away at Puddleduck Farm, Phoebe was chatting to Maggie. They had just walked up to see the donkeys armed with a bag of sliced carrots – Roxy and Neddie went mad for carrots and Diablo was always pleased to see Maggie. He'd have followed her around like a dog if he could have escaped more often.

It was a month since Puddleduck Vets had opened. The article Tori had put in *New Forest Views* had brought in more new business and their database of customers was building.

'I didn't think we'd get this busy until we were maybe six months, a year down the line,' she told her grandmother now.

'That's good news, isn't it?' Maggie stroked Diablo's white nose and he blew on her fingers and half closed his eyes in the morning sunshine. He looked the picture of donkey happiness.

'Well, yes, but I think it's too much for you. You did nearly ten hours last week. And you worked Saturday. I feel as though I'm taking advantage.'

'You're not. Sitting on my backside is a doddle compared to looking after a farm full of animals, which is what I've been doing for the last six decades. Or had you forgotten that?' She smiled serenely. 'Seriously, darling, there is no comparison.'

'OK, but the whole idea of employing Natasha full-time was so you could retire properly and put your feet up. Relax and enjoy yourself.'

'I am enjoying myself. I'm perfectly happy answering the phone. I don't see what the problem is. I really don't. The customers are happy too, aren't they? I haven't missed any appointments.'

'Not that I know of...' Phoebe hesitated and her grandmother, who had a radar more sensitive than a military submarine's, dived into the pause.

'Hang on – is this about that dodgy cocker spaniel woman?'

'She wasn't dodgy. I told you. She's a very responsible breeder. We've been through that. She was Kennel Club registered.'

'Pah,' Maggie said. 'They've been responsible for all manner of health issues across the years because of their ridiculous breed standards.'

'The point is that we can't let our personal opinions impact on customers. We shouldn't be giving unwanted advice.'

'I thought that's why people consulted their vets.'

Phoebe bit her lip. 'As Jenna and I get busier, we'll need a full-time receptionist.'

'A *proper* receptionist.' Maggie sounded hurt. Her voice was clipped and her usual sparkle had gone.

'That's not what I meant.'

Maggie fed Diablo a carrot while Neddie and Roxy jostled for position. 'Don't worry,' she said, pointedly not looking in Phoebe's direction. 'I won't be offering any more unwanted advice. From now on, my lips are sealed.' She made a zipping motion across her mouth with her hand. 'You can rely on that.'

Phoebe nodded. 'OK.' She felt as if some of the sunshine had gone out of the morning. She knew Maggie was disgruntled. But she didn't want to backtrack. Maybe it was one of those situations where it was least said, soonest mended.

* * *

For the next week or so the practice ran like clockwork. Despite the fact that Jenna had taken a couple of days off, which meant Maggie was doing more hours than usual.

Phoebe administered annual vaccinations, sorted out a golden retriever's sprained paw and diagnosed a stomach infection in a cat. She was still seeing new customers, so one morning when Maggie had booked in a new patient appointment for a greyhound called Boris and his owner, a Miss Connor, she wasn't expecting any big surprises.

Phoebe would have put Miss Connor at a similar age to herself, mid-thirties, although it was hard to tell. Maybe it was her clothes. She was wearing a white floral pinafore-style dress, dotted with pink and grey flowers which was very pretty but quite old-fashioned, and a single strand of pearls. Miss Connor could have stepped out of a 1950s film. She had an air of what Phoebe could only have described as 'other-worldliness'. She was very pale-skinned, her eyelashes were almost transparent, and her hair was so fair, it was almost white.

Phoebe introduced herself and Miss Connor shook her hand. She had beautiful pink painted fingernails.

'It's so good to meet you, Miss Dashwood. This is Boris. Named after the former prime minister. I was so sad when the party ousted him – he did such good work, I always thought.' Her voice was girlish and breathy.

'Good morning, Boris.' Phoebe bent to pet the dog's head and he wagged his thin tail politely. His coat was smoky grey. He was a beautiful example of the breed. 'Boris is very handsome,' she told his owner, avoiding any discussion of politics. 'So, is there anything you're worried about or shall I just do a general check-over? I see his vaccinations are all up to date.'

'Oh yes. They're all done. He's my first dog. I haven't had him long. He belonged to a neighbour who died suddenly.' Miss Connor cleared her throat. 'This is rather delicate, but as I mentioned to your receptionist, I'd like to have him – er – sorted out. You know. Castrated. I believe that's best – isn't it? Before he starts getting romantic feelings towards, er, lady dogs.' Two dots of pink appeared on her cheekbones. It was clear she wasn't comfortable talking about such things.

This wasn't unusual, although in Phoebe's experience it was men that tended to skirt around the subject of neutering. Women were usually more down to earth.

'Absolutely.' Phoebe crouched in front of her patient, ran her hands over the dog's coat, and then listened to his heart with her stethoscope. For a few moments, there was silence as she monitored the steady, regular beat. No problems there. She checked his teeth, which were gleaming. Then she glanced at his nether regions, aware that Miss Connor was looking more uncomfortable as her examination progressed.

But now it was Phoebe's turn to feel uncomfortable. What she'd been expecting to see there was missing. Boris had already been neutered. Not recently either, as far as she could tell. She glanced up at his owner. Had she really not known this? Had she perhaps not actually looked? This seemed highly unlikely. Greyhounds were short-coated enough for their state of entirety, or not, to be fairly apparent. Then again, Miss Connor clearly found the subject difficult.

Before Phoebe could say anything, her client continued, 'It's not a major operation for dogs, so I'm told. It's just an in-and-out thing, isn't it? Not like males, you know, where I believe it's quite a thing and only done in extreme cases to prevent harm to society. Men, I mean. Not male dogs.' She was flushing scarlet now. Heat radiating from her cheeks. The temperature in the consulting room had rocketed up by several degrees.

Phoebe stood up and met her eyes. Using her best no-nonsense voice, she said, 'Boris has been castrated already. Maybe you hadn't checked.'

They both glanced at the dog's nether regions and she saw an expression of complete mystification spread across Miss Connor's face.

'But I don't understand. How can he have been castrated? It's still there.' Miss Connor waved vaguely with her hand. 'His... you know. His, er, little pecker.'

Catching up with her client's train of thought, Phoebe suddenly realised that Miss Connor had totally misunderstood what castration meant. Oh gosh. How to explain.

She cleared her throat. 'When a male dog is castrated, it means that his testicles are surgically removed, which removes the testosterone and hence the ability to reproduce.'

'I'm not entirely sure I follow you,' Miss Connor said.

It was Phoebe's turn to blush furiously. Nothing in her experience had prepared her for this. 'To be clear,' she said. 'His, er, his little pecker stays put. That's not the bit that's removed. He needs that bit for...' She broke off because she could see the light had finally dawned. Miss Connor's face was a picture of slow-growing realisation and embarrassment.

'Oh golly. I'm so sorry. I've got completely the wrong end of the stick, haven't I?' She looked at Phoebe wide-eyed, before grabbing the greyhound's lead. 'Come along, Boris. Let's go. We've wasted quite enough of the lovely vet's time.'

She turned her back on Phoebe, and headed for the door, hauling the amenable Boris with her. She clearly couldn't escape fast enough.

'Any problems, please don't hesitate to phone us,' Phoebe called after her.

Phoebe closed the door and leaned back on it with a sigh. Jeez. That had to get the award for the most embarrassing consultation of her career. She fanned her face. She still felt hot.

She gave it a few moments. When she finally risked emerging, the waiting area was empty and Maggie was writing something on one of her index cards. Phoebe strolled across and leaned over to see what it was.

No Balls Boris was the heading.

Beneath it, Maggie was just finishing a sentence.

Alice Connor ghost lady and Boris, the greyhound with phantom balls.

'Hang on a minute.' Phoebe looked at her grandmother suspiciously. 'You knew she'd booked an appointment to talk to me about neutering her dog, didn't you? Why on earth didn't you say something to her? Or me, for that matter?'

'You told me not to give any unwanted advice.' Maggie's face was poker straight. 'So I haven't. Zipped lips. Remember?' Her eyes sparked with amusement and she snorted with laughter. She'd never been able to hide her emotions. Not from Phoebe anyway.

In the next moment, they were both convulsed with laughter and for a few seconds they couldn't stop. It was Phoebe who recovered first.

'OK,' she said. 'Point taken. You can give advice when it's wanted and needed and you judge it to be in the patient's best interest. Or mine...'

'I wouldn't dream of doing anything else,' Maggie said, with a glint of satisfaction in her eyes, and Phoebe knew she'd been outmanoeuvred. No change there when it came to her incorrigible grandmother.

8

At Easter, which was late this year, Phoebe took the chance to catch up with her parents who had invited the whole family over for Sunday lunch at Old Oak Way, Phoebe and Frazier's childhood home. Family lunches had got a lot more hectic since the twins had arrived as, naturally, the focus was on the babies.

'They already have such distinct personalities,' Alexa told the table of adults which included Maggie and Phoebe, as well as Louella and James. They had just polished off a roast dinner and were sitting around the long dining table in the conservatory which came into its own on special occasions. 'Bertie is the quiet one,' Alexa continued. 'He's quite content to sleep for hours and even when he is awake, he's happy to sit and watch everything, aren't you, my lovely little man.' She pulled a face at her son, who was nestled peaceably in her arms, dressed in a navy stripe romper suit, and he giggled.

'Whereas this little madam,' Frazier bounced Flo on his knee as he took up the story, 'might be dressed the same, but she's his polar opposite. She hardly sleeps at all, and she already knows how to get everyone to leap to her beck and call.'

'Tell me about it,' said James. 'Earlier on, I picked her toy elephant up off the floor eleven times. Every time I gave it to her, she giggled and threw it out of her cot again, the little monkey.' He didn't sound as though he minded one little bit.

'Oh, she can play that game for hours,' Louella joined in, laughing. 'I must have picked it up a few times myself. I'm getting too old for all that bending.'

Maggie shook her head in mock disapproval as she glanced at her daughter. 'You're too old. Wait until you get to my age, love. Then you'd think twice about kowtowing to her every need. If you're not careful, she'll turn into an entitled princess before you know it.'

'Too late,' Frazier muttered.

Everyone laughed. Everyone could also see that Maggie had a twinkle in her eye. Earlier on, when Maggie hadn't thought she was being watched, Phoebe had seen her partaking in the 'please pick up my elephant' game too. She might be in her mid-seventies, but she certainly hadn't had any trouble bending.

The conversation turned to other things, such as how Puddleduck Vets was going and how long Maggie was planning to stay on as receptionist. This was from Louella, who had expressed concern to Phoebe earlier about Maggie overdoing things.

'Don't forget how old she is, love.'

'I shall stay on as long as my boss thinks I'm the best person for the job,' Maggie said now to Phoebe with a challenge in her voice. 'However long that might be.'

'I definitely couldn't have a better receptionist,' Phoebe said. 'Although we are going to need an extra one very soon. Business is booming. At the moment, I'm using an agency for holiday cover.'

'Holidays. Pah! I haven't had a holiday.' Maggie looked outraged.

'Doctor's appointments then,' Phoebe countered smoothly.

'And chiropodist appointments, and sorting out things with Natasha and the animal adoption scheme and wasn't there that time you shot off to see Eddie for a coffee?' Eddie was Maggie's ex-farmhand who now lived with his son but still visited Puddleduck occasionally.

Maggie was nodding slowly. They'd had this conversation before, but Phoebe knew her grandmother still wasn't keen on getting another receptionist in – she saw it as a black mark on her abilities. Which it wasn't at all.

'It sounds as though you're a victim of your own success,' James said and Phoebe saw her father was nodding thoughtfully. 'Well done, angel. We're really proud of you.'

'Yes, well done,' Frazier echoed and suddenly the attention was on Phoebe.

For a while, they talked about the practice. Phoebe told them about some of the funnier stories like No Balls Boris and also about a goat called Gonzales she'd gone out to see for Seth.

'She'd cut her leg whilst attempting to climb out of her field,' Phoebe explained, 'but that didn't affect her mobility too much. I soon found out why she was called Gonzales. It took the owner and I forty-five minutes to catch her. She was charging around her field faster on three legs than most goats manage on four. Seth laughed his head off when I told him about it.'

Her family laughed too and then the talk turned to lop-eared rabbits and the problem with breeding them with flatter and flatter faces.

'We had another one in last week,' Phoebe told them all. 'From what I could work out, it was from the same breeder as the first one I saw. I know that all lop-eareds can have their problems but hers do seem to be particularly bad.' She explained about the teeth and ear issues.

'Good for business though, isn't it?' her father said. 'Sorting out their teeth and suchlike on a regular basis.'

'That's true, Dad, but we don't want to be profiteering from animal cruelty.'

'Hear, hear,' Maggie said. 'The owner of Bates Bunnies should be made to spend a day with a plastic bag over her head. See how she manages when she can't breathe properly.'

'Could you involve the RSPCA?' Louella asked, looking worried. 'It does sound very cruel.'

'Breeding animals with genetic defects isn't considered to be cruel,' Phoebe said. 'Not legally anyway. Although it should be. There have been similar problems with dogs. There was a big thing a while back about flat-faced dogs like pugs and the breathing difficulties they can suffer.'

'There was a ruling in Norway,' Frazier said suddenly. 'I read about it in the news. Didn't they bring in a ban on breeding them.' He frowned and Phoebe knew her brother was filtering through his near photographic memory. He had a gift for retaining seemingly irrelevant facts. 'English bulldogs and King Charles spaniels,' he announced triumphantly. 'It was opposed by the Norwegian Kennel Club.' He glanced at Phoebe. 'That's right, isn't it? Why did they oppose it?'

'Because they thought it would drive the whole breeding thing underground. That it would just create a black market for breeding brachycephalic dogs. That's the official term for flat-faced.' She sighed.

'It's a flaming disgrace,' Maggie said.

'Most people just don't realise what the consequences are for their pets,' Phoebe countered. 'If they did, I truly don't think they would buy them in the first place.' At least Max and Milo were getting the right treatment. Thank goodness for lovely owners.

'I still think we should start by stopping the Bates woman,' Maggie added stubbornly. 'I think I might pay her a visit with a bag.'

Phoebe shook her head.

'I am joking,' Maggie said. 'I do know, it's illegal to put bags over people's heads. However much they deserve it.' She shot a glance at Phoebe. 'Besides, I'm too old to be an activist.'

Flo, who, up until that moment, had been distracted by a dummy she had in her fingers, began to squawk and the conversation was interrupted.

Frazier glanced at Alexa. 'Do you think they need feeding, love?'

'It's about that time,' she said. 'If it's not feeding, it's changing.' She glanced apologetically around and Louella jumped up.

'I think there's still a made-up bottle in the fridge.' Louella raised her voice to be heard above the squawking because Bertie had now joined in with his sister. 'Alexa, shall I see about heating some water?'

From the sideboard, Alexa the virtual assistant sprang into action, 'The water temperature of the sea is variable depending on location and time of year.'

'Alexa, be quiet,' Maggie shouted gleefully. Maggie had only recently got involved in the fun and games that having a real Alexa in the house as well as a virtual one could produce.

'I think that only works if Alexa is playing music,' Phoebe told her, laughing. 'Presuming you were talking to the virtual Alexa and not the real one.' She had to raise her voice too to be heard. And instantly the sounds of classical music filled the conservatory.

James leapt to his feet. 'Sorry, guys, I forgot I'd moved that blasted computer in here. Where is it anyway?'

'In the drawer,' Louella told him. 'I thought it was turned off.'

'It's impossible to turn off electronic spying devices,' Frazier said. 'We're all being spied on by the Chinese, aren't we?'

For a few seconds, there was chaos and Phoebe took the opportunity to slip out of the room and read a text that had come through on her phone earlier from Tori. Tori's relationship with Harrison was going well. She sent Phoebe regular updates. Tori and Harrison had just spent the Easter break together and, by the sound, of it she was having a great time.

H has invited me up to the manor for a private tour. How cool is that. I shall report back later.

The message was followed by a smiley face emoji and Phoebe found herself smiling too. Tori was obviously in her element. She'd always been fascinated by stately homes and Beechbrook House definitely fell into the category of stately with its quarter of a mile drive and its parapet, chimneys and paned windows. Not to mention the real-life lord in situ and his two generations of heirs.

Tori had wanted to get a look inside Beechbrook House for as long as Phoebe could remember. Her mind flicked back to last year when they'd gone up to speak to Rufus about Archie's unauthorised recces down to Puddleduck Farm to visit the donkeys. They'd been shown into an office just inside the huge oak front door, Phoebe recalled, which meant that aside from the odd ancestral portrait they hadn't seen much, but she could clearly recall Tori's words. 'I'd give anything for a proper look around a place like this,' she'd said, her eyes wide.

Fleetingly, Phoebe wondered just how much of Harrison's attraction lay in the fact that he could grant Tori's wish and just how much of it was for the man himself. She chided herself for being cynical. Tori must really like Harrison; they'd been seeing each other for about five weeks, which had to be some sort of record for Tori. She loved the very early stages of a relationship, but Phoebe couldn't remember her best friend dating anyone longer than a month for a very long time.

She sent back three emojis in reply – a thumbs up, a heart and a smiley face – and went to see if she could help with the washing-up. The twins were quiet now; they were both being fed in the conservatory by each of their parents and she found her mother stacking the dishwasher.

'I wondered where you'd got to,' Louella said. 'Are you OK, darling? I'm really pleased Puddleduck Vets is doing so well.'

'Me too, Mum. Hey, I can do that. Shall I see if there's anything else on the table? Or shall I wash the pans?'

'Your father will do them. No, love, stay and talk to me. We've hardly had the chance for a proper conversation lately. Aside from your new business, how's everything else going? How's Maggie really? Is she overdoing it?'

'You know, Maggie. I do restrict her hours, but she's in her element.'

They were both very aware of the mini stroke Maggie had had last year, and her stubbornness.

Louella nodded slowly. 'I'd hate to lose another parent to overwork. Your grandfather's accident with the tractor was considered to be what caused his death, but I've always suspected that overwork was a contributory factor too.'

'Don't worry, Mum, I won't let her overdo it. I've already broached the subject of getting a full-time receptionist.'

Louella nodded, satisfied. 'Good. I will stop worrying. How's your love life? Do you have a love life?'

'The short answer to that question is no.'

'Is there a longer answer?' Her mother eyed her keenly. 'Or is that just a turn of phrase?'

'It's a turn of phrase.' Phoebe smiled, and to divert her mother from asking any more questions about her non-existent love life, she told her about Tori's new relationship with Harrison. 'I haven't met him yet, but she's obviously pretty enamoured. They've been seeing quite a lot of each other.'

'I'm very pleased for her. Let's hope this one works out.' Louella knew as well as Phoebe did about Tori's track record for relationships.

'There's nothing wrong with playing the field, Mum.'

'I didn't say there was, love.' There was a little pause and then Louella added idly, 'Sam's got a new girlfriend, I hear. Have you met her?'

'Er no, I haven't.' Phoebe felt a little jolt of something she couldn't quite identify. 'I didn't know he'd started seeing someone. Although I must admit, I haven't seen much of Sam lately.'

'I met Jan the other day for a coffee and she was telling me all about it. Apparently it's the mother of a little girl he teaches at Brook.'

'Good for Sam,' Phoebe said. 'I'm pleased for him.' And she was, despite the tiniest twinge of emotion. Not quite jealousy, but something had jolted her.

'Yes, it's nice to see you youngsters pairing off.' Her mother gave another meaningful pause. 'Are you completely over Hugh now?'

'I am, Mum. Yes.'

'That's good to hear. You know I don't like to interfere, darling, but I would like to see you happy and settled.'

At least now Sam had a girlfriend again, her mother wasn't likely to mention the fact that she'd hoped he and Phoebe might one day have a romance.

Phoebe felt a sudden urge to cry. Where had that come from? She was happy that Sam was dating.

Her mother looked at her meaningfully. 'Tell me to butt out and mind my own business if you like, but you won't leave it too long, will you. Or all the good ones will be gone.'

'I promise I won't leave it too long,' Phoebe said. 'And you don't need to butt out.' Just for a moment, she was tempted to confide in her mother about her feelings for Rufus, but something stopped her.

Nothing had happened between her and Rufus and despite the fact that all her friends seemed to be happily pairing up, there was a very big part of her that knew nothing was likely to happen either. It was all in her head.

She'd told no one, not even Tori, but she'd had an erotic dream about the lord of the manor a couple of nights back. They'd been in her consulting room and she'd just asked him to unbutton his shirt so she could listen to his heart with her stethoscope.

'Only if you go first,' Rufus had said, and his dark eyes had held hers flirtatiously. 'Or maybe I should do it for you. Allow me.'

He'd leaned across the examining table and his eyes had never left her face as he'd started to undo her buttons, one by one. After each button, he'd bent forward to kiss the part of her he'd just exposed, and she'd moaned as his lips left a trail of goosebumps on her over-sensitised skin.

Phoebe had woken up with her heart pounding and the memory of his lips on her skin as real as if he'd actually been in the bed beside her. She didn't know what was wrong with her. Thank God it had just been a dream.

It had played on her mind ever since. Lately she'd begun to wonder if part of the reason she was so obsessed with Rufus lay in her reluctance to get back into the real-life world of dating. If she didn't date anyone, she couldn't get hurt again.

Phoebe might be over Hugh, but he had hurt her badly and she was in no hurry to risk repeating that kind of heartbreak again.

Then, one Wednesday lunchtime, about ten days after Easter, just as Phoebe's dream had faded into a more manageable part of her mind, Rufus turned up in her surgery. Phoebe had just finished cleaning the consulting room. She'd expected to find reception empty. Technically, they were closed, Jenna had gone for lunch, but she must have forgotten to turn the sign around. Maggie had gone off to talk to Natasha about a problem on the farm.

Rufus was sitting on a chair. A cardboard box with the top taped up was on the floor beside him. When he saw her, he got to his feet.

'Apologies for calling on spec, but I've just seen Mrs Crowther and she suggested I came in – as I was here. I hope you don't mind?'

Phoebe wasn't surprised Maggie had sent him in. She was always keen to stay on the right side of their neighbours.

'I don't mind at all. Please, do come in. Is this the patient? Is it Elastigirl?' The box had air holes, she was relieved to see.

Rufus picked it up and they moved into the examining room and suddenly in the confined space it was impossible not to be hyperaware of him. Echoes of Phoebe's dream were flying at her thick and fast. Rufus was wearing a white shirt, open at the neck, as he had in her dream, and Phoebe had to drag her eyes away from the top buttons.

Aware that he had answered her question but that she had no idea what he'd said, Phoebe focused on his face. 'If you'd like to tell me about her symptoms please, that would be great. Er, what seems to be the problem?'

'She's a him. Did I not say that? His name's Bob. We're still on a theme, despite the species change.'

He didn't seem to have noticed how flustered she was. Thank heavens for small mercies.

'*The Incredibles*. Yes.' Species change? What on earth was he talking about? She couldn't see anything through the box. But she could feel her face getting redder.

'Symptoms. Well...' He frowned. 'We literally only got him at Easter, but he seems to have a cold. He's sneezing, he has gummy eyes, and he seems to be feeling a bit sorry for himself. He's very quiet. Shall I get him out?'

'Yes please. Let's have a look-see. I'm sure we'll soon find out what the problem is.'

Oh my God, now she was babbling.

But Rufus just nodded. He was carefully untaping the masking tape and then he gently removed a ball of white fluff and placed it on the table. Phoebe was rocketed into the present.

It was another lop-eared white rabbit. A young one by the look of it. And, yes, he did have a problem. She felt her heart sink as she examined the listless baby rabbit who also had a slight discharge from his eyes. 'How old did you say Bob was?'

'I didn't, but the breeder said he was eight weeks old.'

Phoebe doubted that. This rabbit was tiny. She wasn't an expert, but not more than four weeks she'd have said.

'It may sound a silly question. But there was no sign of this when you bought him? Nothing in the mother.'

'I wasn't there,' Rufus confessed. 'Emilia took Archie to get the rabbit from a place in Burley. The breeder already had him boxed up. She said he was the last one of the litter. All the others had already gone to their homes. Emilia seemed to think we were lucky to get one. The woman had told her there weren't any other good breeders of lop-eareds in this area, hence the price.'

'Do you remember what that was?'

Rufus frowned as if trying to recall it. 'About a hundred pounds, I think.'

Phoebe blinked, almost as shocked by the overinflated price as she was by Rufus's indifference to it even being high. How the other half lived.

'The breeder said she'd send the paperwork on as she was in a hurry to go out. Apparently her rabbits were registered with the BRC.'

'Did she send the paperwork on?'

'To be honest, I don't know. I could check. Why? Do you think the breeder wasn't reputable?'

'I don't know. Do you recall her name?' Phoebe felt a surge of foreboding.

'Yes. Belinda Bates. Burley Bunnies. I could find you the address too if you like. She advertised online.' He broke off suddenly. 'Why? What's wrong with him?'

'I think he has a respiratory infection which possibly comes from mouldy hay. We see this sometimes when lots of rabbits are kept together, or occasionally if the hay isn't of a suitable quality. Is he in contact with any other rabbits?'

'No. He just has the guinea pigs for company. Do you think that's enough?'

'Truthfully, both rabbits and guinea pigs are better off with their own kind. Especially when they're young.' She looked at him and he nodded. 'I'm going to give you some antibiotics for him. It's a good job you spotted it so quickly and brought him in.'

'Is he going to survive? Archie will be heartbroken if he dies.'

'I hope so.'

With her examination complete, she paused to look at Rufus. All echoes of the dream had gone now. He was just another client worried about an animal. Although she sensed he was more worried about his son than the rabbit.

Then he did something that shattered this assumption. He stroked the rabbit's soft fur very gently with the back of an index finger. 'I like rabbits. I had them when I was a kid. I must admit I prefer the old-fashioned look. I'll see if I can talk Archie into getting a straight-eared rabbit – sounds like Bob here could do with a companion and it's not as if we don't have the space. Archie's great – he does all the cleaning out himself.' Suddenly his face closed down as if he'd become aware that he'd been showing a softer side of himself that he preferred not to reveal.

Or maybe you're overthinking this whole thing, Phoebe told herself. She didn't even know this man. Yet she'd already created a persona for him. Most of which was based in her imagination.

She turned away from him to update the system and order the medication.

A few minutes later when they were back in the waiting room once more, she said, 'I can email the bill to you if you'd prefer to settle up later?'

Rufus shook his head. 'It's fine. I'll settle up now.'

Phoebe presumed – correctly – as it turned out, that Maggie hadn't had a chance to make up an index card for Rufus. That was probably just as well. Lord knows what she'd have put on it. Lord being the operative word, she thought wryly.

* * *

Rufus paid his bill, put the boxed-up rabbit carefully in the footwell of the Land Rover, beside the package of antibiotics, and drove the short distance back to Beechbrook House.

He was beginning to think that Phoebe Dashwood was a bit of an enigma. She was certainly a contradiction. The two times that she'd come up to the house (three if he counted the time he'd caught her in his back garden in pursuit of her donkeys), she'd been feisty and sure of herself. Yet both times he'd seen her on her home ground, she'd been the opposite.

He'd have expected it to be the other way round. For her to be more confident on her home territory, not less. Today she'd given him the distinct impression that she was flustered and unsure of herself. She'd reacted as though she was his subordinate – in the same way as people occasionally did around his father when they found out that he was a lord. Almost starstruck. It was something Rufus disliked about the title. He didn't want people to treat him differently, just because he lived on a huge estate and was the son of a lord. He wanted to feel 'a part of', ordinary, but it was something he never really had felt. Despite the fact that he spent much of his time doing a job that was, when it came down to it, pretty ordinary. He did all of the paperwork for the estate management, and he was also taking over more and more of the financial side from his father, who was semi-retired. Keeping an eye on the family's investments alone took up an inordinate amount of time and energy.

Arguing with his father about the way things should be done also took a lot of energy. Alfred was old-school and traditional. Pheasant shoots and fox hunts had been part of his upbringing and he saw no reason to change this.

Since he'd been diagnosed with PTSD, Rufus had managed to

persuade his father to stop the hunts' access across the Beechbrook estate. They had mostly been drag hunts since the ban, so this hadn't been too difficult. The pheasant shoots still happened, even though Archie hated them. He loved all creatures and it had broken Rufus's heart when he'd found his son crying one day after he'd found an injured bird that had somehow managed to get halfway up a tree and was stuck.

Emilia and Rufus had sneaked it into an outbuilding and it had actually recovered, much to their relief. Rufus knew his father would have been furious if he'd found out. 'The boy needs to toughen up and learn the facts of life,' was what he would probably have said.

Rufus and his father had different views on things, which made Rufus feel even more an outsider. He knew he'd never be a traditional lord of the manor, despite being heir to the title. He didn't fit the role. Neither did he seem to fit in anywhere else. The only time Rufus had come close to feeling 'a part of' was when he'd met Rowena. One of the things that had attracted him most about his late wife was the way she'd worn her wealth and privileged background so lightly. Her parents, who'd been wealthy bankers, were far richer than his own family had ever been. They'd owned half of Berkshire. But Rowena hadn't ever taken this for granted – there had been nothing 'entitled' about her, but neither had she let it dictate who she spent her time with or how she spent her time. She didn't act as though she had anything to prove.

Once, when they'd been at a top London restaurant that had double-booked them, near to her father's London offices, Rufus had been about to give the new maître d' a piece of his mind. The words 'do you know who I am?' weren't in his vocabulary, but he'd been very tempted to point out that Rowena's father brought so many clients there he practically kept the restaurant afloat. It had been Rowena who had stopped him.

'We can always go to McDonald's,' she'd said in a stage whisper.

'McDonald's.' Rufus had stared at her in horror as she'd grabbed his hand.

'Yes, I've always wondered what it's like there. Why don't we go and find out?'

'Seriously?' He had let her lead him out of the restaurant, aware of the maître d's look of surprise, and they'd spent what had turned out to be a brilliant evening in the fast-food chain. They'd eaten Big Macs and drunk copious amounts of milkshake and they'd laughed and laughed. When they'd left, Rowena had given their server a generous tip and she'd flushed scarlet and tried to give some of it back.

'I don't think you meant to give me so much, ma'am?' she'd said.

'I did. Go and do something fun,' Rowena had told her. 'We've had such a great time. Thank you.'

The incident had made a big impact on Rufus. It had also been one of the most memorable dinner dates of his life. It was odd that – they could eat at the best restaurants in the world, but an evening in a fast-food venue stood out. It had made him think that Rowena was right: the best things in life weren't about money, they were about something less easy to define.

He came back to the present with a start. He realised that he was still in his vehicle outside his house, sitting beside the boxed-up baby rabbit. He glanced at his watch. He'd been going to task Emilia with the job of administering antibiotics to Bob, but she wouldn't be around until later. Archie wasn't due to finish school till four and then he'd be at one of his after-school clubs. Rufus was pretty sure the sooner he started the medication, the better it would be for the patient.

He took the syringe and the rabbit back to the spacious hutch and run in the garden and then carefully lifted the rabbit out, sat on the ground with it and administered the medicine.

Bob rewarded him by pooping on his lap. Rufus suppressed a frown. He imagined Phoebe would have laughed her head off. Rowena would have laughed too.

It wasn't the first time he had found himself comparing the two women, he realised with a jolt of surprise. How odd.

* * *

In between work, Phoebe spent the afternoon thinking about Belinda Bates. She knew she couldn't carry on ignoring what was becoming increasingly apparent – there was a totally irresponsible rabbit breeder in the local area. There must be something she could do to stop her. It might not be a crime to breed flat-faced rabbits, but it was possible there were other rules the breeder was breaking. The only way to find out was to go and see. But she was also aware that she needed to tread carefully. She couldn't just go blundering in and start hurling accusations.

At closing time, she left Jenna to clear up and then she went to find Maggie to talk to her about it and finally tracked her down at the furthest edge of Five Acre Field talking to Natasha. That was odd. They used the smaller field for the neddies in spring. Five Acre Field was too big and too much spring grass could lead to laminitis. A small stream ran across the land. A winterbourne that often dried up in the summer completely, although it had water in it now, because there had been so much rain lately.

Maggie was deep in conversation with Natasha, close to the stream, but they both glanced up as she approached.

'Hi,' Phoebe looked at them curiously. 'What are you doing up here?'

Maggie's face was worried, and she answered with a question of her own. 'What do you make of this?' Her grandmother gestured towards the stream and Phoebe took a step closer to see what she was talking about.

There was nothing immediately obvious, but then she saw two tiny dead voles laid out on the bank.

'Dead voles?' she queried. 'Is that what you mean?'

'Water voles,' Natasha said. 'I found one yesterday too. I thought it was a coincidence at first, but now I'm not so sure.'

Natasha might be young, but she was pretty savvy and observant. Her attention to detail was second to none and now her dark eyes were worried.

'It's not just the voles,' Maggie said. 'Natasha found a couple of dead frogs earlier too – only they were further upstream.

'I was checking the fences,' Natasha explained. 'Or I wouldn't have been near the stream.'

'She was worried, so she came to see me,' Maggie went on. 'We're wondering if there's been some sort of a contamination incident.'

'Oh my God.' Phoebe looked from her grandmother back to Natasha. 'That does sound worrying.'

'We'd need to do some kind of water test to see if we're right,' Natasha continued. 'It's easy enough to get hold of a test. One of my friends goes wild swimming and they often test water to check it's safe.'

'Every day's a school day,' Phoebe said. 'What do they check for? Do you know?'

'Bacteria, I think. Heavy metals maybe. I'm not a hundred per cent sure, but I could find out.'

'Do you know where they get the tests?'

'Online. I can check. I think if we're worried we could maybe also call the Environment Agency. They'd know what to do. They might even send someone out to test the water.'

'That's probably a better plan,' Phoebe said. 'It would be more conclusive that way. More accurate than a home test.'

'In the meantime,' Maggie said, 'we could do a spot of investigation ourselves, couldn't we.' She glanced up the slope towards Beechbrook House. The stream meandered up to the belt of woodland and disappeared. The strip of woodland hid the house from view, but Phoebe knew from experience how close their neighbours were if you didn't take the official route in.

There was a silence as they all took in the implications of this. The contamination was likely to have come from their neighbours and landlord. That could be very awkward. Especially if they had to go up to tell them. But neither could it be ignored.

10

'We could follow the stream back and see if we can see anything obvious,' Natasha suggested, looking at Maggie. 'I haven't quite finished walking the kennel dogs, but...' She sounded wistful, as though she'd rather be hunting down the mystery of a polluted stream than walking dogs, but Maggie looked troubled.

'I think it's best if you focus on the dogs. Also, don't we have an appointment today with Catty the cat?'

'Catty who?' Phoebe asked.

'Catty the cat whisperer.' Natasha grinned. 'She's coming in to give Saddam an assessment. I'd better go and check he's not holed up somewhere we can't find him.' She shrugged good-naturedly and headed back across Five Acre Field in the direction of the kennels, leaving Phoebe and Maggie standing in the afternoon sunshine.

'What does a cat whisperer even do?' Phoebe asked Maggie.

'Lord knows, but Natasha said she had excellent reviews.' Maggie shook her head. 'How did you get on with Rufus? Sorry I didn't warn you. He just turned up and I thought it would be quicker if he came and found you than have me messing about.'

'Of course. Rufus was fine. He brought a baby rabbit he'd just got for Archie. It had an eye infection. I'm glad I could help.'

'Who flogs baby rabbits at Easter?' Maggie tutted disapprovingly. 'Oh, don't tell me. It was that bloody Bates woman again.'

'Yes, I'm afraid it was.'

'We need to do something about that woman.' Maggie's eyes flashed fire. 'If it's not the RSPCA, then another welfare organisation. Do rabbit breeders have to be licensed? Dog breeders do.'

'I don't know, but I will find out.' Phoebe understood her grandmother's angst perfectly. She touched her arm. 'I'll make it a priority. Don't worry. If nothing else, I can go and see her. Maybe it's just a question of education.'

'Education with one of my baseball bats is what she needs,' Maggie said, sounding scarily serious.

Phoebe shook her head. 'Often, people just aren't aware of the problems they're causing. They don't think things through.'

'Pah,' said Maggie and although Phoebe didn't want to admit it, she thought the old lady was probably right. Selling bunnies at Easter that were too young to leave their mothers, for ridiculously overinflated prices – none of it looked good. And that was before you even got started on the genetic defects and the animal husbandry. All of it looked like the business model of someone who was far more interested in profit margins than pet welfare.

'Meanwhile,' Phoebe added, glancing back at the deceased voles, 'we have a more pressing issue to deal with.'

'Yep. Let's get on with it. At least we can rule out the fact that something's been dumped on the land I'm responsible for.'

They walked one behind the other alongside the stream. In places where it was narrow enough, you could cross over it, but it didn't seem necessary, Phoebe thought, as you could see both sides.

'What kind of thing are we looking for?' she asked her grandmother. She had visions of barrels of toxic waste marked with a skull and crossbones lying on the riverbank, but she didn't really think they'd find anything that obvious.

'It's hard to tell, to be honest.' Maggie paused to glance back at her. 'Anything out of the ordinary. We had an incident about twenty years ago on the farm: similar result – dead wildlife. It turned out that an overload of slurry had been washed off the land into the watercourse. There had been much more rain than usual. That's possible, I suppose. There was a lot of rain in February and March.'

'Although not so much, lately.'

'No.'

For a few minutes, they walked in peaceful silence. There was just birdsong and a faint breeze that tugged at Phoebe's plaited hair. The stream looked perfectly normal to her. Flies buzzed over the top of it. She was beginning to hope that the frogs and the voles Natasha had spotted had just been an unfortunate coincidence, when they found a dead robin. The tiny bird was on the edge of the water, almost invisible against the mud, but its red breast caught Phoebe's attention.

'Maggie,' she called, bending down to scoop up the bird. 'Look.'

Maggie caught her arm. 'It's probably best not to touch it, love. Something's killing the wildlife and until we're sure what it is... Hang on, I've got a plastic bag here.' She produced one from her pocket and Phoebe took it and bagged up the robin.

'Yes,' Phoebe said, becoming fully aware of the seriousness of the situation. 'And if it really is some kind of toxic waste...' She paused. 'Thank goodness Natasha spotted it.'

They kept walking and a few minutes later they reached the boundary between their fields and the Holts' land. To Phoebe's relief, there were no more dead animals, but neither was there any evidence of anything that could have killed them.

For a few seconds, they stood by the edge of woodland. The stream ran through it but then disappeared into the trees and thick undergrowth. It would have been difficult to follow it any further even if they had wanted to trespass.

'We need to speak to the Holts as a matter of urgency.' Maggie looked at Phoebe and squared her shoulders. 'On the plus side, at least relations are warmer than they used to be. Now you're their official vet.'

'Yes. That's true. I'll go round, shall I?'

'Do you have time? Have you finished for today?' Maggie looked relieved.

'I have as it happens. I'll go up to the house. No problem.'

* * *

Half an hour later, Phoebe was in her Lexus turning right out of Puddleduck Farm and driving along the high red wall that bordered the Holts' land. As she turned right again to go beneath the stone archway with the life-size sculpture of a stag standing on top, looking out across the fields, she felt a flicker of déjà vu.

She drove past the gatehouse, which didn't seem as gloomy as the first time she'd seen it, and started up the quarter-mile drive that led to Beechbrook House. Making this trip was beginning to feel, if not exactly a regular event, at least a little less intimidating than it had once been.

Perhaps this was because she had met Rufus a few times now and, on some of those occasions, particularly today, he'd seemed less like the arrogant lord of the manor he'd first appeared and, in fact, quite human.

She parked beside the fountain and the two tasteless white

cherubs that adorned it, noticing that only the Land Rover was in situ. The silver Mercedes was missing. She presumed Rufus had brought Bob the Bunny in his car, but maybe not.

She walked up to the huge oak door, feeling a flutter of butterflies. So maybe she was more anxious than she knew. Her body certainly was.

The bell jangled, but no one came.

Phoebe left it half a minute or so and then tried again.

No answer. Rufus must have gone out again. Maybe he was picking up Archie from school. But surely Emilia would do that.

Phoebe was just about to give up and go back to her car when a tall figure walked around the side of the house. He was silhouetted against the sunshine and for a moment Phoebe thought it was Rufus. She started towards him, smiling, but then stopped when she realised she was facing a stranger.

A pretty grumpy one at that. The man, who was almost the same height as Rufus but stockier now she could see him properly and a lot scruffier, was scowling.

She guessed it must be Harrison. The object of Tori's affections. Wow, Tori hadn't been exaggerating. Given what he was wearing, he wasn't her usual type at all. For some reason, she was put in mind of *Lady Chatterley's Lover*. Not that Tori was in any way like Lady Chatterley, but the contrast between this man and the usual smoothies she went for was so marked.

Momentarily thrown, Phoebe hesitated before gathering herself and saying politely, 'Good afternoon. I was hoping to see Mr Holt.'

'I think he's out.' The man had stopped scowling, but he wasn't smiling either. 'His car's not there. Can I help. I'm Harrison, his estate manager.'

'Yes. In fact you're probably the best person to speak to. I'm from Puddleduck Farm. I'm Maggie Crowther's granddaughter. We think we've got a contaminated stream.'

'You think this because...' Although, this was technically a question, his voice was very flat. His face still almost expressionless.

'Dead wildlife.'

'There's loads of reasons for dead wildlife.'

'Yes, I know that.' Phoebe could feel an edge creeping into her voice in response to his non-committal tones. 'I'm a vet.'

'You've done a post-mortem, have you?'

Was he taking the mickey? 'No, of course I haven't done a post-mortem. But we've found a couple of dead voles and a robin this morning. Look – I'm here as a matter of courtesy, that's all. I'll be reporting it to the Environment Agency. I just thought you should know.'

Harrison's eyes narrowed. 'All right. I'll take a look round the estate.'

'Good.' Phoebe turned on her heel. 'You're welcome,' she muttered under her breath as she headed back to her car. What was it with the men at Beechbrook House? Were they all just arrogant nobs or was it something in the water? That would be ironic.

She got back in her car, glancing in her rear-view mirror as she did up her seat belt. And what the hell did Tori see in Harrison? She didn't get that at all.

* * *

Phoebe drove back round to Puddleduck Farm and told Maggie what had happened.

The old lady nodded thoughtfully. 'I've met Harrison before. I think his bark's worse than his bite. He'll have a proper look, I'm sure. It would be more than his job's worth not to. I just telephoned the Environment Agency. They've got a hotline.'

'What did they say?'

'I got one of those ridiculous monotone voices. Press one for this, two for that. I tried pressing buttons, but I didn't get very far.' She looked at Phoebe hopefully. 'I don't suppose you could...'

'I'll give them a call. Don't worry.' Phoebe knew how much her grandmother hated phones. She had only just got her head around answer machines. If she could talk to a person it was fine, but if she was sent around in circles and had to press buttons, she lost patience and gave up.

Sometimes Phoebe wondered how many other phone-phobes there were out there like her grandmother who would rather give up and just abandon the whole idea of contact if companies made it too difficult for them. Probably there were thousands of people who would never deal with being lost in the automated voicemail mazes of big corporations, no matter how urgent their issues were.

Phoebe tried the number again and was put on hold with some music. She'd been holding on for twelve minutes when another call came through to her mobile from a number she recognised as one of her client's.

She abandoned the call and answered it and was relieved she had because it was the owner of a bitch that needed help with a whelping.

'I'm needed,' she told Maggie. 'I'll try phoning the Environment Agency again later.'

* * *

To Phoebe's relief, after a worrying start, she managed to free a stuck pup and deliver seven more healthy puppies and left them with their exhausted, relieved mother and very pleased owner.

'Thank you so much for getting here so promptly,' the woman said, offering her tea and cake, which Phoebe accepted. 'I think we might well have lost them all without you.'

'My pleasure,' Phoebe told her before finally driving back to Woodcutter's Cottage. That emergency had been a wake-up call for her. So far since she'd opened her practice, she'd been lucky she'd had no emergency calls that clashed. If that had happened, she'd have needed to prioritise, which would have meant putting an animal's health, perhaps even their life, in danger.

* * *

Her phone was ringing again before she reached home and she pulled over to answer it. This time it was Seth.

'Phoebe, could you possibly do something for me. I know you're not technically on call, but I'm at The Ellison Stud. A difficult foaling.'

His voice was brusque but hopeful and Phoebe heard herself say, 'Of course I can. What's the call?'

'Elm Tree Farm, the place where we went for the lambing. They've got a sick ewe and if old man Dean thinks it needs a call-out, it must be urgent.'

'I'm on my way,' Phoebe said, trying not to yawn.

'Thanks. I think I'm going to be stuck here for a while.'

* * *

Two hours later, Phoebe was home again. The ewe sadly was too far gone to save and had needed to be put to sleep. She hated that part of her job, but it had been the only option and the shepherd had been pragmatic. 'She had a good innings,' he'd said to Phoebe. 'Thanks for coming out so late.'

She'd finally got home just before ten. There were good days and bad days in this job, but one thing she could count on was that there was never a day that was the same.

Her last thought as she fell asleep was that she might have to take on another vet, as well as a new receptionist, sooner rather than later. Perhaps even before Christmas. Being her own boss was immensely satisfying. But it was much harder and more tiring than she had ever imagined it would be.

11

Thursday began badly. Phoebe's first appointment of the day ended with her putting a chicken with heart failure to sleep. It was an old ex-battery hen called Mabel and the bird's owner was philosophical.

'She's not been laying for a while. As I see it, she's had a good couple of years of extra life – and I don't want her to suffer and have to linger on.'

Neither did Phoebe. But it was still hard playing God. Heart failure was treatable in chickens, but the owner was right, Mabel's days were numbered and the treatment might not work for long. When to call time was always hard with pets.

At lunchtime, Phoebe finally managed to get through to the Environment Agency and was told that they'd send an inspector out to assess the situation as soon as one was available.

'Do you know when that's likely to be?' she asked.

'It depends how busy they are with other incidents,' she was told. 'All reported incidents are assessed and prioritised, according to risk to the public. But it shouldn't be long. I can ask whoever gets assigned to keep you posted if you like?'

Phoebe knew she would have to be content with that. Chances were they would have to contact Maggie anyway, as they'd need to access her land to check out the incident.

She passed this on to her grandmother, who shook her head and looked resigned. 'I guessed as much,' she said. 'It's all cost-cutting these days. I didn't think we'd be top of their list. That stream probably doesn't pose too much of a risk to humans. Although that very much depends what's in it. Which they won't know, of course. Unless they come and test it. Maybe I should get one of those water test kits Natasha mentioned.'

'Maybe.' Phoebe's mind was on her afternoon appointments. A dog with a dermatological condition, a cat for a post-operative check after spaying and a cat with a bad breath issue.

Her very last appointment of the day was another sad one. A very old cat called Garfield who had advanced cancer. His owner, Tom Long, was bringing him in for what would probably be his final appointment.

Phoebe could see immediately that Tom Long, who was in his early twenties and had a piercing in his nose, was heartbroken. Garfield had been a lifelong companion to him.

'I don't want him to suffer,' he said, not meeting Phoebe's eyes as he lifted his beloved cat gently out of the cat basket and held him in his arms. 'I don't want to keep him alive just for me. Do you think it's the right time to let him go? Do you think he's in pain?'

Phoebe examined the old cat. She'd already seen him several times and she confirmed what she suspected Tom already knew – that despite the painkillers and all of their best efforts to make him comfortable, Garfield didn't have much quality of life left.

'I think he's had enough,' Phoebe told him as gently as she could. 'I'm afraid I do think it's the right time to let him go.'

'Can I stay with him until the end?'

'Of course you can.'

'Do you promise he won't know what's going on.'

Tom's dark eyes met hers and a tear rolled down his face and fell into Garfield's soft amber fur.

'He'll just go peacefully to sleep,' Phoebe reassured him. 'And he'll be out of pain then.'

'Do you think I should do it today. Like, I mean... now...?'

He was clutching at straws. But she knew how hard it was for people to make this decision. Some of them wanted her to make it for them, but she tried not to do that. She could tell them the best course of action on medical grounds, and on humane grounds, but they had to make the decision that was emotionally right for them too.

'If he was my cat, I would say that today was the right time...' She paused and swallowed as Tom's face screwed up in pain and determination before he finally made the decision and signed the consent form.

Phoebe gave Garfield his final injection as swiftly as she could, explaining to his heartbroken owner that he wouldn't be aware of what was going on. All he would know was that he was with the person he loved. 'Keep talking to him,' she murmured. 'We think that hearing is the last sense to go in animals as well as humans.'

Then she left Tom alone with his much-loved pet's body to grieve for as long as he needed. She'd deliberately made him her last appointment so he could do this undisturbed. She would stay at the surgery for as long as it took.

Back in reception, she and Maggie talked in quiet voices about the pain of endings, however merciful they were.

When Tom did finally come out with the deceased Garfield in the cat box to take him home to bury in his garden, he was dry-eyed but still clearly upset as he headed for reception.

'What do I owe you?'

'Don't worry about that now. We'll send the bill on,' Maggie told him.

'Thanks,' he said gruffly, as he headed out of the main doors.

'Poor chap,' Maggie said, looking after him. 'That's the worst bloody part of having an animal, isn't it?'

'Always,' Phoebe said. 'I know it's for the best putting them to sleep when they're in pain, but it's still so very difficult playing God. It's the only part of my job that I really dread. I don't think it will ever get easier.'

'And if it did,' Maggie said, her own eyes soft, 'then you wouldn't be the woman we all know and love.'

Phoebe glanced at her watch. It was only four thirty, but it felt more like seven. It had been a long day. Or maybe she was still tired from the previous one and the sadness of having three euthanasias in a row.

One more day and then they had a long weekend. The first May bank holiday. Time to catch up on her paperwork, look into Bates Bunnies properly and do some long overdue chores. She was also seeing Tori on Saturday night for a girlie catch-up. Tori had texted her and suggested they meet at The Brace. Phoebe hadn't told her she'd met Harrison and was feeling slightly awkward, in view of the fact that she'd been so unimpressed.

'I'll get cleared up,' she told Maggie, then I'll head off home. 'I'll lock up if you like.'

'OK, darling, if you're sure?'

'Before you disappear, though, how did it go with Saddam?' Phoebe asked suddenly remembering Catty the cat whisperer. 'Did he have his assessment?'

'He did indeed. I didn't see the woman. But, according to Natasha, she was only here for about five minutes. Apparently she was wearing a skirt and high heels and tights. Natasha asked her if she'd like to borrow some overalls – you know how handy

Saddam is with his claws – but she declined. Was quite snooty apparently.'

'Ah.'

'Ah indeed. So that was the first red flag.' Maggie rolled her eyes. 'Then Natasha showed her where Saddam was and offered to help, but she said it was usually best if pet owners stayed out of the way while she assessed the patient. The words "pet owners" was the second red flag. I mean, Natasha did tell her that we were an animal shelter and that Saddam wasn't exactly a cute pet.'

'Mmmm.' Phoebe waited, fascinated. 'So what happened next?'

'Suffice to say she didn't stay in the barn very long. She came out at top speed with a bleeding leg and a broken heel.'

Phoebe winced. 'Ouch.'

'Natasha said she did offer her a plaster, but she wasn't keen on hanging around. She was off in her 4x4 like a bat out of hell. Said she'd email her report.'

'I bet you can't wait.' Phoebe suppressed a smile and her grandmother harrumphed.

'We live and learn. It was worth a try.'

* * *

Maggie had disappeared and Phoebe was about to go out back to wipe down the consulting rooms when she saw a figure heading towards the glass doors.

Not another client calling on spec, she thought, wearily, feeling a sense of déjà vu from the day before when Rufus had turned up with Archie's baby rabbit. Before she could gather herself, the door opened and she realised that it was Rufus. Although today he was minus a cardboard box, which was a relief.

Her next observation was that he didn't look very happy.

'Is everything all right?' she asked as he came in. 'How's the patient?'

'The rabbit's fine. I'm not here about that.' His eyes were dark and angry and she took an involuntary step back into the surgery. 'Harrison said you have a complaint about us polluting a stream.'

'I didn't say that.' At least she didn't think she had. 'I said we'd got a contamination incident.'

'And that it's come from our land.'

'I didn't say that either. Although, as far as we can tell, it hasn't come from ours.' She really wasn't in the mood for this. She felt too sad after Garfield's appointment.

She especially wasn't in the mood for a game of Chinese whispers passed on by his unhelpful estate manager.

'What exactly is the issue then? Perhaps you can clarify things for me in words of one syllable.' His face was the picture of antagonistic impatience.

Phoebe took a deep breath and then said very slowly, as if she was explaining something difficult to a child, 'A member of our staff found some dead wildlife up by the stream, which led us to think there may be some kind of contamination. This is the stream that runs over your land on to ours. Is that enough clarification for you?'

'Yes,' Rufus said, and he looked so cross that for a moment she expected him to stamp his foot. He didn't. He seemed to gather himself and she caught another glimpse of that icy control she'd seen once before when she'd been retrieving Maggie's donkeys from his private terrace. 'I'm sorry.' He lifted his hands up, palms facing her. 'I may have come across as a little abrupt. I've only just been told this. It worries me – this kind of thing. We had an incident once which resulted in the loss of some sheep owned by one of our tenant farmers and there was a large compensation claim –

my father was upset. We're all a bit sensitive about contamination incidents.'

That probably explained Harrison's reaction too, Phoebe thought. She nodded.

'Apology accepted.' She hesitated. 'I'm sorry too. It's been a difficult day. Maybe we should start again.'

'Yes. We probably should.' He met her eyes. 'Could you show me the stream you're concerned about? At a convenient time.'

She hadn't expected that. 'I can show you now if you're free.'

He glanced at her shoes and she followed his gaze. Smart flatties for seeing patients, but not very suitable for tramping along by streams.

'I'll just get my boots.'

12

Five minutes later, they were heading across Five Acre Field. They didn't see Maggie en route so Phoebe assumed she must have gone back into the farmhouse to get something to eat. It was probably just as well. Maggie might worry if she saw Rufus. She denied it emphatically, but Phoebe got the feeling her grandmother would definitely prefer to avoid all contact with her landlords if possible. Mind you, Maggie preferred avoiding contact with most people if she got the chance. She was much more comfortable in the company of animals.

It was warm for an end of April evening. A faint breeze ruffled the spring meadow and sent a wave rippling through the long grass across Five Acre Field. Spring flowers dotted the ground and Phoebe was reminded of the time she'd walked across this field a year ago with Archie. It felt strange to be walking across it now with his father.

Rufus was dressed for tramping around the countryside, boots, jeans, some country jacket that looked mega expensive, although she didn't imagine he spent much of his day walking round fields. She envisaged him sitting in an office signing eviction orders with a flourish of his fountain pen, like some sort of modern-day Scrooge. She smiled to herself. Where the hell had that image come from? They weren't living in the dark ages.

'What's so funny?' Rufus asked and Phoebe, surprised by the question – she hadn't realised he was looking her way – answered without editing her words.

'I was just thinking that this probably isn't how you spend your time. Walking across fields, I mean.'

'How do you think I spend my time?'

'Sitting in an office – signing... er... things.' She'd almost said eviction orders.

He laughed. Another surprise. 'That's pretty spot on. I do spend a lot of time in the office. Reading through tedious tenancies. Answering emails, going to Zoom meetings, a slave to my computer.'

She glanced at him. 'It doesn't sound as though you like it much.'

'I don't.'

There was a pause and Phoebe assumed the conversation was over, but then he said, 'I assume you do like your job. But then I guess being a vet is more of a vocation.' He narrowed his eyes and looked at her. 'Or are you going to tell me you just do it for the money?'

He was very direct. That was rare in a person, especially a lord-of-the-manor type. Phoebe wondered if he was like that with everyone. Maybe he was. Maybe it was partly what made him come across as bad-tempered.

'I've wanted to be a vet ever since I was a little girl,' she told him. 'I used to do pretend operations on my collection of toy animals. Then I spent a lot of time on this farm. It was full of animals in those days, of course.' She gestured around her at the fields, now empty of dairy cattle, and at the farmhouse which lay in the distance behind them with its red roof and smoking chimney. 'As well as the herd, there were dogs, cats, all manner of wildlife. I spent every summer holiday here. I was more familiar with this farm than I was with my own back garden.'

They'd arrived at the edge of the stream where yesterday Phoebe had found Maggie and Natasha talking, but Rufus seemed more interested in what she was saying than looking at the stream.

'I liked being outdoors too. I had a tree house.' His eyes went slightly distant as if he too were taking a trip back into the past. 'I used to sit in it and watch the deer come into the woods. And there was a barn owl. She used to fly like a ghost through the trees. Totally silent. Have you ever seen one up close?'

'Not that close.'

She stared at him fascinated. He was shattering her perceptions of landowners who had big estates. Didn't they spend their time shooting deer and pheasants and gassing badgers? Before he could break the spell and tell her he did – and that the tree house was really a hide where he'd learned to shoot – she changed the subject.

'This is the place where we found the dead wildlife.'

'Right.' His voice became more brusque. 'What did you do with it?'

'I bagged up a robin. It's in my freezer at the surgery. I thought someone from the Environment Agency might want to test it.'

'Yes. Good plan.'

For a while, they traced the stream's course up the slope towards the boundary that separated the Beechbrook Estate from the farmland.

They didn't find any more dead wildlife. Phoebe felt relieved but also a little guilty, as if she'd brought him on a wild goose chase.

They paused at the belt of woodland.

'We can catch up with the stream if we bypass the woodland,' Rufus said, gesturing. 'So, in the interests of transparency, why don't you come with me?'

'All right,' she said.

Phoebe followed him along the line of trees and then there was a gap and suddenly she could see into the woodland, which was full of bluebells. Phoebe was transported back again to when she'd come here with Archie a year ago. How the little boy had told her that his dad always said that in this part of the woods it looked as though the sky had fallen down.

It was exactly like that today; a thick floor of dazzling blue. If anything, nature had put on even more of a show than she had the previous year. There was nothing but bluebells as far as the eye could see, crammed into every space between the silver birches. Their sweet scent was in the air.

'Oh wow,' Phoebe said, temporarily unable to move. 'How incredibly beautiful.'

'Graham Joyce had it right,' Rufus murmured. 'He described it as though the sky had fallen down onto the earth floor.'

'We can't tread on them,' she said.

'We don't need to. Follow me. There's a path.'

She did as he said and seconds later she was walking in his footsteps along a path that was only just discernible, but he was right, they didn't need to tread on the bluebells. And unlike the last time she'd been here when she'd felt the edge of adrenaline because she'd known she'd been trespassing, this time she felt as though she was being taken on her own private tour through the lord of the manor's secret woods. There would be no stroppy nannies appearing to break the spell. They were in a bluebell heaven hidden from the world and accessible only by them.

A few steps ahead of her, Rufus turned left and then right and she saw that he'd been correct. The undergrowth was clearer here and they were back on course beside the stream. He glanced back at her as if to see her response and she smiled in delight. 'What an amazing place to own.'

'Do we ever own land? Or do we just borrow it from the next generation?' His brow furrowed. 'That's a quote too. Although don't ask me who said it.'

For a while they kept going along the stream. And Phoebe couldn't imagine that many places could be more idyllic. But then Rufus found the next dead creature.

The first thing Phoebe knew about his discovery was when he swore under his breath and halted abruptly. Then he hunkered down to look at something by the stream. Phoebe leaned forward just in time to see him poke at a mound of feathers on the ground.

'It's a woodpecker,' he said, glancing back at her. 'That's a shame. I haven't seen many lately. No obvious cause of death. I think you're right. I think there is something going on with this stream.'

She didn't say, 'I told you there was.' There would have been no satisfaction in the words. She just acknowledged him with a nod and watched him pick up the dead bird. He'd come prepared too – with a plastic bag. The type you could seal at the top.

'An occasional dead bird is a coincidence, but the voles as well, and this one, that's too many.' He stared into the stream, which looked clear and innocent. There was nothing else to be seen. 'I suppose this confirms that the contaminant is further upstream. Harrison did have a walk about yesterday. He didn't see anything that set off alarm bells, but we will investigate further.'

'Thank you,' Phoebe said. He was back to being businesslike Rufus. The nostalgia had gone from his eyes and there were no more Graham Joyce quotes. Phoebe wondered for a moment if she'd made up his softer mood of earlier. Maybe she'd conjured it up from her own imagination. 'I think the EA will send someone out,' Phoebe matched his professional voice. 'Maybe if you were to phone them too. You've probably got more influence than I have.'

'Yeah. There is the odd advantage to—' He broke off and then she heard the noise too. The sound of trees snapping underfoot – someone was walking close by, although it wasn't immediately apparent who it was for a moment. They were shielded by woodland. Then she saw the small figure of Archie making his way purposefully towards them.

'Dad... Hey, Dad. What are you doing?'

'Never mind what am I doing. What are you doing up here?'

'I tracked you. You didn't see me, did you? Hello, Phoebe,' he added. 'I tracked you too.' He was wearing camouflage kit which meant he did blend in pretty well with the woodland and he was looking very pleased with himself. 'You didn't hear me either, did you?'

'No. We didn't. And you shouldn't be up here. Where's Emilia?'

'On the phone to the school. Why shouldn't I?'

'Why is she on the phone to the school?' Rufus looked distracted.

'I left my blazer in the gym so she needed to phone up to make sure it's put away safely.' He widened his eyes in an expression that looked far too innocent to be genuine.

Rufus gathered himself. 'Seriously, Archie, I need you to keep out of these woods because I think we have a problem with the stream.'

'What problem?' Archie stepped forward, craning his neck and spotted the bagged-up bird. 'Is that a dead woodpecker?'

'Yes it is. And it didn't die of old age. It's been poisoned and until I find out what poisoned it, you're to stay out of these woods.'

Archie hunkered down to get a better look at the bird. 'Wow. Will it be a police matter? Is it a crime to poison birds? Or is that just if they're endangered?'

'I'll deal with this and let you know what happens.' Rufus sidestepped all of his son's questions and glanced at Phoebe apologetically.

'Thanks. How are the guinea pigs and Bob?' she asked Archie and he reluctantly dragged his gaze from the dead woodpecker and stood up.

'They're all doing well thanks. Bob's getting big. We're getting him a companion, aren't we, Dad?'

'Yes, eventually.' Rufus looked distracted. 'Can you find your way back OK?' he asked Phoebe.

'Yes, of course I can. And I promise I won't tread on any bluebells.'

'Thanks.'

'I'll be in touch about the EA.'

He'd turned slightly away from her now and she had the distinct feeling she was being dismissed. That was fair enough. He was worried.

She gave both father and son a quick nod and retraced her steps back along the stream and onto the woodland path.

13

A few minutes later, Phoebe was back in Five Acre Field and walking down the slight slope towards the farmhouse. At least the problem of the poisoned stream was no longer hers. If the lord of the manor couldn't get the Environment Agency leaping into action, then no one could.

Rufus was still an enigma, though. One minute he seemed to be almost human, and the next he was as cold and as distant as the stars. Phoebe decided to make a conscious effort to put him out of her head. They lived in different worlds. They might be able to connect as landlord and tenant. They might be able to connect as two professionals. But they were never going to be more than that. They were never going to be friends.

She let herself through the stable door into Maggie's kitchen and got an enthusiastic welcome from Buster and Tiny, the Irish Wolfhound who'd originally come in for rehoming but had somehow wheedled his way into the farmhouse kitchen. Which meant he'd also wheedled his way into her grandmother's heart. Any strays who got as far as the kitchen were there to stay.

She stroked both the dogs. There was a pan of something that smelled disgusting, simmering on the Aga. Tripe probably. Maggie cooked it up for the dogs and she didn't seem to be aware of its awful stink. Maggie herself was nowhere to be seen.

Phoebe gave the pan a stir, gagged, then swiftly put the lid back on and moved it to the edge of the hot plate.

She went to find Maggie and discovered her in the room she used as an office, sorting through some adoption cards.

Maggie glanced up as Phoebe went into the room. 'Oh hello, love. I didn't know you were still here.' Her eyes brightened. 'Some good news. Natasha has rehomed Terrence the tortoise and I think we finally have a home for Mutley, isn't that great. I thought our little barker would be here for good.'

Phoebe had thought the same thing. Little barker was an understatement when it came to Mutley, a very cute, but vociferous two-year-old Jack Russell terrier. He'd been given up by his previous owner who'd lived on a housing estate because the neighbours had complained about the noise. Both Maggie and Phoebe had thought that this was probably just an excuse to give him up – all dogs barked after all – but that was before they'd met him.

Mutley was the only dog Phoebe had ever met who actually barked himself hoarse. The slightest thing set him off – noises, imaginary noises, birds, bats, other dogs, people, vehicles, kitchen implements like the coffee percolator or the fridge door opening and shutting.

'I assume you've managed to find someone who's stone deaf and who lives in the middle of nowhere for Mutley then?' Phoebe quipped now. Maggie gave each animal she rehomed an initial assessment, so she had full knowledge of their quirks and foibles, good habits and bad ones, which could be passed on to their forever families. Maggie tended to err on the side of caution, she never played down an animal's bad points, and this meant that very few of her animals, once rehomed, came back again because prospective owners knew what to expect.

'You're not that far off.' Maggie looked very pleased with herself. 'It's a chap called Dusty Miller. That's not his real name, obviously. He lives at White Mill Farm. It's up at Cadnam. It's the last house before you get to the M27, but it's not near anything else and Dusty's very deaf. He's a friend of Eddie's. You remember Eddie? He used to be a farmhand, back in the day.'

'Of course I do. Is he still alive?' Every time her grandmother mentioned Eddie, Phoebe was afraid she was going to say he was dead. He must be at least ninety.

'Of course he is. He's only a couple of years older than me.'

'Is he? He doesn't look it.'

'Well, he is and he's coming down for a visit in a couple of weeks. He wants to see the practice. Well, he mostly wants to see you. He always asks after you.' She smiled. 'He's very fond of you.'

'And I of him. Let me know when he's coming and I'll make sure I'm about. And great news for Mutley. Did you need me to do a home check?'

'No, don't worry. Eddie vouches for Dusty. That's good enough for me. I'll meet him when he comes in next week.'

Phoebe filled her in on Rufus's visit and how they'd found the dead woodpecker. 'I know we haven't resolved anything, but at least it's in hand. And now the Holts can report it too. That might get things moving a bit faster.'

'Yes, the authorities are much more likely to jump through hoops for them, than us,' Maggie agreed. She looked happy.

Phoebe had been planning to raise the issue of needing an extra receptionist, but she didn't want to burst Maggie's bubble. She glanced at her watch. 'I didn't realise it was so late. I'd better get home.'

'OK, love, we can catch up properly tomorrow.'

* * *

They never did get the chance to catch up properly. Friday turned
out to be their busiest day yet and Phoebe hardly saw her grandmother, let alone got the chance to speak to her. Jenna was back,
luckily, and the two of them fielded calls, sorted out medication
and saw patients.

Phoebe was heartily relieved she wasn't on call this bank
holiday weekend. She paid Seth to do two weekends' cover for
her each month and so far it had worked out well. It also meant
she could have a glass of wine when she caught up with Tori on
Saturday night. Phoebe never drank anything when she was on
call. Although it was unlikely one glass of wine would affect her
judgement, it wasn't worth the risk.

* * *

At seven, she met Tori in The Brace of Pheasants. The Brace was a
country pub at Godshill, not a million miles from where Tori
lived – it was mostly frequented by locals as it was a bit off the
beaten track, but it was always busy. It had an inglenook fireplace,
a great pie chef and a range of real ales and fine wines.

Phoebe smelled the delicious aroma of baking pies and saw
Tori as soon as she pushed open the big wooden door. She was
standing at the bar, deep in conversation with a couple, one of
whom turned out to be Sam, Phoebe realised as she got closer.

None of them had seen her, which meant Phoebe had time to
study Sam's companion. Wow. No wonder she hadn't heard from
him lately. The woman he was with was very pretty. Slender, with
blonde hair that hung loose about her shoulders, she reminded
Phoebe of a young Cameron Diaz. She was laughing, her head
thrown back, as Phoebe approached and she had one hand on

Sam's arm. Her blood-red fingernails made Phoebe think fleetingly of her ex-boss, the woman her colleagues had nicknamed Cruella de Vil. She blinked away the images as she arrived at the bar.

'Hi, guys. Hey, Sam. Nice to see you.'

Sam jumped violently at the sound of her voice and his partner looked at him curiously and then a little warily at Phoebe.

'Phoebe – er, hi. Tori didn't say you were meeting.' Sam's face had reddened and he looked flustered.

Phoebe leant to peck his cheek, which felt suddenly awkward.

'I didn't get the chance,' Tori said. 'I haven't managed to get a word in edgeways yet. Hi, Pheebs. We were just talking about the New Forest Show. Sam's entered Ninja in a show-jumping class. As well as babysitting half his pupils, who are also going along, by the sound of it. Isn't that right, Sam?'

'That's right.' Sam seemed to recover himself and remember his manners. 'I'm looking forward to it. Um, Jo, this is Phoebe, a very old friend of mine. Phoebe, this is Jo...' He didn't qualify who Jo was. He'd gone even redder, if that were possible.

'It's good to meet you, Phoebe. I've heard lots about you.' Jo smiled pleasantly but her eyes were guarded and Phoebe wondered what exactly Sam had told her. She was feeling slightly in the dark because she'd have liked to be able to say something light like, 'Ditto, it's great to meet you at last.' But she couldn't because Sam had told her precisely nothing about his new girlfriend. If it hadn't been for her mother, she wouldn't even have known Jo existed.

The atmosphere still felt awkward. Tori had noticed it too. She glanced at Phoebe and then at Sam. 'Right then, I guess it's time we left you lovebirds to it. Much as we'd love to stay and chat, we have urgent girl talk to catch up on.'

'We do,' Phoebe said, noticing that Sam and Jo looked as relieved as she felt.

'Thanks,' she murmured to Tori as her friend picked up two drinks from the bar, which she must have pre-ordered, and glided away towards a table at the far end of the pub. As they sat down, Phoebe added, 'That was a bit awkward. Or am I being super-sensitive?'

'No, I don't think you were. Sam was like a cat on hot bricks.' Tori looked thoughtful. 'He wasn't like it before you turned up. If you ask me, he's still got a thing about you.'

'I don't think so, Tori. Jo's absolutely gorgeous. And she was clearly quite smitten with him.'

'That doesn't mean he hasn't still got a thing for you, though, does it? If you ask me, she's his "get over you" date. Lots of people date someone new to get over a previous relationship.'

'That only works if we'd had a relationship. Which we haven't.'

'Oh, but you have. You've been friends with Sam all your life. I think he's been in love with you for ever.'

'Tori, I was in love with Hugh. We lived together in London for six years. We were going to get married.' She wasn't sure about that last bit, but the rest was true.

'Sam never thought you were going to marry Hugh. Neither did I.' Tori sipped her drink and gave her a candid look. 'At least I hoped you weren't. He wasn't right for you.'

Phoebe felt slightly shocked. She'd suspected Tori felt like that but she'd never said it outright before.

'And you think that Sam is right for me. Is that what you're saying?' Phoebe realised she had lowered her voice, even though Sam and his new girlfriend were at the other side of the bar, and she had her back to them, and there was a Saturday-night buzz in

The Brace so no one at any other table could possibly have heard what she said.

'I think Sam's lovely, but no, I didn't say that, Pheebs.' Tori was shaking her head now and her beautiful green eyes were suddenly serious. 'I'm the last person to give relationship advice. It's taken me until the grand old age of thirty-five to find a man I think I might finally stick with.'

Phoebe could see she meant that. Her face was lit up suddenly.

'I'm so pleased for you.' Although even as she said it she remembered how grumpy Harrison had been.

'I'm pretty pleased for me too. But going back to you, do you really want to know what I think? Or am I tramping about with my size nines, poking my nose in? Just say if you'd rather I shut up. I won't be offended.'

'I don't want you to shut up. And you're allowed to poke your nose in.' Phoebe smiled to soften her words. 'You're my best friend.'

'OK. Well...' Tori took another sip of her drink and went on. 'I think that your uptight ex, AKA Heartbreaker Hugh, did such a hatchet job on your emotions, because he wasn't in touch with his own bloody emotions, that you are too scared to let yourself be vulnerable again. You are too scared of getting hurt to get close to anyone, or even to risk going on a date. You have decided to play it totally safe. Consciously or not. And you've got so used to that feeling of "safe"' – she mimed the inverted commas around the word – 'that it's become the norm. You probably wouldn't recog- nise a pass if one was wrapped up in pink ribbon and roses and lobbed at your head.' Her mouth twisted into a mock smile. 'That's a terrible metaphor for a journalist. But you get the picture.'

Phoebe nodded.

'So how am I doing? Am I anywhere close to what's happening in Phoebe's head?'

'Yes. You're pretty much spot on.' Phoebe could hear that her own voice was husky. She wanted to get up and run away. Or drink a lot more wine. Neither of which was really an option. Not a grown-up option anyway.

'Thought so.' Tori held her gaze. 'The question is, what would you like to do about it?'

14

_____

On the other side of the bar, Sam was feeling unsettled. It had jolted him bumping into Phoebe. He hadn't seen her for ages. Not since he'd been dating Jo. He'd managed to get Phoebe out of his mind in the same way he'd done when she'd been living in London with Hugh. Only it had been easier when she'd been in London. For one thing, he'd been seeing Judy back then. He'd been happy. Not that he wasn't happy with Jo, but it was different since Phoebe had been back. He'd declared his feelings to her – he'd put all his cards on the table and Phoebe had said categorically that she wasn't interested in more than friendship.

Sam thought he had accepted this, but when he'd seen her tonight, when she'd stood opposite him, looking her usual beautiful self, he had felt his heart clench so painfully that he'd known he was kidding himself. He might have managed to bury his feelings, but they certainly hadn't gone.

'Earth calling, Sam. Hey, where are you tonight?' He became aware that Jo was speaking to him and he blinked as her face came back into focus.

'I'm sorry.' He managed a smile, but she didn't look very reassured.

'Sam, you've been acting weird since we bumped into those women. At least that's what it looks like from where I'm sitting. The one that came in – Phoebe – is she really just an old friend? Or is there more to it? Did you two ever have a thing?'

'No, we didn't. Never.' He could feel himself reddening again and he cursed the gene that caused embarrassment to flare on his skin.

'I mean, it's OK if you have, obviously.' Jo was looking at him curiously. 'We don't get to our age without having baggage, do we?'

'There has never been anything between Phoebe and I.' He felt as if he were denying the same thing over and over and he felt guilty, even though it was true. 'We were childhood friends, that's all. Myself, Tori, Phoebe and her brother, Frazier. We grew up together.'

'And are you all still close?'

'Not as close as we used to be. Our lives have gone in different directions. Frazier's married with twins. Tori's the editor of *New Forest Views*, and Phoebe's a vet. She set up her own practice in a barn on Puddleduck Farm, which belongs to her grandmother. Until last Christmas she was living in London with her partner who was also a vet. But they split up and she came home.' He paused. 'My pa refurbished the barn and I saw a fair bit of Phoebe while that was going on.'

'But not in a romantic sense.'

Sam shook his head. He wondered if he should tell Jo that if he'd had his way it would have been romantic. But what was the point? She'd probably walk away there and then and he wouldn't have blamed her.

'Is she seeing anyone else?' Jo asked idly.

'I don't know. I haven't spoken to her lately.' Sam glanced across the pub and saw that, in the far corner, Phoebe and Tori were laughing uproariously at something. They looked as though they were having a whale of a time. He picked up his glass of real ale – Jo, bless her, had offered to drive them and he took a slug. 'I would think she probably is,' he added. 'I've never known her be that long without a partner.'

Jo leaned across and touched his arm and there was such sweetness in her eyes that Sam felt worse than ever. 'Thanks for being honest with me. I know that we haven't been seeing each other very long, but I really like what we have.'

'Me too,' Sam said, meeting her eyes. That was the truth, at least.

* * *

Phoebe was on her third glass of wine. Tori had persuaded her it was high time she let her hair down and had a few drinks.

'I can give you a lift back to yours, or, better still, mine – we can get a bottle from the offie en route and then you can stay over and we can pick your car up in the morning,' she'd said. 'It'll be just like old times.'

For a while when Phoebe had first moved back from London, she'd lived in Tori's flat and her head had flashed back to late-night toast, coffee and gossip, and suddenly the idea of a stopover with her friend seemed very appealing.

After three glasses of wine, she was committed. And she did feel a lot better. Everything had gone slightly fuzzy around the edges. Their conversation was sparkling, everything they said seemed funny and the old wooden tables and mismatched chairs had taken on a rose-tinted hue. They'd ordered pies, which had just arrived, and they had sorted out Phoebe's love life. The answer, at least in Tori's opinion, was for Phoebe to go to a dinner club event at New Forest Diners – this would ease her gently back into the dating scene. Under the influence of her second glass of wine, Phoebe had agreed that she would. They had booked it online before she could change her mind.

Now, over their pies – chicken and mushroom for Phoebe and beef and ale for Tori – they had moved on to Tori's love life.

'I want to know all about Harrison,' Phoebe said.

'Do you mean you want to know if we've done the deed, what it was like? What our intentions are? All that kind of stuff?'

'I want to know every mucky detail.' Phoebe frowned. 'OK, maybe not every detail. But I definitely want to know what it's like inside Beechbrook House.' Where had that come from? She put a forkful of pie in her mouth. It was fun being tipsy. It took all the brakes off her inhibitions.

'OK, I'll start with the house and build up to the exciting stuff.' Tori's eyes went dreamy. 'There are lots of rooms. Think antique furniture, heavy drapes, dust. Loads of dust. And a lot of dingy old portraits. Mostly of serious-faced ancestors. Harrison did tell me some of the history when he did the tour – I think the family were originally investment bankers.' She paused. 'They go back a long way. A monied old family, hence the lordship. But going back to the house, some of the rooms are closed up and a lot of them are hardly used, which is handy, because Harrison and I have made full use of them – if you know what I mean?'

'Are you saying that you've...?'

'Mmm hmmm.' Tori's eyes glittered with mischief. 'If you haven't made love in a four-poster bed, you haven't really lived.'

'That's outrageous. Doesn't anyone mind?' The image of Rufus on a four-poster bed shot into Phoebe's head and she blanked it out.

'No one knows.' Tori grinned. 'Old Lord Holt lives in the east wing and Rufus, Archie and Emilia live in the middle section. The four-poster bed I'm talking about is in the west wing.'

'Is that where Harrison lives?'

'No, he's in the gatehouse. That's a cute house too. But small.'

'I wondered who lived there.' Phoebe blinked away several more images involving four-poster beds she wished hadn't come into her head. 'Don't get caught will you.'

'We won't get caught. It was only the once, to be fair. We're not that disrespectful. I don't think Rufus knows I even exist. Which is how I'd like to keep it.'

'Yes, I can see why. But don't you ever bump into him?'

'No. He's a total workaholic. Not to mention a recluse. His father plays golf and goes off from time to time, but Rufus is holed up in his office. As far as I can tell, he conducts all his meetings on Zoom and the only place he ever goes to is Archie's school if he absolutely has to.' She hesitated. 'If I do see him, shall I put in a good word for you?'

'Ye... No.' Phoebe corrected herself. 'Tell me some more about Harrison. I met him the other day.'

'No way. Why haven't you told me?'

'This is the first time I've had the chance.' Phoebe told her about the poisoned stream and going up to Beechbrook House.

'So you saw him to speak to? What did you think?'

'I thought he was...' She'd been about to say rude. 'Er... a man of few words.'

'Oh, that's Harrison all over. He doesn't say much. He can come across as a bit abrupt when you first meet him, but that's just his manner. He's amazing once you get to know him. I promise you'll agree with me once you know him properly. Did you tell him who you were?'

'Only that I was one of the tenants. Why? Does he know we're friends?'

'I may have mentioned you. I'm not sure. We talk about so many things.'

Phoebe sipped her drink. She was beginning to feel a little light-headed. 'What is it about him that you like so much?'

Tori put down her knife and fork. Her eyes were shining. 'OK. In a nutshell. Harrison is the best I've ever had. Does that sound shallow and sexist?' She grinned as Phoebe nodded vigorously. 'Sorry, but it's true. He's also amazingly thoughtful – very clever too, considering his job, I mean. Did I tell you he went to Cambridge? He comes from quite a well-to-do family. He did the whole public school boarders thing. That's where he met Rufus. He's even Archie's godfather. He and Rufus have been friends since the year dot apparently.'

That made sense, Phoebe thought, fascinated. Everything she knew about lords and landowners, which was, in fact, very little, told her that it was a closed world that began in childhood, if not the womb. Friendships were forged, unbreakable bonds were made, and whatever happened later on, however much lives diverged, these tended to hold fast.

'Harrison graduated with quite a good degree in applied physics. Not a first though, which was what his parents wanted for him. Basically, the story is that they had a big bust-up and he dropped out.'

'He dropped out of university?'

'No, he dropped out of their lives. Just cut himself off from his family. Cut the umbilical cord totally. Travelled around Europe for a few years and then came back and started working for Rufus.'

'That sounds pretty brave. But also a shame.' Phoebe thought of her own family. The warmth and support she always felt when she was in their midst. 'I mean, that he doesn't have a big support network.'

'Not all families are like yours and mine, though, are they? Some families are crap from the get-go. Harrison's parents were all about how things looked. There wasn't a lot of love there. It was all about achieving. Harrison had a younger sister who committed suicide when she was eighteen, because she couldn't stand the pressure.'

'Oh my God.' Phoebe shook her head. 'How tragic.'

'Yes, isn't it. Rufus didn't fare that much better apparently,' Tori went on idly. 'His mum died when he was young and he was never allowed to speak about it again. Like Harrison, he grew up in a boarding school without a lot of love. It's not all that surprising that he grew up behaving like an arrogant dick.'

'He doesn't always behave like that.' Phoebe found herself flying to Rufus's defence without thinking. 'I've seen a much gentler side to him.'

Tori's eyebrows went up a fraction. 'I knew he must have a good side for him and Harrison to be such good pals,' she said. 'But I didn't know you'd seen it. How come? Did you go on that dinner date after all?'

'No.' Phoebe knew she was blushing. The disadvantage of drinking was that it also loosened your tongue and it was ages since she'd been this inebriated. She pushed her almost finished pie to one side. Oh well, in for a penny, in for a pound.

She told Tori about Rufus bringing Archie's rabbit into the surgery. And about him coming back the next day to rant about the stream. About their foray up into the bluebell wood. She even told her about the erotic dream.

Tori didn't interrupt. She listened thoughtfully, her eyes empathetic, and then, when Phoebe finally ran out of things to tell, she leaned forward and touched her friend's hand. 'That explains a lot.'

'Does it? What does it explain?' Phoebe felt vulnerable again and slightly hazy. So much for the pie sobering her up.

'Well, it explains why you turned down Sam when he told you he'd like to be more than friends. It also explains why you haven't dated anyone else. You're too hooked up on the lord of the manor.'

'I'm too hooked up on an impossible fantasy,' Phoebe said sadly. 'I'm not completely deluded. I do know it's not going to happen.'

'But you don't know it's not going to happen.' Tori paused, and her eyes were thoughtful. 'I've noticed the chemistry. I don't think it's one-way. That time at the launch. There was definitely something there. And he didn't have to bring Archie's rabbit in to see you. Or turn up to talk about the stream. He has minions to do that kind of thing. He has Harrison for a start and that snotty Swiss-German nanny.' She knocked back the last of her wine and Phoebe saw that her plate was empty. 'Have you finished eating?' Tori added, glancing at the remains of Phoebe's pie. 'Shall we get going. We need to discuss this further.'

Did they? Phoebe wasn't so sure, but she knew there was no arguing with Tori when she had that determined look in her eyes.

They both stood up and went to the bar together to pay the bill. When Phoebe glanced over to where she thought Sam and Jo had been sitting, she couldn't see them. She felt an odd sense of loss, which was at odds with all the things she'd just told Tori. How could she be hankering after Rufus and yet still feel a sense of loss that Sam had moved on? It didn't make sense. She didn't yearn for her old life in London with Hugh, definitely not, but she did long for a time when everything had been simple. A time when she hadn't felt so conflicted.

15

———

The following morning, Phoebe woke up with the hangover from hell. It also took her a few moments to realise where she was. A room that was familiar, but not familiar. Her eyes slowly adjusted and she recognised Tori's spare room. The blue flower-patterned curtains and white Ikea furniture against cream painted walls. She could hear Tori moving around in the kitchen and she thought she could smell coffee. Then just as she was considering moving, there was a knock on the door and Tori's smiling face appeared. She looked in fine shape for someone who didn't like late nights.

'I've brought you caffeine.' Tori's voice was bright. 'How are you feeling?'

'Awful,' Phoebe told her. 'How come you're not?'

'I was driving. Remember?' Tori bounded in, put a mug of coffee on the bedside table and perched on the edge of the bed.

'You weren't driving when we got back here.' Phoebe had a vague memory of them getting a couple of bottles of Prosecco from the offie. 'Did we drink all that wine?'

'Not all of it, no. But I've had more practice than you lately by the sound of it. You'll feel better after a coffee and some toast. Or, better still, croissants. I've got some in the freezer – shall I get those out?'

'OK,' Phoebe said, sitting up cautiously and realising she had one of Tori's nightshirts on. 'I don't even remember going to bed. What time did we get to bed anyway?'

'About one-ish, I think. I made you drink a pint of water. That should have helped with the dehydration anyway.'

Phoebe glanced at the empty pint glass on her bedside table. 'Thanks.' She groaned. 'Remind me not to do that again any time soon.'

'Au contraire,' Tori said. 'You need to do it more often. You're obviously out of practice. We didn't have that much to drink. And we had a pie too. It was fun though, wasn't it?' She sounded suddenly wistful. 'It's been ages since we caught up properly.'

'It was fun.' Phoebe sipped her coffee. A disturbing memory was flickering in the back of her mind, but she couldn't quite pinpoint it. 'Did I do anything last night that I'm going to regret this morning?'

'Not unless you mean telling me all your secret fantasies about the lord of the manor. But don't worry, that was all strictly off the record. My lips are sealed.'

Phoebe blinked. 'Hmmm, I do have a vague memory of that. Just remember that the word fantasy is key and that if you ever tell anyone, I *will* kill you.' She gulped more coffee. 'Also, remember that I know far too many of your secrets.'

'Oh, I will.' They both smiled at each other. 'And don't forget what I told you – I'm not convinced it's as one-sided as you think. He might be a future lord, but he's still a man, isn't he? And you are a gorgeous, intelligent, warm and lovely woman. Seriously, Phoebe, you're quite a catch.'

Her green eyes were bright with affection and Phoebe was

more touched than she wanted to admit. 'Thanks,' she said huskily. She finished her coffee. 'Oh crap,' she said suddenly. 'I've just remembered what it was I did.'

'What?' Tori looked alarmed.

'I agreed to go on that New Forest supper club thingy. Can I cancel it?'

'You'll lose your money, but yes, you can cancel it if you like. But why do you want to? You might enjoy it.'

Phoebe doubted that very much. But maybe she was being negative.

By the time they'd had croissants and more coffee she felt recovered enough to agree that maybe she would enjoy it. It wasn't until the 21st May, so she had plenty of time to decide.

They went back to collect her car at lunchtime, had another coffee at The Brace and then she finally set off back to Woodcutter's Cottage.

'Thanks,' she said, giving Tori a goodbye hug. 'You're right, we should do this more often. Aside from the hangover bit, I mean. It's been really lovely.'

* * *

Sam was at Brook stables. He'd just finished giving a private jumping lesson to a ten-year-old girl whose parents thought she was destined to be the next Ellen Whitaker. Sam did not share this optimistic opinion. The girl was loud and heavy-handed and didn't listen to much of what he said. Which meant he had to constantly repeat himself. Sam was known for his tolerance and patience with young riders, but today he felt tested to the limit. It had been hard not to let his irritation show.

By the time the lesson was finally over, he'd felt both on edge and relieved. Henrietta Blackstone, aka Ellen Whitaker, had headed off laughing and chatting with her parents while Sam led her long-suffering pony, Benjamín Blackstone, who was at livery at Brook, back to the stable block.

His teaching commitments finished, Sam tacked up his own horse, Ninja, and set off from the stables for a hack. He'd ridden more than he usually did lately because he needed Ninja to be in top condition for the New Forest Show at the end of July, which was now just only eleven weeks away.

It had been a while since he'd done any competing and Sam was excited about it and also a little apprehensive. Jo had been encouraging him – it was one of the things he really liked about her – her passion for all things horse. She didn't ride herself – she seemed happy to do it vicariously through her daughter.

'You should try it,' Sam had said to her once. 'If you learn, then we could all go riding together. You, me and Abi.'

'I think one rider in the family is costly enough,' Jo had told him laughingly. 'I'll leave the riding to you two. I can always follow you on my bicycle.'

'That's true,' Sam had said. 'Bicycles can get to most places horses can.' And they were a lot cheaper. He knew Jo wasn't exactly flush. Unfortunately, neither was he.

Now he turned Ninja along a familiar sandy track that sloped gently upwards. The thud of his horse's hooves was muted on the soft ground. It had rained overnight. Puddles edged the pathway and everything smelled fresh and clear. Sam loved the smell of rain-washed forest. If ever there was a smell of green, that was it.

Maybe it wasn't just Henrietta who'd upset his equilibrium today, he mused as he sent Ninja from a walk into a slow canter. Things had gone a bit pear-shaped last night after they'd bumped into Tori and Phoebe. Despite the conversation he'd had about it afterwards with Jo, Sam had sensed a tension between them that hadn't really gone and they hadn't stayed in The Brace much longer. Jo had said she was tired and so they'd left around nine. On their way out, Sam had sneaked a glance across at Phoebe and Tori and had seen that they were still laughing. Phoebe had looked happy and for that he was glad. Then he'd been aware that Jo had spotted him looking and there had been something in her eyes. But she hadn't said anything.

He came back to the present with a start as Ninja shied at a bird in a gorse bush, jolting him out of the saddle and almost unseating him.

'Whoa there. Steady. Steady, boy. Nothing to alarm us.' He spoke to the flighty thoroughbred cross he'd owned since he was a youngster, as he brought him back to a trot. 'Just a bird. Nothing scary.'

That would teach him to drift off when they were mid canter.

When they were walking once more in the afternoon sunshine along a wide path edged with gorse, Sam let his thoughts drift back to Jo.

She had stopped over at his flat last night. A rare occurrence because of Abi. But the child was with her grandparents for the bank holiday. Although Sam got on well with Jo's daughter and Abi knew he was friends with her mum, Jo didn't want Abi to be party to stopovers. Not yet. Not until she was sure that their relationship was going somewhere. Sam respected that.

He'd really been looking forward to this weekend and spending more time in Jo's company. But seeing Phoebe had thrown him. And he knew his reaction had thrown Jo. She had been distant even when they'd got back to his – even when they'd been making love. But afterwards, when they'd lain in the soft afterglow, and he'd asked her if she was OK, she'd said she was fine. Sam hadn't fully believed her. But he hadn't pushed it. They were at such an early stage of their relationship that he didn't yet know all the rhythms of her moods.

For Sam, everything had rhythms. The seasons, the weather, horses, work, relationships. They all had cycles and seasons. They were all repetitive but subtle. He didn't yet know Jo's rhythms. So maybe he was making mountains out of molehills, reacting to imagined problems. Imagined tensions. He was sure they would sort it out. They spoke most evenings.

And tomorrow was bank holiday Monday. They'd planned lunch together. They could talk then.

But when Sam called to pick up Jo the following lunchtime, he discovered that Abi had come home from her grandparents a day early. She'd felt homesick, Jo explained, and had wanted to come back.

This meant there were three of them for lunch. Sam didn't mind this one bit, he enjoyed Abi's company, but it had meant there was no chance for him and Jo to talk about anything that might be bothering her. So Sam kept his worries to himself and hoped that time would smooth things over.

* * *

A girlie stopover and a heart-to-heart was the perfect antidote to work, Phoebe decided as the rest of the weekend flashed by. She felt lighter than she had for weeks. It was true what they said about a problem shared being a problem halved – Rufus hadn't exactly been a problem, but he'd been a symptom of one. Tori had been spot on about the reasons she hadn't dated anyone. She hadn't wanted to get hurt again. She was beginning to think that fancying Rufus was actually quite a big part of her survival strategy too. While she was busy hankering after some unobtainable man she was oblivious to any available men. That had been a revelation. But now the blinkers were well and truly removed, she had no plans to go diving into a full-on relationship. She didn't want or need one, but it would be nice to have something other than work in her life. Although there were things that needed sorting out at work too.

Burley Bunnies was one of these. Phoebe needed to find out more about them. She wanted to go and see them, maybe posing as a prospective buyer would be good. But she had another more pressing concern closer to home. She needed to talk to Maggie about employing another receptionist. Which she planned to do on Tuesday morning.

* * *

Maggie beat her to it. Her grandmother was already in reception on Tuesday when Phoebe arrived at Puddleduck Vets, half an hour earlier than usual. She was behind the desk writing something on an index card.

'You're early,' Phoebe said, strolling in. 'Couldn't you sleep?'

'Old people don't need much sleep,' Maggie said, glancing up. 'It's one of the perks. There have to be some perks to counteract the annoying things like arthritis and random aches and pains and the increasing difficulty I have with patience and tolerance. I used to have an abundance of patience and tolerance.'

'Only with animals,' Phoebe countered. 'I don't remember you ever having much with people.'

'You know me so well,' Maggie said, with a gleam in her eye. 'Then again, most people are a pain in the backside. Present company excepted, of course.'

'Phew. I'm glad I'm excluded.' Phoebe took a step closer to reception. 'What are you doing anyway?'

'I'm transferring my card index onto the computer system for when you take on a new young thing to do reception duties.'

Phoebe opened her mouth to say something, but before she could speak, Maggie continued.

'I know I've outstayed my welcome, darling. It's OK. I'm aware that I'm not the ideal person for the job. You're trying to build your business up. You don't need a grumpy old woman sitting here glowering at people who don't know how to look after their animals properly, telling them things they don't want to hear. Scaring them off.'

'You don't scare people off.'

'We both know that's not for want of trying.' She lowered her eyes. 'I've come to the conclusion that being a vet receptionist brings out the worst in me.'

Phoebe shook her head. 'OK, maybe it does a bit, but that doesn't mean I don't appreciate you. You've been brilliant. I couldn't have got any of this going without you.'

'You don't need to sweet-talk me,' Maggie said. And then when Phoebe paused, 'Although you could carry on for a bit longer if you like...'

Phoebe realised she had missed this too. The banter they'd always shared. 'I think I've been more stressed than I've realised lately,' she said. 'It's taken me by surprise how fast we've built up a client base and it feels different being totally responsible for a practice. A lot different than just working for someone else.'

'Yes, my darling. It is different. Responsibility is one of those things that's heavier than we realise. I think it maybe gets heavier over time too.'

Phoebe was very aware that her grandmother knew all about responsibility. Not just the decades of running a dairy farm when she'd had Farmer Pete, her beloved husband and Phoebe's granddad to help her, but the years of running an animal shelter, single-handedly. At least until recently.

'Getting the right sort of help is key to managing it,' Maggie went on. 'Taking on Natasha is one of the best things I ever did. The animals are happier, I'm not as tired. And I only did that because I was *encouraged*, shall we say, by my very supportive family.'

'Forced, you mean,' Phoebe said.

'Forced, encouraged, manipulated – all similar words.' Maggie waved a dismissive hand. 'The point is I needed the help. And you lot made me see that I did. To be honest, there are other things I'd like to do with my retirement. I've been thinking about them.'

They were interrupted by the sound of the door opening and Jenna breezed in.

'Morning, ladies, you're early birds. Did you both have a good bank holiday?'

'We did. Thank you.'

They all smiled at each other. And another week had begun.

* * *

On Wednesday afternoon, in a gap between appointments, Jenna, Maggie and Phoebe drafted out an advert for a full-time receptionist to work at Puddleduck Vets.

On Thursday afternoon, Emilia brought Bob, Archie's rabbit, in for a check-over and Phoebe was relieved on two counts. Firstly, that the young lop-eared rabbit was so much better than the last time she'd seen him and, secondly, that it was Emilia who'd come in and not Rufus.

Archie's nanny was formal and polite. Phoebe suspected that some of her brusque manner was probably just due to communication difficulties because English wasn't her first language. She certainly seemed pleasant enough and clearly cared about Bob.

'Mr Holt asked me to tell you that the Environment Agency are coming to see him,' Emilia said. 'He also asked me to give you this.' She handed over a business card to Phoebe, which had the name Burley Bunnies in gold embossed lettering on a white background. There was a picture of a gold rabbit leaping over a ditch.

Phoebe tucked the card into her bag with a sigh of satisfaction. Finally, they had an address. She had no intention of dashing off to visit Burley Bunnies without a proper plan. If she was going to be posing as a prospective buyer, she'd need to wait for the woman to advertise again. But she would be paying Belinda Bates a visit as soon as she possibly could.

16

On Friday afternoon, Dusty Miller arrived to collect Mutley, and Maggie asked Phoebe if she would give the little Jack Russell a quick check-over before he went off to his new home.

'Absolutely,' Phoebe said. 'We'll make it the last appointment of the day if that's OK?' She was thinking of the noise levels. If Mutley was on his usual form, he was likely to bark throughout most of the appointment.

Dusty Miller turned out to be a grey-haired, pink-faced, dapper little man dressed in tweeds who could have been anywhere between sixty-five and eighty. He didn't seem to be wearing a hearing aid, which surprised her.

'He can lip-read,' Maggie told her cheerfully. 'Don't worry. Just make sure you're facing him when you speak and you'll be fine.'

Phoebe showed the pair into the consulting room and asked Dusty if he could lift the Jack Russell onto the table.

A beaming Dusty instantly lifted up one end of the examining table and looked at her for further instructions and Phoebe realised he'd got the wrong end of the stick.

'We need to lift Mutley up,' she told him, enunciating the words as clearly as she could.

'Why didn't you say?' he shouted, his eyebrows raised in bemusement. He shook his head and bent to lift his new dog, who was already barking incessantly, up onto the table.

It was just as well they were relying on lip-reading, Phoebe thought, as she ran her hands over the little dog's brown and white patched coat. It would have been hard to communicate with anyone above the din Mutley was making. She had to dig her fingers in to feel his ribs, but he hardly paused for breath.

'He's a little too heavy,' she told Dusty loudly.

He looked blank, so Phoebe tried another way.

'Mutley's a bit overweight.'

Still nothing. So much for lip-reading.

She pointed at her own midriff. 'Fat tummy.'

Dusty looked shocked. 'No way.' He drew a curvy shape in the air with his hands and shouted at the top of his voice, 'Perfect proportions. You are "*bellissimo*", as they say in Italy.' Still beaming, he blew her a kiss.

'Not me,' Phoebe shouted, thinking quickly. 'But thank you.' She smiled, before she realised that Dusty had only caught the last word she'd said – *you*. Or perhaps, you was the only one she'd said clearly enough for him to lip-read.

'Me?' he asked, before bursting into peals of laughter. 'I know. Too many pies. Hey, fellow.' He glanced with great affection at Mutley. 'Meat and potato pies. They're my favourite, you see. It's OK for him to have the odd pie, isn't it, doc? I'm not a big fan of the tinned rubbish they palm you off with in the shops – load of old slop, not proper food for dogs – but if I just give him the meat. Would that be all right?'

Phoebe made the gesture of small with her finger and thumb and Dusty nodded enthusiastically.

'I won't overdo it. He's a bit on the tubby side, already. Don't you think?'

'Yes.' She nodded in relief.

The conversation went on in this vein for a few more minutes. She would suggest something, Dusty would misunderstand and then they'd get to it in a roundabout way. Mutley barked on and off throughout, but Dusty appeared to be oblivious.

It was one of the most convoluted, not to mention noisiest, consultations Phoebe had ever had with a client. Thank God it was the last appointment of the day and there was no one out in the waiting room to overhear. Maggie may have overestimated Dusty's ability as a lip-reader, but she was absolutely right about one thing, he was the perfect owner for the constantly barking Mutley. It was a match made in heaven.

* * *

Finally, they were done and Dusty took Mutley back out to reception while Phoebe got him some flea and wormer treatment.

When she brought it through, she found him talking to Jenna via a series of hand signals, which seemed to be working a lot better than lip-reading, and then he was finally off with his dog.

'He was a character,' Jenna said as she updated the new patient registration and for a few moments she and Phoebe laughed about the eccentricities of customers. 'It's one of the things I love about this job,' Jenna admitted. 'There is nothing quite as quirky as pet owners. When I was working at Seth's, we had this woman come in with a dachshund one day that had a rash. Seth had just finished examining it when the woman mentioned she had a similar rash. Then before Seth could stop her she whipped off her top and whisked out her boobs to show us the rash. I've never known Seth move so fast. He leapt across the other side of the consulting room in a flash. And his face was the colour of a ripe tomato. It was so funny. Although not at the time.'

'I bet.' Phoebe suppressed a giggle at this vivid evocation of her ex-boss. She could imagine exactly the expression of horror on his face. 'What did he tell the client?'

'That he wasn't qualified to diagnose people, only dogs, and that she'd need to see her doctor. She wasn't a bit bothered that she was standing in our consulting room with her boobs out. She was quite put out if anything. She kept saying, "can't you just have a quick look? My doctor's totally useless. Besides, I thought you lot had to train longer than doctors do."'

'Priceless,' Phoebe said.

'It was. I don't think she ever came back again. Her dachshund was quite old, but for years afterwards we used to wind Seth up and tell him Mrs Radcliffe had booked an appointment and was refusing to see anyone but him. You only had to say "Mrs Radcliffe's here" and he'd be hotfooting it out of the back door.' Jenna chuckled as she finished updating the computer and pressed enter. 'The trials and tribulations of being a vet. Oh, by the way, a man came in for you just now,' she added and glanced at her notepad. 'Rufus Holt. Isn't he the lord of the manor chap?'

'Oh?' Phoebe's heart skipped a beat despite herself. 'Did he say what he wanted?'

'No. Just that he needed a quick word. I couldn't really deny that you were here as we could hear most of what you were saying to Dusty in the consulting room. He said he'd pop back when you were finished. I hope that's OK?'

'That's fine. I'll go and see if I can find him. Are you all right to finish up?'

'Sure I am. You go.'

Phoebe thanked her and went to find Rufus. There had been a

part of her that had truly expected she wouldn't see him again. Tori had been right when she'd said he had absolutely no reason to call round personally. Phoebe was half pleased and half worried that he seemed to have found one.

He was in the car park. Sitting at the wheel of the beat-up old Land Rover that she had presumed belonged to, or at least was used by, Harrison. He got out when he saw her approaching. He was casually dressed – jeans and a leather jacket that looked old and worn but mega expensive. Everything about Rufus screamed class and money – even when it was patently obvious he wasn't trying. Maybe even especially when he wasn't trying.

'Good evening, Phoebe. I hope this isn't a bad time.'

'No, it's fine. I've just finished appointments. Is everything OK?'

He looked serious and she felt a clench of foreboding in her stomach.

'Yes and no.' He shifted from one foot to the other and once again she had the impression of a man who was uncomfortable in social situations. 'I wanted to give you an update on the contamination incident.'

'OK. Have the Environment Agency been out?'

'No, not yet, but... It's probably easier if I show you. Have you got half an hour?'

'Yes. Sure. Shall I follow you?'

'It's probably easier if we both go in this.' He opened the passenger door for her. 'It's cleaner inside than out.'

She climbed in and he got back into the driver's side. He waited for her to do up her seat belt before he pulled away. Phoebe was very conscious of him sitting beside her. The line of his jaw, the curve of his dark hair, his hands on the steering wheel. Strong hands for someone who sat in an office all day.

Neither of them spoke, but Phoebe felt as if the air was crackling with chemistry. There might be absolutely nothing between them. The whole chemistry thing might be totally in her head, but that didn't mean it felt any less real. That was for goddamn sure.

Rufus turned right out of the Puddleduck entrance and then kept going along the high wall of his estate. As they approached the gatehouse, he indicated to turn right and they were through the archway with the stag on top and driving up the long drive. He hadn't elaborated about where they were going and Phoebe, assuming he'd tell her when he was ready, hadn't asked him.

It felt odd being driven up to Beechbrook House by the lord of the manor himself. Phoebe had once been on holiday with Hugh to an Italian castle in Tuscany that had been owned by a count and countess who'd been friends with Hugh's parents. To welcome them, the countess had picked them a basket of figs from a tree in the grounds and Hugh had joked that it wasn't often you had fresh figs hand-picked for you by a countess. Phoebe felt a bit like that now.

She'd expected Rufus to drive straight up to the house, but he stopped at a five-bar gate on their left before they reached it. He hopped out to open the gate, drove the Land Rover through and shut it again.

They bumped off across the field. He was a skilled off-road driver, clearly at ease behind the wheel.

'Are we going anywhere nice?' Phoebe remarked when they reached another gate and Rufus still hadn't said anything. 'Not that magical mystery tours aren't fun.'

He glanced at her. 'Sorry. I didn't say, did I? Don't worry, I'm not abducting you.'

Had he just made a joke? Phoebe mused. If any other man had said that to her in these circumstances, she would have thought so, but it was hard to tell with Rufus. He didn't smile much. Although she was pretty sure he wasn't abducting her.

'ETA's approximately six and a half minutes,' he added, getting out to open the next gate.

Phoebe had always wanted to know what lay behind the high walls of Beechbrook Estate and now she did. Unsurprisingly it wasn't a lot different than the landscape of Puddleduck Farm. Although where Puddleduck Farm had carved grazing land out of the landscape, here there was a lot more woodland. It was mostly plantations, rather than the ancient forest that surrounded them, but it had still lain untouched, she guessed, for generations.

They were now on a track that wound in and out of the silver birch woods and was obviously well used. Rufus drove along it for a few hundred yards and then parked the Land Rover and they both got out. Phoebe realised they must be close to the outer boundaries of the estate. On their left through a gap in the trees, she could see stock fencing curving around what looked like the boundaries of the Beechbrook land. Beyond that were gorse bushes and the undulating familiar landscape of the forest.

There were shaggy brown ponies dotted about and, close to the fence, a foal ambled along behind its dam, seemingly oblivious to the humans.

'Cute,' Phoebe remarked, gesturing towards the foal. Rufus, who was beside her, nodded and she saw the muscles in his face tighten. He wasn't a fan of horses then. She remembered Sam saying he didn't like them much. It must be difficult not liking horses when you lived in the New Forest and were surrounded by them.

Phoebe took a deep breath of the untainted countryside air – the scent of gorse and trees and freshness. 'That's what I love about living here,' she said. 'The smell of the forest. And the peace. Nothing but birdsong.'

'I love that too.' Rufus glanced at her. 'Far from the madding crowd.'

'You're a fan of Thomas Hardy?'

'Yeah, I guess I am. I read all his books when I was a child. We had to read him. Most of the boys complained he was over-wordy and boring. I never let on that I loved the stories. Especially *Under The Greenwood Tree* and *Far From The Madding Crowd*.'

The more she found out about him, the more he surprised her. She wouldn't have had Rufus down as a reader. At least not of classic novels. She had no idea why this was. No doubt he'd have had the best classical education money could buy.

'I loved reading too,' she told him. 'Reading and being outdoors. Did you grow up on this estate?'

'My time was divided between home and school,' he told her. 'I didn't often have friends back so when I was here I spent a lot of time reading.'

For a moment, she imagined them growing up a stone's throw from each other. But whereas she'd had Tori and Sam, not to mention her brother, Frazier, as playmates, it sounded as though Rufus had been very much alone.

As they'd been talking, they'd also been walking, heading into a more densely wooded part of the Beechbrook Estate. They were still on a track, of sorts, but it was the kind only animals used. She could see why they'd left the Land Rover behind. It wouldn't have got much further.

The woods were still dotted with bluebells. Still vibrantly beautiful. In another fortnight, they would start to fade and then they'd be gone for another year. Then Rufus halted so suddenly she almost cannoned into him.

They had just reached a small clearing and through the trees Phoebe caught a glimpse of metallic yellow that was even brighter and more shocking than it should have been because it stood out against the natural browns and greens of its surroundings. There was also, oddly, a gap in the faded bluebell beauty of the forest floor.

Phoebe realised they were looking at half a dozen oil barrels that had been dumped in the clearing, evidently some time ago because the undergrowth had grown up around them. Although not the bluebells. She could see the words, CAUTION. HAZARDOUS WASTE inked in black capitals on one of them.

She gasped, as Rufus turned back towards her.

'Those are most likely the source of our stream contamination,' he said, his face very grave.

Phoebe nodded. She could see rust spots on the barrel closest to where they stood and a thick line of rust around the rim.

'As you can see,' Rufus continued, 'a couple of them have rusted right through and the contents must have been seeping into the ground for some time. We're not very far from the stream. It's a few metres south of where we're standing, so in heavy rainfall whatever was in these barrels would be washed straight in.' He looked grim. 'If I'd known they were here before, we could have done something about it. But as you can see' – he gestured around them – 'you'd be unlikely to happen across them by accident. Which is presumably why they were dumped here. This is just inside our boundary. They must have driven right up to the fence.' He pointed and Phoebe saw the wire of the boundary fence a few metres away. 'We're not far from the road here.'

'So I see.' Phoebe felt a flash of anger at the callousness of the people who'd done this. 'They must have deliberately put them over your fence,' she gasped. 'Why go to the trouble of doing that?'

'Probably because there's less chance of discovery and hence prosecution. Fly-tipping is quite a problem for us, and for the whole forest, as I'm sure you're aware. There is CCTV all over the place. If a truck just dumps stuff at the side of the road, chances are there are cameras it would be picked up on – number plate recognition means that it can be tracked down and the driver prosecuted. Especially as it can be a regular thing – a lucrative little sideline.' Rufus sounded more resigned than angry. 'It costs a lot of money to responsibly dispose of stuff like this.'

'Yes, I know,' she murmured.

'I brought you here because I wanted to let you know that we weren't being complacent. We're never complacent about wanton destruction of the environment.' He held her gaze.

'I didn't think you would be. I'm sorry if I ever gave you that impression.'

'You didn't.' He touched his fingers to his temples. 'But I just wanted to make sure you knew that we are as on board with this as you and your grandmother are.'

She nodded. 'Thank you. From our end, we've made sure none of the shelter animals can get near the stream. We're not using that field at the moment. But what happens now?'

'Harrison has it all in hand. He'll take care of things. He's been to see all the landowners who might be affected. I've reported this to the police and I've informed the Environment Agency. We have photographs. We'll have a crime report. It's highly unlikely the perpetrators will ever be caught – these have obviously been here a while. But you never know. And, of course, I've made arrange-ments for a company to come and remove this lot. They'll be here first thing tomorrow morning.'

'Do you have to pay for that?'

'Yes.' He gave her a rueful look. 'The taxpayer ends up paying for fly-tipping on public land, but we *rich* landowners are responsible for anything that's fly-tipped on our land.' He emphasised the word rich.

Phoebe nodded slowly, thinking of her grandmother and Puddleduck Farm and all of the other farmers she had known when she was younger. There was a common misconception that all farmers were rich, but she knew this wasn't true. 'That seems very unfair.'

'It would be difficult to prove that we hadn't dumped these barrels here ourselves,' Rufus said matter-of-factly. 'Although it wouldn't make a lot of sense to poison our own stream.'

'Yes, I can see that. On both counts.' She sighed, remembering the bagged-up robin in her freezer. There was probably no point in testing it now. 'And on that note, presumably the stream will clear itself once toxic chemicals aren't being leached into it.'

'Correct,' Rufus said. 'We'll do some more water testing to confirm that. Just in case there are any more of these lying about on the estate. Harrison's had a good look around and I've looked too, we don't think there are any more. I've also asked him to arrange for a camera to be put up here. It's a vulnerable spot because we're not that far from the road, and although this was probably a one-off, you never know. Whoever dumped this lot may be tempted to come back one day with some more. Shall we head back?'

'Yes. Thanks for keeping me in the picture.'

'I'm just sorry it was such a grim picture.'

They walked back in silence. The return journey felt sadder. Maybe because of what they'd just witnessed, Phoebe thought. Rufus hadn't spoken again, but just before they got back to the Land Rover, he halted once more on the path. 'Do you remember I told you I had a tree house when I was small?' he asked. 'We're quite close to it. Do you want to see?'

'I'd love to.'

He looked pleased.

A few moments later, they were in another clearing and Rufus pointed up. Phoebe gasped. She wasn't sure what she'd been expecting, but it wasn't this. She had never seen anything like this. It was a king amongst tree houses. It wasn't so much built in one tree as built in between several. Here the tall, skinny-trunked silver birches were clustered close together and a cleverly designed spiral staircase wound up between the trunks, linking two wooden platforms, one above the other. Each platform held a tree house made of slatted wood: the first was about two and a half metres up and the second was a few metres above it. Both of them had pointy wooden roofs and what looked like an open-plan viewing window. They were artfully designed to blend in with their surroundings and looked as though they had been fashioned by some master craftsman.

'Wow,' Phoebe said, craning her neck to take it all in. 'That's the most amazing tree house I've ever seen. Did your father build that?'

'He had it commissioned,' Rufus said. 'By a guy who makes them in Sweden. It's pretty cool, isn't it?'

There was a thread of pride in his voice and something else underlying it. Sadness maybe, which seemed out of place in the circumstances.

'Would you like to go up?' he asked her.

'Is the Pope catholic!'

Now he did smile and he led her across to the foot of the first spiral staircase. 'I haven't been up here for a while, but Archie uses it, so I make sure it's in good order. The ladders are rock solid.' He tested the lowest rung with his foot to show her.

Phoebe believed him; it was one of the most well-made things she'd ever seen.

There was nothing rickety about the ladder at all. He went

ahead of her up into the tree and, relieved she was wearing trousers and sensible shoes, she followed him up. She felt a vague sense of surrealness as they climbed. Was this really happening? Was she really following Rufus Holt up into a tree house?

Moments later, he'd reached the first platform and he glanced back. 'We could stop at this one, but the view's better from the top one. Are you OK with that? How's your head for heights?'

'I'm fine with heights.' This wasn't entirely true, but no way was she about to confess they made her legs go wobbly. Besides, going up was the easy bit. She could worry about how she was going to get down later.

They carried on climbing and, after a few seconds more, Rufus disappeared through the doorway of the top tree house and then turned and offered her his hand.

Phoebe took it gratefully, unprepared for the shock of awareness that jolted through her as their fingers touched. It was impossible to tell if he'd felt it too. But fortunately the touch was brief. He let go of her fingers as soon as she was up and sitting beside him on the wooden floor. There wasn't enough headroom for them to stand. The whole structure was about two metres long and maybe a metre and a half high. It was closed on three sides, but the fourth side had a large open gap that served as a window. It wasn't completely open. A thick lip of wood came up from the floor, so it would have been tricky to tumble out by mistake, but it afforded them a decent view of the forest.

'Wow,' Phoebe said again, feeling slightly breathless. Was that the climb or his nearness or the sheer wonder of it all? The view was beautiful – all around them were trees in leaf, and the smell of wood and mustiness, with a touch of leaf mould. A small spider ran across the floor in front of her, disturbed by the intruders.

Rufus pointed through the trees. 'Do you see the hole in that birch, quite high up, where the branches fork?'

She followed his pointing finger and nodded.

'That's the home of a great spotted woodpecker. Or at least it used to be.' He looked reflective and she wondered if he was remembering the dead woodpecker they'd found by the stream. 'I must check with Archie. He's not been up here as much lately. He spends as much time as he can riding. I think he'd live at Brook Stables if we let him.' A muscle twitched in his face when he mentioned Brook Stables and Phoebe had the impression he didn't approve of his son's hobby. That was odd too. It was one thing that he didn't like horses himself, but not wanting his son to ride was a little extreme.

'I wondered how he was doing,' she said carefully. 'I'm glad he's getting on well.'

'He's amazingly well balanced,' Rufus said, 'considering the circumstances...' He didn't elaborate and Phoebe didn't want to pry. She assumed he was talking about the loss of his son's mother so young.

For a few moments, neither of them spoke. They sat in the peace of the forest, which had gone totally silent for a brief while when they'd arrived, as if all the birds had hushed and were waiting for their next move.

Now they'd been here a while, normality had resumed. Birdsong had begun again and in one of the trees close by a young squirrel had paused on a branch to look at them. It studied them without moving. A frozen statue of a silver squirrel, motionless for a few seconds before scurrying away. A breeze rustled through the leaves at the tops of the trees. Phoebe felt as though she was part of something that was alive and breathing. Not just an outsider observing from a distance, but actually inside the forest itself.

'Are you hungry?' Rufus asked, and she looked at him in surprise.

'Er – why? Do you have a chef up here hidden away?'

'Not quite.' His eyes sparked with amusement and, a few seconds later, he disappeared down the spiral staircase and she heard him rummaging around in the tree house below. Then he was back again, carrying a sealed bag. From within it, he produced a couple of mini bars of fruit and nut chocolate. 'Secret supplies,' he said. 'Not even Emilia knows these are here. Or they'd be gone.' He handed her one. 'If you haven't eaten chocolate in a tree house, then you haven't lived.'

'How could I resist? Thank you.'

And he was right. It was heaven.

Rufus seemed to be in no hurry and Phoebe followed his lead, nibbling the chocolate, half a square at a time and letting it melt on her tongue. If someone had told her when she'd got up this morning that by the end of the day she'd be up in a tree house sharing chocolate with Rufus Holt she'd have told them they were completely mad.

18

Rufus was having similar thoughts. But he couldn't remember the last time he'd felt so at ease with someone. Certainly not a woman. He hadn't been this relaxed with a woman since Rowena. He wasn't entirely sure how it had happened. He just knew he didn't want it to end any time soon, which was crazy.

Earlier on, he'd told Phoebe jokingly that he wasn't abducting her and yet somehow he felt now as though that was exactly what he'd done. He couldn't imagine telling his father or Emilia, or even Harrison, that he'd brought Phoebe up into the tree house. They'd be at best astonished and at worst alarmed.

'It's best not to get too social with tenants.' That was his father's approach. Of course, you had to appear to be sociable. You had to be the image of the benign and friendly landlord, amenable and responsive to their needs. It was the twenty-first century, after all, and good tenants were in shorter supply than they'd once been. Rufus imagined that if his mother had still been alive, or Rowena herself, there would have been a lot more socialising involved too.

When he and Rowena had first moved into Beechbrook

House, there had been talk of them having an annual gathering. Some kind of feast or open day up at the big house. Drinks and food provided. Maybe a tour. After she'd died, it had never been mentioned again. Rufus knew that neither he nor his father would ever get round to doing it. Lord Holt would have found it too exhausting and Rufus would have found it too stressful.

Phoebe was not just his tenant. She was his vet too. Did that make a difference? It put her on more of an equal footing with him. A professional relationship. Dad wouldn't have seen it that way. He was still a snob. Professionals were there to be of service. Relationships with professionals should be kept on an even cooler footing than relationships with tenants.

Phoebe was not just his vet either. She was a very attractive woman. It wasn't just how she looked, although he certainly wasn't immune to those beautiful hazel eyes and her very slightly upturned nose. When he'd known she wouldn't notice, he'd stolen a glance at her slim but still gorgeously curvy figure and he'd let himself imagine just for a moment what it would be like to hold her in his arms.

Rufus dragged his thoughts into a more controllable direction. It hadn't been Phoebe's looks that had attracted him. It had been her feistiness, her total lack of fear when he'd first met her. He'd berated her for trespassing and she'd raised her eyebrows and looked at him as if *he'd* been in the wrong. And he'd known that he had been in the wrong for yelling, which had made it all the worse.

Rufus suspected she'd have been horrified if she'd known he was thinking about her in such terms. He struggled with himself. He should never have asked her to come up here. It was an intimate space, that, prior to this day, had been shared only with his late wife and his son. Not even his father had ever been up here – except once when it was first built – to check it for flaws.

He knew Emilia came sometimes, but that was to keep an eye on Archie. She had never been here with him.

Phoebe's soft voice interrupted his thoughts. 'I'm guessing you must have a lot of memories of being up here.'

That was another thing he liked about her. She was not unaware. And she didn't seem to observe the usual barriers that women did when he met them. She was neither in awe of him nor flirty – he came across flirty all too often. To his surprise, he realised that he saw her as much more his equal than he'd seen anyone for a long time.

'Yes. I do.' He glanced at her. 'But most of them are with Archie. I don't make a habit of bringing anyone else up here.' He felt heat in his face.

'And there was me thinking you conducted all your business meetings in a tree. And served the attendees with coffee and chocolate. Where is the coffee anyway?'

Rufus was momentarily taken aback, but then he realised her eyes were dancing with fun and he relaxed.

* * *

Phoebe could have kicked herself. Why was she taking the mickey when the truth was she felt impossibly touched by what he'd just told her? He was opening up to her, which clearly wasn't easy for him, and she had just knocked him down.

'The chocolate was a lovely surprise,' she added. 'Thank you.'

'You're most welcome.' He sounded formal again, despite their surroundings. And when a few moments later he glanced at his watch and said, 'I guess I had better take you back before the mosquitos decide to join us,' Phoebe wasn't surprised, but she was certainly disappointed.

'OK.'

'Would you be more comfortable going down first or shall I?' Rufus asked. 'I find it's easier to go down the same way we came up – as in facing into the ladder. It's less daunting that way.'

'You go first,' she said, and regretted it almost immediately because she made the mistake of looking down as soon as he'd disappeared down the top rungs of the spiral ladder. They were a long way up and although it would have been hard to fall from the ladder, she could still feel her head spinning alarmingly and her hands had gone clammy with fear.

Don't let me down now, she told her reluctant body as she took the first few steps.

Jeez, she'd made the mistake of looking down again. Rufus was a few steps below her, but now she felt even more vulnerable. The ladder creaked with their weight and suddenly Phoebe was paralysed with fear. Her mouth was dry, her hands completely slippery with sweat and her heart was pounding in a crazy escalating rhythm. She stayed where she was. Frozen. Aware only of a giddy sickness that made the world spin so the forest and trees around her became part of a green whirling landscape.

Then she heard Rufus's voice immediately below her and she realised he must have climbed back up a few steps. 'It's OK. I'm right below you. I won't let you fall.'

She didn't answer. She was gasping for breath.

'It's just a panic attack,' he was saying. 'Your body is reacting to a danger that does not exist. I want you to focus, Phoebe. Pick a spot directly in front of you and focus on it.'

Some part of her was listening, concentrating on the sound of his voice, even if she wasn't yet taking in his words.

'I want you to do exactly what I say. I want you to breathe with me. Breathe in and breathe out. Breathe in and breathe out.'

At first it was impossible to do what he said, but he kept talking and Phoebe focused on his voice until it became more real. Until it filled her head and she found that she could do what he said. She stared at the white papery bark of the silver birch directly in front of her.

'Breathe in and breathe out. Breathe in and breathe out. That's it. Breathe with me.'

It was working. She could feel her body calming down, feel her heartbeat slowing and although her hands were still sweaty, she no longer felt paralysed with terror.

'Now, when you're ready, I want you to move your right foot onto the next rung down. There's absolutely no rush. Keep breathing. I'm going to guide you down. One step at a time. Breathe in and breathe out. I'm right behind you. I won't let you fall. One step at a time.'

And in this way, they went down, as Rufus said, one step at a time. By the time they had got back to the first tree house, Phoebe had recovered enough to speak. 'Thank you,' she said. 'I'm so sorry. If I'd realised that was going to happen—'

'It's no problem,' he said. 'Panic attacks are no fun.'

She managed the final ladder without difficulty and when they were on solid ground again, she faced him, feeling a little bit foolish.

'I bet you're regretting inviting me up there now,' she said, knowing her cheeks were burning. 'After that little performance.'

'Not at all.' His eyes were gentle.

'How did you know about panic attacks? How to deal with them. Have you ever had one?'

'Oh yes. I've had plenty.' He paused and she waited. They stood in the leaf-rustling stillness of the forest – even the birds had gone quiet again now – and eventually he continued. 'It was after my wife died. I saw a therapist about them. I still see him sometimes. It helped me a lot to know how to breathe through them, but it wasn't easy at first. I had to learn techniques.'

His voice was a mixture of matter-of-fact and surprise as if he couldn't quite believe what he'd just confessed. He sounded impossibly vulnerable and Phoebe caught hold of his hands and pulled him closer to her. It was an impulsive, instinctive gesture and she wasn't sure whether she wanted to give or to receive comfort. Perhaps it was both. But he reacted to her touch and then they were in each other's arms, which felt totally right, and the kiss when it came was as natural and as inevitable as her putting one foot at a time on the rungs of the spiral ladder.

His lips were soft and he tasted of chocolate and warmth and Phoebe felt as if her legs had gone weak all over again, but it was not fear that was buckling them now. Oh my God, this was nothing like her fantasies. This made the imagined chemistry seem tame. This made her erotic dream feel like a teenager's fumbling first experience. It was the kind of kiss that sent all her senses rocketing into orbit and she never wanted it to end.

It was Rufus who finally broke it. Just for a second as they drew apart, she saw that his expression mirrored her feelings. A mixture of shock, lust and desire. The shock was winning though.

'Forgive me. I think I just took advantage—'

'You didn't,' she interrupted him. 'I wanted that too.'

They stared at each other. She could see him consciously trying to distance himself and she wanted to tell him to stop it. Tell him it hadn't been a mistake. But already she found she was doing the same thing. She was telling herself the only reason it had been so impassioned was because they'd just gone through such an intense experience together. That it was terror and adrenaline that had heightened their senses, not chemistry.

'We should get back,' he said, stepping away from her, straightening his shoulders, moving purposefully back in the direction of the Land Rover.

A few minutes later, they reached it. As before, he opened the passenger door for her, then leaped into the driver's seat and they headed back the way they had come. Phoebe opened each gate. He thanked her. Nothing else was said. She wanted to say something about what had happened between them, but she couldn't find the words. She would say something when they were back at Puddleduck.

But in no time at all they were there, and she still couldn't find the words. It seemed he couldn't either.

'Thank you for today,' she managed, glancing at him.

'You're welcome.' His voice was brusque. 'I... should get back.'

'Of course.' Clearly he couldn't wait to get rid of her. She jumped out of the Land Rover. 'Good luck with the Environment Agency.' This was in her cheeriest voice. She held up crossed fingers.

He nodded and then he was driving away.

Phoebe waited until he was out of the gate and then she swore. 'For fuck's sake. What was that? What just happened there?' She wanted to scream very loudly. To scream and shout and yell away the overrun of adrenaline up into the infinite sky.

But decorum and the fact that Maggie and Natasha were probably somewhere about stopped her. Pulling herself together with a huge effort, Phoebe walked slowly back round to the vet unit to make sure everything was locked up for the night.

19

Phoebe knew Tori was seeing Harrison that weekend, but she could not keep her churning thoughts to herself. As soon as she left Puddleduck, she phoned her friend from the car.

'Tori, what time are you off to see Harrison? Are you still at work?'

'Yes, I'm just finishing a magazine and, re Harrison, I'm not sure yet. We said we'd play it by ear. What's up?'

'Nothing's up exactly. I just need to talk to you.'

'OK. Give me half an hour. Where are you?'

'Just on my way home.'

'Well, if you shoot by the office instead, I should be done and we can grab a quick coffee. How's that?'

'Perfect.'

Tori rented office space in Bridgeford, but she was the only one still there by the time Phoebe arrived.

'No one else is crazy enough to work late on a Friday night,' Tori said, patting the seat of a swivel chair beside her. 'Is this a quick chat or more involved? Do we need more than a coffee?'

'A coffee is fine.'

While Tori put a pod into a machine on the side, Phoebe sat on the office chair and twirled. She could see why Maggie did it so often behind reception. It beat sitting still when your head was overflowing with thoughts.

'What's happened?' Tori asked, bringing back the coffee and putting it on the desk nearest to Phoebe. 'You're never this fidgety.'

'I kissed Rufus.'

'What? Where?' Tori clapped her hands. 'So I was right. That raging chemistry we spoke about wasn't just one-way.'

'It would seem not. We'd just been up a tree. Well, to be more specific, we were in a tree house.'

'Oh my God. This gets better and better. What tree house was this?' Tori sat down and gave Phoebe her full attention. 'Details, please.'

Phoebe told her about Rufus's impromptu visit, about the oil drums and about the tree house and then as she was describing the panic attack she'd had and the way he had talked her down, she realised that if she wasn't very careful, she'd betray his trust. Rufus was a very private person, and she had no doubt he'd have hated anyone to know he'd had therapy for panic attacks. He probably wouldn't be that keen on anyone knowing about the kiss either. That amazing kiss that had sent her heart rocketing into orbit. But it was too late to bury the kiss now. Besides, Tori might be a journalist, but she was also her best friend and Phoebe would have trusted her with her life.

'That sounds lovely. Very romantic,' Tori said. 'What's the problem?'

'I think he regretted it the moment it was over. Which probably sounds nuts because...' She broke off and did another twirl on the chair. 'Well, I don't know what I expected to happen.'

'I do.' Tori smirked.

'No. Not that. I wasn't expecting him to cart me off to his boudoir at the big house and ravish me. Do men even have boudoirs? That word's always struck me as feminine.'

'It is. It's from the French word *bouder*, "to sulk". The implication being that a female could withdraw there to sulk,' Tori said helpfully. She was like a walking dictionary. 'Rufus probably has a four-poster bed. But I know what you mean. Why weren't you expecting that? If kissing isn't foreplay, then I don't know what is.' Her eyes went dreamy. 'Harrison's a fabulous kisser. We can kiss for hours. Sorry. Too much information.'

Phoebe shook her head. 'Because usually there are first dates involved. Then second, then third and, I don't know, maybe a lot of dates. Yes, I think that's what I was expecting. I think I was hoping he might ask me out – or at least refer to it, but he couldn't get away quick enough. He actually said, "forgive me". He seemed to think he'd taken advantage.'

'Did you tell him he hadn't? That you've wanted to snog his face off for weeks – not to put too fine a point on it?'

'Yes. Well, I told him the first bit. But it didn't make any difference. He was just distancing himself as fast as he could. I could see it happening before my eyes. He was thinking, oh shit, I've just kissed a commoner.'

'Phoebe, my darling.' Tori put on her sternest voice. 'Sometimes you can be a complete doughnut. You cannot possibly know what he was thinking.'

'No. That's true. You're right. I can't.' She spun the chair again.

'And please stop doing that – you're making me dizzy. Stop fiddling with the buttons too. It's Laura's chair and she'll notice if any of the settings are changed.'

'Sorry.' Phoebe gulped down half her coffee and put the mug down. 'I'm gathering myself. This is me gathering myself.' She spread her fingers in front of her and breathed deeply a couple of

times. 'You know what you said when we went out, about relationships, well, you were right. I've been avoiding getting involved
with anyone for ages because of what happened with Hugh. And
I think you were right about Rufus too.'

'The chemistry not being one-way – clearly.'

'Yes, but that wasn't what I meant. For ages I've been so caught
up fantasising about scenarios I didn't think would happen that I
wasn't prepared for how I'd feel if they did.'

'That makes total sense.' Tori looked at her thoughtfully. 'How
do you feel?'

'I don't know. Anxious. Scared. A bit overwhelmed.'

'The question is – are you scared because you think there
won't be a repeat performance or because you think there will?'

'I'm not entirely sure.' Phoebe burst out laughing. 'Listen to
me. That's a complete lie. I'm still in denial, aren't I? Of course I
want a repeat performance. Who wouldn't? It was lovely. I must
be worrying there's *not* going to be one, mustn't I?'

'I'd think so.' Tori clicked her tongue. 'You do know you don't
have to wait. This is the twenty-first century. It's not as though you
don't know where he lives.'

'You're suggesting I rock up on his doorstep and ask him if
he'd like to carry on where we left off?' Phoebe had a vivid image
of parking in front of Beechbrook House, walking past the fountain with its tasteless naked cherubs and jangling the doorbell.

'Mmm, I guess it's a bit more difficult when a man lives with
his father,' Tori said, winking.

'It is when his father's Lord Holt.'

'Not to mention you'd have to get past that snobby, overprotec-
tive nanny who definitely doesn't like letting in attractive women
to see her boss.'

'You're not helping,' Phoebe said.

'I know. I'm sorry. But what's the alternative?' She glanced at her watch. 'I'll need to get going soon. Hey, maybe we could have a foursome. I could get Harrison to arrange it.'

'You are not to breathe a word of this to Harrison.'

Tori's face dropped.

'Swear to me,' Phoebe said. 'If Rufus thinks I've kissed and told, that may be the last I ever see of him. I'd hate him to think I'd been gossiping.'

'OK. Don't worry. Your secret is safe with me. I won't tell a soul.'

'And definitely not Harrison.'

'Definitely not Harrison.' Tori's face sobered a little. 'To be honest, Harrison still hasn't introduced me to Rufus, although I think he did tell him he was seeing someone. Maybe I should be worried about that. Perhaps he's ashamed of me. Although I've met a couple of his other friends.' She brightened again. 'We bumped into them at a restaurant the other day.'

'Now who's being a doughnut? Of course Harrison's not ashamed of you. He's probably just being a typical man. They don't talk much to each other about relationships, do they?' To be fair, this assumption was based on Hugh, who'd never discussed his emotions with anyone.

'You are so right,' Tori agreed. 'That'll be it. Try not to stress about Rufus. It will work out. You'll see. Have a great weekend.'

'You too,' Phoebe said, but as she drove home with the prospect of the weekend yawning before her, she found herself wishing she could time-travel into a future where she knew which way it was going to work out. She hated uncertainty.

* * *

Rufus had back-to-back meetings all day Saturday. This was a relief. Work always focused him. Or at least that was how he viewed it. Work was one of the things the therapist – he still couldn't bring himself to say *his* therapist – had suggested they talk about.

Bartholomew Timms, the therapist in question, was a golfing buddy of his father's. He had white bushy eyebrows, an intense stare and a nose with exaggerated flared nostrils. Or maybe he just flared them a lot. Rufus hadn't decided. He didn't like the man much, but he did respect him on a professional level. Even so, he'd been shocked when Bartholomew had suggested he might be avoiding his feelings by being overly busy.

'Some people use work in the same way that an alcoholic uses alcohol or an addict uses drugs to change the way they feel,' Bartholomew had told him at their last session, leaning back in his chair, nostrils wide.

'You mean me?' Rufus had said.

'Do you think that's something you might do?' Why did therapists always answer everything with a bloody question?

'No. I just work a lot. There's a lot to do.'

'Do you think you have enough work/life balance? How's your social life?'

It was non-existent. Bartholomew probably knew that already. His father had probably told him when they pottered about on the golf course.

'When I'm not working, I like to spend time with my son. And Dad too.' He had seen Bartholomew's eyebrow twitch. He probably also knew he and Alfred didn't spend much time together that didn't involve work. Unless you counted arguing – they argued a lot. That wasn't usually about work – they disagreed about the way Rufus was bringing up Archie. They had very different views on parenting.

'But you don't have any hobbies as such?' Bartholomew had pressed.

'Not, as such.' Rufus had glanced at the clock and willed the session to be over so he could get back to work. Maybe Bartholomew had a point, he had thought, feeling a stab of irony.

He'd thought a few times since that Bartholomew might be right about him trying to avoid feelings. But never more so than this weekend. No matter how busy he was, no matter how much he tried to focus on work, images of Phoebe kept slipping through the gaps.

The memories were disturbing because they were so conflicting. He'd wanted her. There was absolutely no doubt about that. There was a raging chemistry he'd never in his life felt before. And thereby lay the conflict. He hadn't even felt it with Rowena. His wife had been his soulmate, his best friend and his lover. He'd worshipped the ground she walked on in the same way his father had done with Rufus's mother. But Rufus had never felt that mind-blowing, rocket-fuelled, dazzling chemistry with Rowena that had been simultaneously ignited and raging through him when he'd kissed Phoebe.

Or when she had kissed him? He wasn't sure who'd kissed who. It didn't matter. The outcome had been the same. He'd wanted her totally. Right there on the forest floor and never mind the consequences. It had taken every bit of his iron will and steely self-control to stop when they had, and to step away from her.

Back in the present, he put down the contract he was looking at, or rather, not really looking at, and got up from his desk. He had to get a grip. Maybe a walk would help. He'd just finished his final Zoom meeting of the day. It was now 4 p.m. and everyone else was out. Archie was at the stables with Emilia. His father was seeing a tenant.

Rufus changed his indoor shoes for outdoor ones, strolled down the long hall and out of one of the back doors. A few minutes later, he was outside in the fresh air. Archie had left his chessboard on the table on the terrace. He was halfway through a game. The black knight sat in the centre of the board. There had been a time when Rufus couldn't look at the knights with their proud equine shapes without triggering an attack of PTSD. That hadn't happened lately. He must be improving.

If he could get a lid on the PTSD, would that mean he was getting over Rowena's death? And if he was getting over it, did that mean he no longer loved her as much? It was a question that had bothered him lately. He'd wanted to ask Bartholomew, but he couldn't find the words.

He crossed the lawn which had just been mowed. The scent of cut grass was in the air and there were tulips in one of the borders. Pops of cream and red with golden narcissi sprinkled amongst them, Rufus could smell the sweetness of the narcissi. They had a great gardener who knew how to get the right mix between formal and meadow. Rowena had employed him when their old gardener who'd worked until he was about eighty had finally announced he was ready to retire.

The cherry trees were in blossom. Rufus paused to take in their beauty. Rowena had always loved spring. She'd had big plans for this garden. She had talked about a trellis of climbing pink roses over stone steps that led up to a bench beyond or maybe a love seat, somewhere they could sit in an evening with a glass of wine. A hidey-hole from the world. But they had barely been living here a year when she had died. And the garden plans had died with her.

He hurried past the place where the bower would have been and on along a path through the birchwood. The bluebells were at their peak. The forest floor a vibrant blue, which was deeper the more distant it was. Close up, the flowers were more individual, each one alone – it was only at a distance they gave the impression of being one mass of blue.

His thoughts drifted back to Phoebe. He hadn't planned to kiss her. Showing her the tree house had been spur of the moment. Although it was true what he'd told her – he had never taken anyone else there apart from Archie, and Rowena, of course. His late wife hadn't been scared of heights. But she'd never stayed in the tree house long. Rowena hadn't stayed anywhere for long – she was the eternal fidget. Quickly becoming bored of views, experiences, food, places, people. When they'd got married, he'd wondered if he would be enough for Rowena. If they would manage a long marriage, break the chain of bad luck that had haunted the Holts for the last few generations. Rufus had wondered if his marriage to Rowena would herald a time of peace and happiness instead of turbulence and drama. When Archie had been born he had felt for a while that it would.

Rufus had only the sketchiest memories of his own mother. She'd died when he was three and a half. He could remember the smell of her hair, her laughter, her warmth and the feel of her arms, but he couldn't remember her face. He knew what she looked like, of course. There were photographs of her in albums, looking a little stiff. There weren't many of her smiling, but he couldn't connect his sensory memories to her visual image. It was as if he was remembering two different women.

Inwardly, he had rejoiced when Archie had celebrated his fourth birthday with his family, and then his fifth. They'd had a cake in the shape of a green smiling dinosaur for his fifth – Archie had been going through a dinosaur phase. Rufus had taken dozens of photographs of Archie in his school uniform on his first day at school – a huge milestone – which he was determined none of them would ever forget. He couldn't remember what they'd done for Archie's sixth birthday party. He had a feeling they hadn't made as much fuss as previous years. They'd been busy, having recently moved into Beechbrook House to start a new phase of their lives. Archie had been six and a half when Rowena had died. He'd had three years longer with his mother than Rufus had had with his.

When they'd lost Rowena, Rufus felt as if his world had ended. As if he would never be happy again. Times were different now. It was perfectly acceptable for a widower to remarry – especially one as young as him, yet he couldn't see himself following that path. He couldn't imagine dating again. He couldn't imagine even wanting to try.

Against his will, Phoebe came back into his head. He blocked her out. He had no intention of dating Phoebe. It was too soon. Too painful. It was... He didn't know what it was.

He was through the woods now and onto the track they'd walked yesterday. He retraced their steps up to the barrel dumping site. They'd been removed this morning. Only the flattened poisoned ground where they'd lain remained. It wouldn't be long before nature reclaimed that too. The cameras were yet to be installed, but Harrison had assured him it was in hand. If anyone fly-tipped here again, they would catch them on film. That didn't mean a prosecution would follow, but at least they'd have a chance.

Rufus stood for a while.

Even Harrison, the eternal bachelor and his biggest ally, had met someone and was considering settling down. Maybe it wasn't so wrong to want some happiness for himself, a mother for Archie. Wouldn't Rowena want that too?

20

May was whizzing by. It was another busy week at Puddleduck Vets and Phoebe was relieved on two counts. It confirmed that her decision to employ an extra full-time receptionist was the right one. Their advert was now live online, and they'd had seven applications already. But it would be another week before it closed and she, Jenna and Maggie began sifting through the hopefuls.

It also meant she hadn't had much time to dwell on Rufus. The tree house, her panic attack, that kiss, all of it was beginning to feel slightly surreal, as though it had happened to someone else.

She had heard nothing from him. And despite Tori's gently prompting messages to take the bull by the horns herself, Phoebe had resisted the temptation to contact him. She could deal with Rufus's silence. What she could not have dealt with was a concrete rejection.

No doubt he was finding the whole thing embarrassing and awkward and had decided it was a case of least said, soonest mended. That was the conclusion Phoebe had finally come to.

It was now Friday afternoon and she was finishing up at the unit. Jenna had already left and Maggie had asked her if she'd like to pop in for an early supper. Phoebe, who had no plans except work for the weekend, had said she'd love that. She locked up and walked round to the farmhouse. There were a few ducks in the yard, enjoying the balmy evening, and as she passed, a white puddle duck, which may or not have been Jemima, quacked at her loudly and came waddling across. Phoebe was not entirely convinced that Jemima remembered her because she had once saved her life. Despite the fact that Maggie swore blind she did.

Not that Maggie was in the habit of telling lies, Phoebe mused. Except when it came to her health and her energy levels, both of which she insisted were always perfectly fine.

'Hello,' Phoebe said, bending slightly. She was never sure how to greet ducks. They didn't appreciate being stroked like dogs.

Jemima waggled her behind, which meant she was happy. At least that was something they had in common with dogs.

Phoebe carried on to the house. Tiny and Buster, who spent their time between the farmhouse and various sunny spots around the farm, came to greet her as she walked in through the stable-style kitchen door, both halves of which were already open.

'Hello, guys.' She stroked the dogs' heads, shaggy grey and soft black, laughing as they shoved and vied for her attention. 'Where's the boss then?'

'I'm here,' Maggie called out. 'Sweating over a hot stove.'

'To make my supper? Oooh, I'm honoured.' The delicious smell of bread permeated the kitchen and Phoebe spied some on the worktop next to the Aga. Her grandmother did look hot. She was in her scruffs. Ancient faded black jeans and an oversized olive green T-shirt. 'You've been making bread?'

'Not much gets past you.' Maggie paused from stirring a pan,

'And I'm just heating some soup to go with it. Cooking is something I'd like to do more of when I retire.'

Phoebe looked at her in surprise. 'I didn't think you were that keen. I thought that's why you cooked everything in batches so you didn't have to do it very often.'

'That's true. But I do enjoy baking. I've made some cookies for Eddie's visit and I've also made some for the dogs.'

'Better not get those mixed up!'

'It wouldn't be the end of the world. The ones for the dogs have bacon and peanut butter in – perfectly edible for humans.'

'No wonder these two are hanging about then.' Phoebe glanced at Buster and Tiny, who were both sitting within a stone's throw of the Aga, looking expectant.

'Yes, they do like them.' Maggie looked smug. 'And so do the rest of the kennel dogs, not that we have very many in at the moment. Natasha's rehomed a lot lately – she's very good at it.'

'That's great news. When's Eddie coming to visit? And where are his cookies and do they have chocolate in and can I have one – in the interests of testing them out, obviously?'

'One question at a time. I'll answer the most pressing one first. Yes you can. They're over there on that plate. Don't eat too many or you'll ruin your supper.'

'No chance of that,' Phoebe said. 'I'm starving.'

'That's good to hear.' There was another little pause. 'I must admit I've been a bit worried about you this week. You haven't seemed your usual bubbly self.'

'Haven't I?' Phoebe helped herself to a cookie from a plate on the wooden worktop that ran around the perimeter of the large kitchen. They did have chocolate in – oh God – they were the kind that were slightly soft and bendy and very sweet with big chunks of chocolate in. How did her grandmother do that without it melting?

'When is Eddie coming?'

'Next Wednesday afternoon. You haven't answered my question.' Maggie turned fully from the stove. 'Are you OK, darling? I was starting to worry that you might have man trouble – except, of course, you don't have a man in your life.' She held Phoebe's eyes. 'Or at least not one you've told me about.'

Phoebe stopped mid chew. How on earth did her grandmother do that? How could she possibly have even guessed?

'Mmmm, so you do have a man.' Maggie frowned. 'Not that it's any of my business, of course, unless he's messing you about. Tell him if he does that, he'll have me to answer to.'

'There isn't really a man.' Phoebe decided half a story was better than none. 'There was just a kiss. One kiss.'

'OK.' Maggie moved the soup pan off the Aga hot plate, then ladled it into two bowls. 'Would you like to take these over to the table and I'll bring the bread.'

A few minutes later, they were sitting at the solid old farmhouse table that hadn't been moved in a generation with a bowl of spiced vegetable soup in front of them and chunks of home-made bread and the butter in a dish at just the right temperature because it had been softened on the back of the Aga.

Her grandmother was amazing at soups. This one was red and had sweet potato, green beans and red pepper in and Phoebe could taste paprika, fenugreek, nutmeg and garlic.

'This is gorgeous. How do you get it to taste like this?'

'Go overboard on the herbs,' Maggie said, which was what she always said if asked because she didn't use recipes or even the same ingredients. She just flung in whatever was at hand when she was cooking.

For a few moments, Phoebe just relished being in the peaceful ambience of her grandmother's kitchen, eating soup and home-made bread, feeling surrounded by love. It had been the same for as long as she remembered. Beams across the ceiling and a dark grey flagstone floor that was immune to spills and animals' paws – or even neddies' hooves. A Belfast sink, and an oak French dresser hung with dusty cups that no one ever used. And of course the Aga, with copper pans hung on nails behind it and terracotta pots of herbs everywhere.

The dogs were lying down again now. Neither of them scrounged from the dinner table, both were secure in the knowledge they'd get something at the end of the meal if they didn't pester.

'I have two questions,' Maggie said, when she'd finished her soup. 'The first is would you like some more? And the second is, was it a good kiss and if it was, why are you so sad?'

'That's three questions. But yes please to the first one. I'll get it.' Playing for time, Phoebe took their bowls back to the Aga, refilled them and came back. When she was sitting down again, she said, 'Yes it was a great kiss. The best.'

'And it wasn't with Heinous Hugh, I take it?'

'No, it wasn't.' It hadn't occurred to Phoebe that Maggie might think she'd rekindled something with her ex. 'And no the guy isn't married or attached.'

'I never thought for a second that he would be,' Maggie said with a sweet smile. 'That's not you, darling, is it?'

'No.' Phoebe felt near to tears. She hadn't realised her emotions were so close to the surface. She also knew there was no point in having this guessing game with her grandmother – not when she knew she would tell her eventually. 'I kissed Rufus Holt. That sounds wrong. It was a mutual kiss. I didn't throw myself at him and he didn't seduce me.' As she spoke, she held her grandmother's gaze and she saw a flicker of something in her eyes. Alarm perhaps, apprehension. It was hard to name it because it was gone almost immediately, but it had definitely been there. 'You don't approve?'

'You don't need my approval, darling. But why the sadness? What's happened since?'

Phoebe stirred her soup disconsolately, then put down her spoon. 'A wall of silence is what's happened since.' She filled in the details she'd missed. Not that there were many. Her grandmother listened patiently, her face becoming more serious as Phoebe mentioned the tree house, their closeness, the kiss and then Rufus's sudden switch of mood. And then nothing. 'Tori thinks I should go round and ask him out,' she finished. 'But that's not really my style. What do you think?'

'I think your instincts are right. There's a lot you don't know about the Holts.' She shook her head and looked troubled, and Phoebe felt a jolt of foreboding.

'I know the Holts used to own Puddleduck Farm way back before it was called Puddleduck,' she said slowly. 'Didn't our family win it in a poker game or something crazy like that?'

'Yes, that's right. My grandfather won it.'

'And didn't the name get changed by our family?'

'Yes. It was originally called Forest Farm. My mother changed the name to Puddleduck Farm when she and Dad inherited it. The story goes that she was a fan of Beatrix Potter and because her maid of honour bought her and my father a pair of ducks for a wedding present they decided to change the name to Puddleduck and always make sure we had a Jemima.'

Phoebe knew that too. It was a family legend. 'But there's more to it?' she prompted.

'Yes, but my memory is a bit hazy. This is what my mother told me – I'll see if I can get the dates right.' Maggie frowned. 'My grandfather fought in the Boer War. Not the first one but the second one, which was a conflict between the British Empire and the Boer republics. It was a conflict over gold, I think.' She waved a hand. 'The details aren't important. The important thing is that my paternal grandfather, that's your great-great-grandfather, Henry Pettifor, fought as a boy soldier in that war. Or at least in the last year of the war, which was 1902, when he was just about old enough. He served under Lieutenant Walter Holt, who would be Rufus's great-great-grandfather.'

'I see.' They'd both abandoned their spoons now, the soup forgotten as Maggie got into the story.

'The war finished in May 1902. Everybody went back to their normal lives and that would have been the end of that, had not Walter Holt decided to have a reunion of his section at Beech-brook House three years later. Walter was, by all accounts, a bit of a daredevil, reckless and no doubt courageous, which served him well during the fighting but could make life difficult for him in peacetime.'

'How do you mean?'

'He liked nothing better than a good party. He was a womaniser. He liked to drink and he liked to gamble. Henry went along to the reunion, of course he did. It was a chance for free food and drink. There weren't many opportunities for parties like that in those days and he wanted to see his war cronies, the ones who were left. He was also probably quite keen to see how the other half lived. He'd only just married my grandmother. They rented out a farm cottage at the time, not a million miles from here.'

'And the poker match took place at the reunion?' Phoebe breathed, fascinated.

'Correct.' Maggie gave her a wry frown. 'From what I've been told, Walter was so blind drunk he didn't even remember he'd put up the farmhouse and land on a hand of poker. But Henry won it fair and square and there were so many witnesses that even though Walter tried to back down, he couldn't. They'd shaken on it, you see.'

'Wow.'

'Yes. Walter's father, who was the resident lord at the time, and not a bit like his wayward son, made him honour the bet. But he was furious that Walter had been so irresponsible. He'd gambled away a war medal too. I think they got that back, did some sort of trade with the soldier in question. Even so, Lord Holt wasn't over-pleased about giving up the prime farmland they'd previously rented to a tenant. For the next few decades, the Holts didn't speak to the Pettifors. They planted that strip of woodland so they didn't even have to look at the land and the farmhouse that had once been theirs.'

'The strip of woodland that's still there today,' Phoebe said, thinking about Rufus's tree house. She'd always assumed the woodland was there to give Beechbrook House privacy, not to block out the sight of Puddleduck Farm.

'Yes. Walter Holt was eventually cut off by his father, presumably to stop him playing fast and loose with any more of the family assets. I think he died in a hunting accident.' Maggie hesitated. 'Events like that are never totally forgotten. They leave a dark shadow, a long shadow. As far as the Holts are concerned, we took a large chunk of their property and I doubt they've ever really forgiven our family for that.'

'No.' Phoebe's mind whirred with thoughts. 'But they do have the land back now.'

'They had to buy it back,' Maggie reminded her. 'It was part of the reason your grandfather and I sold it to them. Not that we dealt with them directly. You might remember me telling you – all negotiations were done through a representative.'

Phoebe did remember. This story also explained why her

grandmother was always so reluctant to have any direct dealings with the Holts.

Reading her mind, Maggie said, 'It's not the Montagues and the Capulets exactly, but I can't see a Holt ever welcoming the idea of our families being on any more than nodding acquaintance.'

'But I've seen Rufus a few times and he's always been civil. Actually, no he hasn't, has he? He was furious when the neddies escaped that time and were tramping around on his garden. Do you think the family grudge was behind that? Could that be why he was so angry?'

'I don't know, love. But my mother grew up being told to stay well away from the Holts and she passed that on to me. Farmer Pete was more than happy to steer clear of our neighbours too. We just never engaged.'

Phoebe found her mind flicking back over every interaction she'd had with Rufus. There had been more lately than ever. He'd come to the launch of Puddleduck Vets. He'd brought the baby rabbit to be treated. And it had been Rufus who'd asked her to go and look at the fly-tipping site. He certainly hadn't needed to do that. And yet...

'You think Rufus kissed me and then had second thoughts because of bad blood between our families in the past.'

'I'm not saying that. Times have changed. I don't even know Rufus. He didn't seem to have a problem with you being his vet. His father, though, is a different generation. Maybe a different mindset. He may have talked to his father.'

Phoebe gathered up the soup bowls and took them back up to the Belfast sink.

Maggie tore up a piece of leftover bread from her plate and gave half each to Buster and Tiny.

For a few moments, neither woman said anything else. It was

just gone eight and the light was beginning to fade outside the windows.

Phoebe stood at the sink, her shoulders tense. She had no doubt Rufus had felt the same chemistry she had. That kind of feeling couldn't be one-sided, but that didn't mean he hadn't instantly regretted acting on it.

She washed up the bowls and her grandmother joined her and wiped them up. 'I may be talking a complete load of old twaddle when it comes to Rufus, darling. All I'm saying is that I don't want you to get hurt. I just wanted you to be aware of what's gone on in the past.'

21

Phoebe thought about her grandmother's words a lot over the next few days. Maybe she was right, maybe not. But whatever the reason for Rufus's radio silence, she sure as hell wasn't going to be the one to break it. He knew where she was. He had her number. If he wanted to contact her, he could. In the meantime, she had a business to run. She had a list of applicants to shortlist and interview for the position of receptionist, she wanted to pay the owner of Burley Bunnies a visit now she had the address. Not to mention the event at New Forest Diners was looming fast on the horizon.

There was also Eddie's visit on Wednesday afternoon. Maggie had the afternoon off for this. Eddie was arriving at three. His son was dropping him off and then going into Ringwood, where he had an appointment. Eddie and Maggie would be having coffee and cookies in Puddleduck Farmhouse and then she would bring Eddie round to the vet unit for a tour. By which time Phoebe hoped she'd have almost finished for the day.

Her last client on Wednesday, booked in at three thirty, was a Miss Alice Connor who had a cockerel acting out of character. Phoebe felt a twinge of foreboding when she remembered her last appointment with no balls Boris. Maybe it was a different Alice Connor.

She checked the system to see. Jenna had transferred most of the information from Maggie's index card system onto the computer. It appeared to be the same Alice Connor. But she was definitely bringing in a cockerel. According to the system, its name was also Boris. That was peculiar. Maybe she named all of her animals after their erstwhile prime minister. Phoebe seemed to remember she'd been quite a fan.

Phoebe decided she'd just have to wait and see. At least this appointment couldn't possibly be as embarrassing as the last one.

Alice Connor arrived bang on time with a brown cardboard box punched with air holes and sat in the dog end of the waiting room. Phoebe didn't keep her waiting long.

Jenna was in the back consulting room clipping a dog's claws, so Phoebe took Alice into the same room where she'd examined the canine Boris.

'Please do come in,' she said, in her most professional voice. She had no intention of referring to anything that had happened previously, but it would have seemed rude not to ask after the canine Boris. 'I trust your lovely greyhound is well?'

'Boris dog is fighting fit, thank you,' Miss Connor replied. 'We've joined an obedience class on Tuesday mornings. He's doing extremely well.' She coloured slightly as if she too was remembering their previous visit. She was dressed in the same old-fashioned clothes as before – an ultra-feminine white dress dotted with strawberries, but definitely from another era – giving her that look of someone who didn't belong in the twenty-first century.

'But today we have Boris cock… er, cockerel,' Phoebe amended hastily. Was she for ever doomed to have difficult conversations with this woman? 'What seems to be the problem with him?'

'Boris cockerel won't come out of the coop unless I physically move him,' Miss Connor said. 'It's most odd. He's acting more like a broody hen than a proud cockerel.'

'I see, and how long has this been going on?'

'A few days. At first, I thought he may be injured. But I can't see any injuries. Hence, I really thought I should get him checked over.'

'Absolutely,' said Phoebe. 'Right let's have a little look-see.'

She untaped the lid of the cardboard box and lifted it carefully so she could see her patient. Her heart sank. She could see immediately why Boris was acting like a broody hen. As far as Phoebe could tell, and she was the first to admit she wasn't a seasoned expert, Boris was not a cockerel. Boris was, in fact, a broody hen. He certainly looked like a hen anyway. A Rhode Island red that wasn't very big and didn't have the brightly coloured comb and wattle of a cockerel.

'How old is Boris?' Phoebe asked, hoping for a miracle. Maybe this chicken was just very young and not fully developed.

'Boris is nine months old,' Miss Connor replied, shattering this hope. 'I've had my flock for a few months now, but Boris is the only cockerel.'

Phoebe lifted the chicken out. It was plain to see now that she definitely wasn't a he. There were no saddle feathers, there was absolutely nothing to indicate the misnamed Boris was a cockerel at all.

Phoebe was just trying to fathom out how she was going to break it to her client that they seemed to have a gender issue here when Alice spoke again.

'Another odd thing Boris does is to break the other hens' eggs. Is this normal behaviour for a cock... er, male bird?' It seemed she wasn't too keen on the word cockerel either.

Phoebe knew she needed to take the bull by the horns. 'Boris is not a cockerel. Boris is a Doris. What I mean is that Boris is a hen.'

Alice Connor's mouth dropped open. 'I'm afraid that's not possible. I know you were right last time over the matter of Boris the dog's, er, pecker, but this time I have definitely not got it wrong. Boris crows every morning. It's driving my neighbours to distraction, moreover he's never laid an egg.'

Her pale face was a defiant red and she was standing very straight, her shoulders thrust back. Phoebe had an overwhelming urge to agree with her. It would be so much easier to just usher her out with some vitamin pills and reassurance that Boris was probably just a lazy kind of cockerel and there was no reason to worry, than it would be to stand her ground and insist that Boris was a Doris. But she knew she couldn't do this. Her integrity wouldn't let her.

'Cockerels and hens have a few distinctive differences,' Phoebe began, knowing her own face was flaming red now too but determined to get through this. 'For example, the cockerel has a much brighter comb and wattle than the hen. They also have different tail feathers and they're much bigger than this little bird.'

There was a squawk of agreement from the examining table.

'What about the crowing?' Alice clearly wasn't up for being talked out of this. 'Everyone knows only the cockerels crow.'

'That's not entirely true. Occasionally, if there is no cockerel present, a dominant female may take over the role of protector and then they can crow.'

Alice's eyebrows shot up in disbelief. She frowned. 'Are you sure about this?'

'Yes,' Phoebe said. 'I've heard of it happening a few times and it's terribly confusing for poultry keepers. I've even heard of neighbour disputes over exactly this. One neighbour insists that a crowing cockerel is disturbing their peace and the other neigh-bour insists they don't have one.'

'Oh,' Alice said. She pursed her thin lips.

'Regarding the egg breaking,' Phoebe ploughed on, 'some-times a young female might break the eggs of another bird or even their own, and this can unfortunately become a habit.'

There was a silence, apart from the soft clucking of Boris, aka Doris. Phoebe hoped fervently that she might lay an egg there and then and resolve the issue absolutely and irrevocably, but she did not oblige.

'So you're saying there's nothing wrong with him... her?' Alice queried.

'Not as far as I can see. She looks like a perfectly healthy chicken.'

'That's good then.'

Phoebe lifted the hen back into her box, but not before the bird had pooped all over the table and on Phoebe's gloved hands. Thank heavens for surgical gloves.

Alice didn't say another word. She taped up the box, lifted it up carefully and strode towards the door.

'There won't be a charge for today,' Phoebe called after her and she saw her client's shoulders tense slightly, but she did not look back.

* * *

Phoebe stayed in the consulting room for a few minutes. At least she had the excuse of cleaning up. Then, when she was absolutely sure that Alice Connor would be gone, she ventured out.

Jenna had finished with her patient too and was updating the computer.

Phoebe told her what had happened. 'I didn't know whether to laugh or cry,' she said at the end of it.

'I'm not surprised.' Jenna shook her head in disbelief. 'What are the chances? Do you think Miss Connor will ever come back?'

'I really hope not,' Phoebe said. 'I know we shouldn't say that about anyone, but sometimes I pray very hard that I'll never see a client again...'

The door opened and Phoebe, who was standing with her back to it, jumped out of her skin. Thankfully, it was not her client coming back for something she'd forgotten, it was Maggie and Eddie, both of them smiling.

'Here she is,' Eddie said. 'Look at you. You're a sight for sore eyes, you truly are.'

To Phoebe's pleasure and amazement, Eddie had hardly aged at all since the last time she'd seen him. Mind you, he'd looked very old for as long as she could remember. With his shock of white hair, white beard and twinkly blue eyes, he could have played Father Christmas if he'd padded out his tummy with a couple of pillows. He'd always been more wiry than well built. He was leaning heavily on a wooden walking stick and Phoebe remembered what Maggie had said about him being not so steady on his feet these days, but other than that he looked exactly the same as she remembered.

She went to meet him. 'Eddie, it's wonderful to see you. Have a seat?' She pulled out a green chair.

But he brushed it away. 'I don't need to sit down. I need a look about the place. I need to see where the action happens.'

'I'll show you—'

He cut across her and she remembered Maggie had said he was getting a bit hard of hearing too. It must be difficult when he got together with his friend, Dusty Miller. They'd have some interesting conversations.

For the next half an hour, she showed him around and he was fascinated with everything. He might be displaying a lot of the physical signs of age, but his mind was still as sharp and enquiring as a child's. He wanted to know how the instruments worked – he tried out her stethoscope on himself. He looked with interest at the drugs cabinet and remarked that it was almost as comprehensive as his at home. 'A perk of old age.' He was fascinated by the operating theatre and Phoebe explained how she only performed minor surgery at the moment but was hoping to expand that in the future when they had more staff.

Phoebe noticed that he and Maggie communicated in a mix of sign language and words and she guessed they must have built this up over their many years of friendship. It certainly seemed to work for them. They both laughed a lot. It was clearly as much a tonic for Maggie to see Eddie as it was for him to see her and it gladdened Phoebe's heart. It was a shame he'd had to move away and live with his son, she thought, more than once.

They finished the tour by going up to see the neddies and Phoebe left them to it. Eddie might not be as mobile as he'd once been, but that certainly didn't seem to stop him getting about.

Phoebe finally said goodbye to them both around six and she headed for home. Seth was doing cover for her this weekend and she was on a mission. Well, two to be precise. She planned to pay a visit to Burley Bunnies. She'd compiled enough evidence to have a proper chat with Belinda Bates. Plus the breeder had just run another advert so the timing was perfect. It was also this Saturday that she'd booked to go to New Forest Diners.

Despite Phoebe's assurances to Tori that she was definitely up for dating and moving on, and that she was looking forward to the New Forest Diners supper club, Phoebe wasn't sure which of these two events she was dreading the most.

22

Phoebe had made an appointment with Belinda Bates to call at Burley Bunnies at around ten on Saturday morning to look at a rabbit. She was posing as a potential buyer. That way she could have a good nose about and ask lots of questions perfectly legitimately without arousing too much suspicion.

She had also arranged for Tori to go with her. 'If the conditions the rabbits are kept in are as bad as I think they might be, I'd really like some evidence,' Phoebe had told Tori. 'I know we can't just go around taking photos, but I was hoping that if you came too, we could take some surreptitious ones.'

'I am totally up for being an undercover reporter,' Tori had said. 'You keep her talking. I'll do the rest.'

Phoebe had a few reservations about this plan. If they weren't careful, it could all go horribly wrong. But she couldn't think of a better one, so at just before ten on Saturday morning, she parked her Lexus outside an ordinary-looking detached bungalow in a residential street on the outskirts of Burley. Tori was sitting in the passenger seat beside her.

They got out of the car and walked towards the front gates,

which had a small plaque next to the number that said, Burley Bunnies. From the street, the bungalow looked like any other. The bottom half was red brick and the top half white render There was a patch of front garden, but most of the front was slabbed over and a grey Mercedes was parked there. To the left of the bungalow was a high double gate that appeared to be bolted shut from the other side.

'The rabbits must be out the back,' Tori remarked.

'But we have to go through the house to get a look at them?' Phoebe said. They glanced at each other and she knew they were thinking the same thing. It wouldn't be easy to make a quick getaway.

Before either of them could say anything else, two things happened. The first was the sound of movement behind the high gate and Phoebe heard the metallic clink of a bolt being drawn. The gate was shunted open a bit, so there was a gap to walk through. The second was that a couple with a child had just arrived behind them.

'Can we get a white bunny like Lily's, Mum?' said a child's plaintive voice.

'I'm sure we can if the lady has them.'

So they weren't the only ones interested in bunnies, Phoebe thought with a flicker of relief. That would make things easier. Belinda Bates couldn't possibly be everywhere at once. It struck her suddenly that maybe she wouldn't even be here. At the prices she charged, she might have minions to sell her rabbits. Phoebe could feel herself getting angry, which was crazy. Over the last couple of months, partly thanks to Maggie's colourful opinions, she had built up a picture of the breeder as a callous money-grab-bing person who was indifferent to her rabbits' welfare and was interested only in making profits, but she didn't know this was the case. Belinda Bates might be an overenthusiastic amateur who just didn't realise the consequences of her actions. The reality was probably – as Tori had sensibly said – somewhere in the middle.

'Come in, come in, don't hang about in the drive,' a brusque voice from the other side of the gate called out and Phoebe, who was closest, stepped through.

The woman who'd spoken was casually dressed, grey-haired and hard-faced, even though she was smiling. Age-wise, she could have been anywhere between fifty and seventy. Beside her was a younger man, about a foot taller than she was, with a half shaven head and a ponytail, possibly her son but almost certainly her minder, he certainly had the stance of a heavy. He was not smiling.

'This way,' the woman said, ushering them down the side of the bungalow, past several rabbit hutches, most of them occupied, and into a back garden. On the far side of the garden was a long oblong shed with big windows that were too grimy to be able to see much of what lay beyond them and a door that was closed.

But they were headed for a wire run in the middle of the grass. This contained five white lop-eared baby rabbits.

'Bunnies,' called the child, a small girl in a blue coat, running ahead of her parents and crouching down by the run. 'Aren't they cute. Can I hold one?'

'Oh, look,' Phoebe heard the mother say. 'They are cute, aren't they? Look at their lovely ears.'

Phoebe felt her stomach clench. This was exactly the problem. The cuteness factor. And most people simply just didn't realise what it meant. And by the time they did, it was too late. Every instinct she had urged her to tell the woman right now what she was letting herself in for, but she couldn't do that. Not when she was posing as a buyer herself.

The breeder was already bending over the run and expertly scooping up one of the babies, which she handed to the child.

'Adorable, aren't they?' she said. 'Have you decided what you're going to call him?'

'How old are these rabbits?' Phoebe interrupted. 'They look very small. Are you Mrs Bates?'

'Belinda Bates, that's right.' The breeder was busy catching another rabbit and she didn't so much as glance in Phoebe's direction. 'The kits are eight weeks. That's the earliest they leave the doe. Lop-eareds of this type are always small. Are you buying for yourself or a child?'

'Myself,' Phoebe said.

'This is the last one I have available. The rest are sold. You can reserve and collect in a couple of weeks if you like. But I'll need a deposit to keep it.' As she spoke, she held the bunny out towards Phoebe, who didn't really have much choice but to take it. One of its eyes was a little gummy she saw and she pointed it out to Belinda, who waved a hand dismissively.

'Sleepy dust. I've just woken them up. It's common.'

Jeez, this woman was full of crap.

Phoebe bit her lip as she stroked the little creature that was trembling slightly in her hands. It couldn't be more than five weeks old. And already it looked as though it had a respiratory infection, the same as Archie's baby rabbit had suffered from. Almost certainly from bad husbandry.

Even giving Mrs Bates the benefit of the doubt, this did not look like a case of misguided ignorance. She must know how old her rabbits were at the very least.

Phoebe very much wanted to tell her that what she was doing was cruel and very wrong, but she needed to keep this on an even keel. At least for now.

Tori had edged away from the group and was heading for the shed. No doubt she was of the same opinion as Phoebe, who guessed the shed was the centre of Belinda's breeding operation.

At the moment, the minder was talking to the father of the child, answering questions about the size of hutch needed for a rabbit. But he wasn't going to be oblivious for ever.

'What do they eat?' Phoebe asked Belinda.

'Grass. Commercial rabbit food. Carrots.' The woman broke off. 'Hey!'

For a moment, Phoebe thought she was still talking about rabbit food, but she wasn't. She was staring in the direction of her shed. 'Hey. Get out of there. That's private property.'

Tori, to whom this was presumably directed, ignored her. She must be inside the shed.

Belinda was now hurrying across the lawn, as was the minder, who'd leapt into action pretty promptly.

Phoebe followed them more slowly, still carrying the rabbit. 'Excuse me,' she called, hoping to stall at least one of them. 'If I had two rabbits for company? Or maybe three, could I get a discount for cash?'

Belinda slowed down – clearly tempted by the talk of cash. The minder didn't. Just as he reached the shed the door opened and Tori popped her head out.

'Hello,' she said cheerily. 'What a beautiful bunch of bunnies. I just wanted to see the mummy and daddy bunny. Are they in here somewhere?'

She was smiling her sweetest smile and using her dumbest, most innocent voice. As if she was completely oblivious to the fact that anyone minded her going into the shed. Tori was very good at playing dumb.

'You shouldn't be in there,' the minder said. 'That's private property.'

'But aren't the parents of the baby rabbits in here?' Tori brandished her phone and stepped back inside the shed. 'I'd love to get a picture of the mummy and daddy. So I know what mine's going to look like. I think I might need the flash.'

'That's not allowed.'

Belinda, whose body language was furious, stormed across. 'No photos without my permission. The rabbits will look exactly like they do now. Only bigger.'

'I'm so sorry. I'll put my phone away.' Tori held it up in front of Belinda and brazenly pressed the button. 'Ooops. I am such a technophobe. Putting it away now.'

Phoebe was torn between snorting with laughter and bursting into tears. This whole thing would have been funny if the circumstances weren't so sad.

Back on the grass by the rabbit run, the parents were staring at the unfolding scenario with various expressions. The woman's was one of disbelief and the man's was curiosity.

'I'd like to see the parents,' he said, strolling across. 'We should see the parents, shouldn't we? Or does that just apply to dogs?'

'We should definitely see the parents,' Phoebe said to them. 'And we should also check that the breeder is affiliated with the BRC. That's the British Rabbit Council. They help to promote welfare and breed standards.'

'The rabbits are very expensive,' the woman said uncertainly, 'which made us think it was all right.'

'Are you affiliated with the BRC?' Tori directed this towards Belinda. She'd dropped her dumb voice now. 'Can we see paperwork to prove it? And I'd like to see your health and breed standards.'

Belinda Bates had had enough. 'Get out,' she said, whirling around in the middle of her lawn. 'All of you. Get out now. I'm not selling any of you a rabbit. Just leave.'

The minder clapped his hands and attempted to gather them

up. 'Come on. You heard the lady. No rabbits for sale today. Put the rabbits back in the run. Chop chop. Quick as you can.'

Tori had disappeared again and as he spoke, he was looking around for her anxiously.

The little girl, realising she was not going to get her cute baby rabbit, began to cry.

Her mother comforted her. 'We'll get you another rabbit, love. A better one.'

Phoebe, realising that Tori had probably headed back the way they'd come in and was taking more photos, waylaid the minder by handing him her rabbit, leaving him no choice but to pause and put it back in the run.

Regretting that she couldn't take the tiny bunny with her, Phoebe reluctantly headed towards the side of the house. 'Time for us to go,' she hissed at Tori, who had a cage open and looked as though she was taking a video.

'I'm right there. Almost done.' Tori stopped filming just as the minder shot into view. But other than forcibly removing Tori's phone, which he'd have had to do in front of three witnesses, plus a child, there was nothing he could do about it.

Seconds later, they were all outside the gates once more.

'Are you with the RSPCA?' the woman asked Tori, beginning to cotton on to what had just been happening.

'Trading Standards,' Tori lied glibly. 'We'll be taking this further. Did you hear that...?' she shouted back over the fence. 'Trading Standards will be hearing about this. *And* we'll be reporting you to the BRC.'

'We had no idea.' The woman looked upset. 'We wouldn't have realised there was any problem with those rabbits if you hadn't been there.'

Phoebe walked out of the garden onto the road with the parents. 'I'm a vet,' she said, and she started to explain some of the

reasons why it wasn't a good idea to breed rabbits with flat faces
and bent ears, but she could see the woman's eyes starting to glaze
over. What she was saying clearly wasn't going in – or maybe the
woman just didn't want to know. Sometimes it was easier to stay
in comfortable denial than get painfully disillusioned.

23

A few minutes later, back in the car once more, Phoebe and Tori talked about what had happened.

'I know you wanted to be more subtle than that,' Tori said as they drove back through the picturesque town of Burley with its fudge shops and New Forest ponies roaming freely around the streets. 'But I didn't really know what else to do. That shed was rank, Pheebs, even from my uneducated perspective. It was crammed full of hutches. It stank to high heaven. The hutches by the side of the house were spacious and clean compared to the ones in there.'

'No wonder they're getting eye infections, poor little mites,' Phoebe said, gripping the steering wheel tightly, even though the traffic was moving at a snail's pace. It was a beautiful warm May day and Burley was packed with tourists, who were nearly as bad as the ponies for stepping out into the road without warning to take pictures of the pretty town. Not that this mattered too much at the moment. The traffic had pretty much ground to a halt in the centre of Burley. 'Did you get many shots?'

'Yes a few. Although it was dark. I'm not sure how much is

going to show up on the pictures. Can we report them to the RSPCA?'

'Yes we can and I will. But I'm not sure how much good that will do. For a start, those two can clean up their act before they arrive. The RSPCA inspector might not see the same picture as we did.'

'You're right. I shouldn't have shot my mouth off quite as much about Trading Standards. I'm sorry. I was so bloody incensed.'

'It's all right. I was too. And I didn't even go in the shed. Bloody people. How can they do it? How can they think it's OK to exploit animals like that?'

'Money.' Tori's voice was grim. 'It's always about money. Do you think the heavy was her son?'

'I'd guess so.'

'Trading Standards is an option, I think,' Phoebe went on. 'The rabbits she was selling definitely weren't the age she said they were. Also Trading Standards probably have more teeth than the RSPCA do, if you'll excuse the pun. Trading Standards is all about selling the same product as you've advertised. At least I think that's what it's about... Whereas the RSPCA,' Phoebe continued thoughtfully, 'is about proving that animal cruelty is taking place.'

'There must be some other law she's breaking. Don't you need a licence to breed rabbits?'

'Yes, if you're doing it commercially, which she obviously is. But Maggie was telling me about an unlicensed dog breeder she got involved with once, years ago. The RSPCA couldn't get the woman on cruelty, despite the fact her dogs had all sorts of breed-related illnesses, not to mention the breeding bitches being in urgent need of veterinary attention. In the end, they took her to court for breeding without a licence and she was fined. But she didn't care. She just paid the fine, which was less than the value of a litter of puppies, and carried on breaking the law.'

'Yes, unfortunately I can believe that,' Tori said. 'Do you know how the Bates woman advertises?'

'Both of the people I know who've bought a rabbit from her said it was online in Free Ads. That's how I found her too. I had to wait until she was advertising in order to avoid suspicion.'

'Which is another reason I should have kept my big mouth shut,' Tori said. 'Doh. What is wrong with me?'

'You care,' Phoebe said. 'Don't beat yourself up for that.'

'Yes, but I haven't helped, have I! Argh.' Tori banged her fist on the dashboard. 'I am so sorry, Pheebs. Look, why don't we go for an early lunch seeing as this traffic's not moving anywhere fast. The Burley tea room's just up here on the left. My treat. And we can have a look at the photos I did get on my phone.'

'Yes. Good plan.'

* * *

Ten minutes later, they were seated in the Burley tea room, which had once been a cottage. It had a thatched-roof and beamed ceiling, and a huge old open fireplace, currently not in use but piled high with logs. Phoebe and Tori were sitting at a white-clothed table beside it. They had just ordered paninis and were sipping coffee and looking at Tori's photos while they waited for the paninis to arrive.

Unfortunately, Tori had been right about the pictures in the shed not showing much detail. It was just too dark. The fact that the rabbits were white hadn't helped. The camera had either focused on the white coats or the dim interiors, but the contrast was too great to get decent pictures.

'It would have been a different story if I'd had my cameras,'

Tori said, stirring two sugar lumps into her coffee. 'I could have got all the detail we needed. I should have thought it through better.'

'You didn't know the rabbits were going to be in a dark shed. Stop beating yourself up. At least you have some pictures. And the video isn't bad.'

'I know but that isn't nearly as damning. It just shows a cute rabbit in a hutch that's maybe a little small. But that's not a crime.'

Phoebe knew she was right, but Tori was beating herself up too much already – she wasn't about to make her feel even worse. 'I'll report her. My profession might help. At least they'll know I'm qualified to judge. And I've treated three of her rabbits in the practice. That's got to help. That's evidence of malpractice.' She wasn't entirely sure of this, but she was relieved that Tori was looking less upset.

'At least we stopped that family buying a rabbit from her,' Tori remarked. 'That was a plus.'

'It was,' Phoebe said, deciding not to tell Tori about the conversation she'd had with the woman. She had no doubt at all that the family would simply buy another lop-eared rabbit from somewhere else. What was really needed was a big push in raising people's awareness of the potential problems with breeding extreme features into animals. 'Baby steps,' she told her friend. 'We've made a start. That'll do for now.'

The paninis arrived. They'd both ordered brie and red pepper and they were delicious. Then their conversation moved on inevitably to men. Tori already knew that Rufus hadn't been in touch since what Phoebe had begun to refer to as 'that stupid kiss', and she also knew that Phoebe had no plans to make the first move.

Phoebe hadn't yet told her about Maggie's revelations about the poker game, but she did that now, a little sadly.

Tori listened, occasionally shaking her head. 'I get what Maggie's saying, but I'm not sure that I'd put too much stock in that being the reason Rufus has backed off so completely.'

'No? What then? You think he's got another reason to completely ghost me?' Phoebe could hear the hurt in her own voice.

'No, but he isn't ghosting you. He just hasn't made contact. That's not the same thing. You haven't made contact either. It's only been a couple of weeks.'

Two weeks and one day, Phoebe thought, not that she was counting, but she said, 'That's true. You're right. Maybe I'm reading too much into it. And I guess our paths will cross sooner or later – I'm still his vet. And he's still Maggie's landlord. Anyway, enough of Rufus. I want to hear about Harrison. Is that still the love affair of the century?'

'Yep, it is. We're going on holiday. Did I tell you? We're flying to Venice for a short break. In the last week of June. We want to go before school holidays start and it gets too busy.'

'Wow, no you did not tell me that. How brilliant. You've never been, have you?'

'I haven't but Harrison has. He's been pretty much everywhere in Europe, but he worked in Venice for a while. On a gondola – do you believe that?'

Nothing that Tori told her about Harrison would have surprised her these days.

'That is pretty cool,' Phoebe said. 'Did he do it for long?'

'Not that long. He said he got fed up with ferrying loud, obnoxious tourists up and down a smelly canal and that it may look romantic on TV but the reality couldn't be further from the truth.'

'I can imagine.'

'Plus he doesn't like people very much.'

'That's the impression I got when I met him.'

Tori didn't look in the least put out to hear this. 'If he'd known we were friends, he'd have been much more sociable, I'm sure. I'd still love you to properly meet up. It's crazy that you haven't met the most long-term boyfriend I've ever had. I need to invite you round for drinks. Maybe I could have a drinks party, then I could invite Rufus too.'

'No,' Phoebe said more loudly than she'd intended, causing the customers on the next table to glance curiously across at them. She lowered her voice, embarrassed, 'What I mean is yes I'd love to meet him, but please don't ask Rufus. Maybe I'll meet someone at New Forest Diners. I could bring them.'

'Yes, that's tonight, isn't it?' Tori eyed her speculatively. 'I hadn't forgotten. But I thought I'd wait until you mentioned it. You're still going then?'

'I'm looking forward to it,' Phoebe lied.

'No you're not.' They both laughed.

'OK, I'm not, but I am going and I'm trying to keep an open mind. It's step one to getting back into dating. A very gentle step one. I might not like anyone I meet.'

'I thought you were keeping an open mind.'

'I am. I promise.'

'Excellent. So we need to discuss what you're going to wear.'

Phoebe rolled her eyes.

* * *

They had discussed what she was going to wear for so long that Phoebe hadn't ended up with very much time to get ready. Not by the time she'd phoned both the RSPCA and the Trading Standards Office. She hadn't managed to speak to a person in either case, which hadn't surprised her very much for a Saturday, but at least she'd started the ball rolling.

She'd also updated Maggie to tell her what had happened and her grandmother had sighed, but she hadn't sounded surprised. 'Thanks for letting me know, darling. Fingers crossed, eh, but I know what you mean. We are billed as a nation of animal lovers, but we bloody shouldn't be.'

They didn't talk for very long about Belinda Bates. Phoebe knew it would just enrage her grandmother more – she'd had years of first-hand experience with people who'd either deliberately or unthinkingly hurt animals by their actions.

It was now six on Saturday evening, which was half an hour before she was due to leave for supper club and Phoebe stood in front of her bedroom mirror studying her reflection. She was wearing a dress. She didn't have many, but this was her 'go-to' outfit for occasions when she wanted to make a good impression without overdressing.

It was a midi T-shirt dress, polka dot burgundy and it clung in all the right places and was very flattering. It also wouldn't show if she spilled anything down it, Phoebe mused. She could get clumsy when she was stressed and she had visions of spilling soup down her front. Tori, who was a supper club expert, had told her the dinners were three courses and often started with soup.

It wasn't quite warm enough in the evenings yet for no jacket, so Phoebe had chosen a navy lightweight linen one that went well with her dress and she was wearing court shoes with a tiny heel. She'd contemplated flats, but if she did meet anyone she clicked with, she wanted to know straight away that she wasn't going to tower over them. She had never been out with anyone who was shorter than her – it was the only dealbreaker. Everything else was up for discussion, except for a love of animals, which went without saying, but height was important too. Phoebe came from a tall family. Maggie was the only one of them who'd missed out on the height gene – Phoebe didn't want to go out with a man who was shorter than her.

Just for a second, an image of Rufus sneaked into her head. Her mind flashed back painfully to them standing beneath the silver birches, the rustling of a breeze through the tall trees, the scent of the forest, the scent of him, and the taste of chocolate and warmth as they kissed.

Phoebe dragged herself forcibly back to the present. Who knew what would happen tonight. Maybe she would meet the man of her dreams. This had worked for Tori – albeit in a slightly roundabout way, Phoebe reminded herself, as she went downstairs, picked up her purse from the kitchen worktop and went out to the Lexus. She had contemplated getting a taxi, but she wanted to stay sober, so there wasn't much point. She did not want the disadvantage of wine-tinted glasses. She wanted the crisp clarity of truth. After eighteen months of getting over Hugh, and of the short but sweet fantasy of the lord of the manor, she was finally ready for full-on reality.

24

The supper club was being held at the Rhinefield House Hotel, which was a stunning country house hotel, set in forty acres of its own grounds in the New Forest.

According to Tori, it was one of the nicest locations they used. Phoebe was aware of its existence. It was hard not to be when you lived in the New Forest, and one of her favourite places, the Tall Trees Walk, was within a stone's throw of Rhinefield House, but she had never been there for a meal.

Also according to Tori the house had been built in 1887 by Mabel Walker Munroe whose family owned Eastwood Colliery, which had featured in several of DH Lawrence's novels.

'How do you know that?' Phoebe had asked her in surprise. 'Did Harrison tell you?'

'I'm a journalist,' Tori had said huffily. 'It's my job to know. But, as it happens, I read it in *The Telegraph* online the other day. One of their journos had done a review of the place. It's probably still there if you want to have a look.'

'Have you ever been there for a meal?'

'No,' Tori had confessed. 'I've missed the ones New Forest

Diners have held there for various reasons. I wouldn't mind going there, though. I might see if Harrison fancies it. They're open to the public when they're not doing a function. They do a lot of society weddings,' she had added thoughtfully. 'It's very posh.'

Posh was an understatement, Phoebe decided as she went up the long drive bordered by azaleas and rhododendrons and found a wooded car park, surrounded by tall trees and huge shrubs. Before she'd left home, she'd sneaked a look at the review Tori had mentioned. The journalist had described the Rhinefield House Hotel as 'grandeur on an epic scale'. They were right about that. At the end of the drive, she was confronted with a magnificent grey building with mock-Tudor turrets and a crenelated parapet; it made Rufus Holt's house look shabby.

How had he crept back into her head? She shoved him out.

She was feeling nervous enough already. Not just at the prospect of dining out with a bunch of judgemental strangers, all of whom would be sizing her up, but also because being in places like this made her feel slightly intimidated. She preferred the wild and untamed grandeur of the natural world to the engineered carefully constructed and architectured grandeur built by men.

Phoebe parked, then, clutching her bag, she walked back round to the entrance. The instructions on the email had said they were dining in the conservatory restaurant, which was less formal than either of the main restaurants. They were to meet in the bar. Even so, she was tempted to flee. Butterflies flicked like crazy around her stomach. This was madness. Wasn't this supposed to be fun? It didn't feel like it. She had reached a door in a glass walkway, of what was obviously a much later addition to the main house, and just as she did so, she became aware of a man walking beside her.

'Allow me,' he said, opening the door for her.

'Thanks.' She had an impression of brown hair, and a nice face, just before she walked ahead of him.

'Are you here for New Forest Diners?' he asked when they were both inside and she glanced at him in relief.

'Yes, I am. Are you?'

'Yes, I'm Steve. I haven't seen you before. Are you new?'

'First time,' she told him. 'I'm Phoebe.'

'It's good to meet you, Phoebe. This is my third event.' There was a warmth about him that was very genuine. What a pity he was shorter than her by about two inches. 'I believe it's round to the left,' he added. 'I've not been here with New Forest Diners, but I came here once for a murder mystery evening.'

'Really? I bet that was fun.'

'It was. The food's good too.'

He was an easy conversationalist and a few moments later they had gone through a beautiful orangery where Phoebe could see several tables laid up for dinner, before they stepped down a level into a bar.

'There's our lot,' Steve said. 'Come on, I'll introduce you.'

They headed towards a table where a small group of six or seven people were already sitting, sipping drinks and chatting animatedly. They all smiled and stopped talking for a few moments while Phoebe was introduced and then they were off again and she found herself at a table on the outskirts of the group with Steve.

He was very chatty and keen to share details of his life. He told her he was a structural engineer and had recently moved to Southampton; he was a great fan of cities.

Phoebe quickly discovered he was also a great fan of red wine. He downed a large glass of it while they were chatting – and his confidences became swiftly more personal.

'I haven't had the need to do much dating. I married my childhood sweetheart, but I was widowed a couple of years ago. Louise, my wife, had a brain haemorrhage.'

'How terrible.' Phoebe looked at him in shock. 'She couldn't have been very old.'

'Thirty-seven. Same as I am now, God rest her soul.' He paused, the light going fleetingly from his brown eyes. 'I miss her desperately. But I also think it's time to move on. Which is why I joined New Forest Diners.'

There was a gap in the conversation while Phoebe struggled to think of the right thing to say, finally settling on, 'Did you and your wife have any children?'

'No, we didn't, which is both a big regret and a big relief. I'm not sure I'd have coped very well with being a single dad. Not that I don't like children. We had just not gone in that direction. We were thinking about it – Louise wanted one of each at least.'

Their conversation was interrupted by a woman with a clipboard called Marsha, who was clearly in charge, telling them it was time to go through to the restaurant.

This turned out to be the orangery they'd walked through to get to the bar. They were on a long table, set up for eight by one of the glass walls. The orangery overlooked a man-made oblong water feature that looked a bit like a very long, oversized swimming pool. Beyond that, Phoebe caught a glimpse of formal gardens – topiary and lawns.

Steve sat next to Phoebe. 'Don't worry, you won't be stuck with me all evening,' he quipped. 'Marsha makes us all swap around between courses, so we get the chance to meet each other.'

'I'm happy to sit next to you,' she said, regretting it slightly when she saw his eyes brighten. He was pleasant enough, but there was no chemistry there at all. Not for her.

He gestured out of the windows beside them. 'It's worth having a stroll around the grounds if you get the chance. They specialise in water features and formal gardens – I think they're a nod to the great French and Italian gardens of the period. I can tell you all about the history of this place. I can give you the full lowdown of the architecture. And I can run you through every detail of the building materials – dates, names, the whole shebang. It's my specialist subject.'

'Wow,' she said politely.

Their soup was lovage with crusty brown rolls. It was delicious. Phoebe concentrated on listening to Steve and eating it without talking with her mouth full. Not that there was too much danger of that happening because Steve had plenty to say for both of them.

He spent most of the soup course telling her about the building of the house and about the fact that it had been a private school for a while, before finally asking her, just as the waiter was collecting their bowls, what her story was.

'You must have been married. You're far too pretty to have escaped.'

'Thank you.'

'Sorry to interrupt your conversations, ladies and gentlemen, but it's time to swap places.' Marsha's voice was accompanied by the tinging of a spoon on a glass.

Phoebe got to her feet without having to answer Steve, quite relieved when her next dining companion turned out to be much quieter and was apparently drinking orange juice.

'I'm Henry Willoughby-Smythe.' He shook her hand. 'Why aren't you drinking? Are you an ex-alcoholic?'

'Er, no.' She met his deadpan blue eyes and took in his bulbous red nose. 'Are you?'

His face cracked into a leer. 'No. I'm jesting with you. I'm not drinking because I'm out in the Aston. One can't risk scratching one's Aston.' Now he'd put on a silly voice too. 'Have you ever been in one? Phoebe, wasn't it? Do you shorten that? Phibs? Phee? Fee-fee?'

'I don't shorten it,' she said, disliking him immediately. Bloody hell. Why hadn't Tori warned her? She'd said the New Forest Diners were a really nice bunch of ordinary people.

'Have you attended one of these gigs before then?' He raised his eyebrows. He had curious eyebrows. Almost white although his hair was dark. Perhaps it was dyed. It didn't look dyed.

'Tonight's my first.'

'A virgin.' He chortled again. 'I do like a nice juicy virgin.'

She was really tempted to slap him. That probably wouldn't be a good move on her first outing, no matter how rudely he was behaving. 'Wanker,' she muttered, just loudly enough for him to hear.

'Steady on. That was a bit uncalled for, Fee-Fee.'

There was nothing wrong with his hearing then.

The beautiful Asian woman who was sitting opposite Phoebe had clearly heard her too because she leaned across the table. 'Well said. Henry gets off on being offensive. He doesn't come to supper club very often, thankfully for the rest of us.' She glared at him and, to Phoebe's surprise, Henry actually looked chastened and didn't argue. 'I'm Catherine,' she added, looking at Phoebe. 'I arrived late, so I missed the intros.'

Phoebe introduced herself, feeling very grateful to have someone in her corner.

Henry didn't say anything else throughout their main course. The choices on the à la carte menu had included cider-braised rabbit with apples and crème fraîche and Henry had chosen this. Of course he had. He was picking salaciously through the small bones and dripping sauce onto the white tablecloth.

Phoebe glanced at his plate and thought of the tiny lop-eared bunny that had trembled in her hands at Burley Bunnies and she felt ill. She'd chosen chicken breast, but suddenly she didn't feel much like eating that either.

She excused herself and escaped to the ladies', where she WhatsApped Tori.

Gorgeous venue. Wish I could say the same about the guys! On the main course. Two no hopers so far.

Tori typed back immediately.

There's still dessert. Hang on in there.

Phoebe wondered if she could break with tradition and sit next to Catherine for dessert. She looked more fun. Or maybe she should just sneak away now. Unfortunately, she'd left her jacket on the back of her chair. She considered sacrificing it in a good cause but berated herself for being a coward. The evening was almost over. She didn't need to stay for coffee.

Dessert, as it happened, turned out to be by far the best part of the meal. Maybe Marsha had got wind of what had gone on, because Phoebe found herself sitting next to a self-deprecating, silver-haired man called Luke Harding who couldn't have been more charming.

By some fluke of fate, he was a vet in Bournemouth and, she discovered once they got chatting, also a friend of Seth's.

'I think Seth may have mentioned you,' he declared, over a deliciously light lemon posset. 'Weren't you the young vet who once brought a crayfish back from the dead?' His eyes glinted with amusement.

Phoebe blushed. 'Reports of it being dead were greatly exaggerated,' she said, warming to him straight away. 'But, yes, that was me.'

'It's a real pleasure to meet you. Seth told me you were going to set up on your own last time we spoke. How's that going?'

She told him and for the next ten minutes they talked shop. He was charming. He was younger than he looked, despite the silver hair. Although he was still fourteen years older than she was.

'I'm on the outer edge of the age limit,' he told her. 'Which is forty-nine. Between you and me, I've been forty-nine for the last three years. They can't get rid of me.'

She laughed. 'You haven't met anyone special here then?'

'I've met lots of special people. But I'm not looking for romance. I just like the fine-dining aspect. This isn't just a dating outfit. We have a few people who pair up and leave, but lots of people just come because they like the social side.'

Phoebe stayed for coffee. Right at the end of the evening, she told Luke she was just in the process of looking for a full-time receptionist and ultimately another vet and he promised to put the feelers out for her.

'I was going to ask Seth,' she confided, 'but I already have his ex vet nurse, Jennifer Aniston. I don't dare poach any more of his staff.'

'I know Jenna,' Luke said. 'Lovely girl. OK, leave it with me. It's always better to have a recommendation, isn't it?'

* * *

As Phoebe drove back along the darkening New Forest roads, images of the evening flicked in and out of her head: Steve and his self-obsessions, Henry and his crassness, and finally the lovely Luke. It had been memorable, that was for sure. But she had absolutely no intention of going to another one, despite Luke's assurances that most of the meals were superb affairs and they didn't often have what he had called 'your more barbarian types' in attendance. Apparently Marsha did quite a good job of wheedling them out.

Just as Tori had invited her, most people came by recommendation, Luke had told her. Unfortunately, Henry, who'd been coming for years had joined before Marsha's time and they put up with him because he came so infrequently. Most people had either left since his last visit or, if they hadn't left, they'd forgotten how much of an arse he could be by the time he came to the next one. Phoebe was pretty sure she wouldn't forget!

Phoebe put both Henry and the drunken Steve out of her head. Tonight had been an experience, that was for sure, and if she'd achieved nothing else, she'd made a new friend in Luke. They'd swapped business cards and agreed to keep in touch. Who knew, she might even get a recommendation for a new vet or receptionist. Fingers crossed.

25

Phoebe spent the first part of June on a mission. She had several conversations with an RSPCA inspector about Burley Bunnies and her concerns that the breeder was keeping rabbits in unsanitary conditions, which was causing health problems from the beginning. She told him about the baby rabbit she'd seen that was showing symptoms of a respiratory infection and about her concerns the rabbits were leaving their mother far earlier than was good for their welfare. She also told him about the owners of rabbits she'd seen at her practice who had come in with problems which had alerted her to the breeder in the first place. 'I'm sure they would both be happy to talk to you,' she had added, knowing even as she spoke that she'd rather have walked over hot coals than phone Rufus about Bob – but then she could always get Jenna to do it.

It had been a month now since that stupid kiss. Rufus's silence had been all the evidence Phoebe had needed to prove that Maggie was right. The lord of the manor did not want a repeat performance. Phoebe was certainly not going to give him any indication that she felt any differently.

The RSPCA inspector had told Phoebe he'd come back to her if he needed any of her clients' details. He was a nice guy, who'd been in the job for years, and he'd promised to go personally to see Belinda Bates and to keep Phoebe updated on his progress. Trading Standards were also helpful when they finally got back to her – but, as Phoebe had suspected, rabbits being sold a week or two earlier than they were supposed to be weren't a top priority.

Phoebe had a strong urge to do more, but she didn't think there was much more she could legally do. Although Maggie had some ideas.

'We could arrange for a late-night rabbit liberation visit,' she had suggested in front of an interested Natasha, who had nodded vigorously.

'No we could not,' Phoebe had told her grandmother, slightly shocked, despite herself.

'I'm joking,' Maggie had said, rolling her eyes. 'I'm far too old to go climbing over six-foot-high fences in the middle of the night.'

'I'm not,' Natasha had said, a little too enthusiastically in Phoebe's opinion.

'If you get yourself arrested, who's going to look after all the animals here,' Maggie had said to her, shaking her head. 'No, love. I think that, much as it irks me, Phoebe is right. We have to do things totally by the book. We need to let the authorities handle this. At least for now,' she'd added in a muttered aside that made Phoebe give her a second glance.

But Phoebe didn't really think Maggie would do anything illegal, no matter how strong her opinions on animal welfare. There was too much at stake for Puddleduck Farm.

* * *

Phoebe and Jenna narrowed down their shortlist and started interviewing for the receptionist job during the second week of June. There were only three people on the final interview list and they were all great candidates. Two were women and the third unusually was a guy. The women, both in their mid-thirties, had the most experience. One had two children both school age, the other described herself as a bachelorette, but they'd both worked at practices before. The bachelorette had just moved down from London, having come out of a long-term relationship. Her name was Kat and Phoebe was tempted to choose her because she reminded her strongly of herself.

'That's probably not a very good reason though, is it?' she said to Maggie and Jenna on the day that they'd been interviewing all three candidates.

'If she has your work ethic it is,' Jenna said.

'What did you think of the young man in the suit?' Maggie said, reaching over to pick up the CVs. She had been covering reception while they interviewed, so she'd only met the candidates briefly.

'More to the point, what did you think of him?' Phoebe asked, recognising her grandmother's thoughtful expression.

'I liked him. He was the only one who engaged with anyone in the waiting room,' she replied. 'The other two played with their phones.'

'I didn't know there was anyone in the waiting room,' Phoebe said. 'Being as we were busy interviewing.'

'Well, that's where you'd be wrong. A few people came in. A man to pick up a prescription and a couple to buy some of that overpriced specialist dog food you flog. The women barely glanced up. They were all very polite to me, of course. Very chatty when they arrived. But I noticed he made a point of being chatty with everyone. Natasha came in as well – he was very chatty with her.'

'I bet he was. Natasha's gorgeous,' Phoebe remarked.

'That's true,' Maggie acknowledged. 'But young Marcus was more interested in the duck she brought in to see me. Natasha thought Jemima was getting bullied,' she explained.

'Was she?' Phoebe asked, getting instantly sidetracked.

'I'm not sure. Maybe. We're going to keep an eye on her. Going back to Marcus though – he was very interested. Said his gran used to keep ducks. He clearly had a soft spot for them and then we got chatting about why this place is called Puddleduck Farm. He was fascinated about that.'

'Sounds like you had a soft spot for *him*,' Phoebe said curiously.

'I did a bit. He was different from your usual lad of that age. Thoughtful.' She put her head on one side. 'You're invisible when you're seventy-three. Especially to the younger generation. And he was very smart.'

'Are you saying he's your favourite candidate?' Phoebe asked, picking up the three CVs and riffling through until she found Marcus's.

'Yes, I think I am. Subject to him having the right qualifications and experience. Obviously.' She arched her eyebrows. 'Like I did.'

They all smiled. Maggie's experience and qualifications for being a vet receptionist were precisely zero.

Phoebe glanced through the CV in her hand. Marcus Peterson was very personable. Maggie was right about that. She'd warmed to him in the interview. But he was the youngest, twenty-seven, and had the least experience of the three. He'd only worked in one practice – a well-respected place in Bournemouth, but that had been for a brief eighteen months a couple of years ago. He hadn't worked at a vet's since then. She had pencilled in a question mark beside that and when she'd asked him about it, he'd said he'd left for personal and professional reasons. His eyes had clouded and she and Jenna had exchanged glances, but neither of them had pursued it.

Now, she looked at his references. Notably he hadn't listed the Bournemouth practice as a referee, but one of the names he had listed as a referee sprung out at her – Luke Harding.

'I've just realised I've met one of Marcus's referees,' she said, pointing out the name to Jenna and Maggie. 'I met Luke Harding socially a few weeks ago. Apparently he knows Seth. Maybe I should give him a ring and get some information. I'll ring both of them. I need to catch up with Seth anyway about work.'

* * *

When Phoebe spoke to Seth, who was on fine form, he said that he didn't know Marcus Peterson. 'Although the name rings a bell,' he added thoughtfully.

They were on the phone and Phoebe could almost hear the cogs whirring in his brain.

'Some kind of scandal,' Seth went on. 'A couple of years ago. Although I might be wrong about that. If he's put Luke Harding down as his referee, then definitely ask him. Luke's one of the good guys.'

'Oh,' Phoebe said. 'A scandal doesn't sound good.'

'I might be remembering that wrong. Don't take my word for it. Ask Luke.'

'Thanks, I will.'

Phoebe phoned Luke as soon as she'd finished catching up with Seth and he sounded delighted to hear from her.

'I'm phoning you in a work capacity,' she said quickly before he got the wrong idea. 'I've been given your name as a reference for a receptionist I'm thinking of hiring. Marcus Peterson. I'd love to know your thoughts.'

'Ah, Marcus.' Luke obviously recognised the name immediately. 'Yes I know exactly who you mean. Nice guy...'

'But...?' Phoebe prompted.

'He has a chequered past.'

'What kind of chequered past are we talking about?'

'Would you like the official version or would you like my considered opinion?' Luke asked her.

'I think I'd like both,' Phoebe said, now totally intrigued.

'OK. The official version is that Marcus got into a slanging match with a high-profile client at a practice where he was working in Bournemouth. The slanging match turned physical and Marcus gave the client a left hook in front of several witnesses and laid him out on the practice floor.'

'Jeez. Did he?' Phoebe hadn't been expecting that at all. 'He didn't seem the violent type.'

'I don't think he is. I've known Marcus since he was a teenager. He's a friend of my youngest daughter. I have never known him to be anything but a polite, gentle and mild-mannered young man. Although he can get passionate about animal causes.'

'So what happened?'

'I have it on good authority that the client was being obnoxious. He was a breeder. Persian cats – the type with a pedigree as long as your arm that sell for very high prices. He'd come in to make an appointment for some kittens to be humanely destroyed. He was the kind of breeder who'd have kittens put to sleep rather than take lower prices for them. We're talking kittens which have minor breed imperfections.'

'Sounds like a lovely guy,' Phoebe said with heavy sarcasm.

'My sentiments precisely.' Luke paused. 'The story I heard was that Marcus refused to make the appointment. Things escalated and got physical and the upshot was that Marcus delivered a knockout punch.'

'I can't say I blame him.' Phoebe shuddered.

'Again, my sentiments precisely. I also have it on good authority that the client got physical first. He grabbed Marcus by the collar and threatened him. Marcus lashed out in self-defence and got lucky. Or, as it turned out, unlucky – because the guy was furious – once he'd got up from the floor that was. He said he'd make sure Marcus lost his job and that he'd never work in the industry again and several other similar threats.'

'But didn't you say there were witnesses?'

'There were, but one of them was the client's son. He swore blind that his father hadn't touched Marcus. That the attack had been unprovoked. And the other two were young women who worked at the practice. I heard they were bullied into keeping quiet.'

'Bloody hell,' Phoebe said. 'That's terrible.'

'It is. And, unfortunately, it gets worse. Marcus got the sack on the grounds of gross misconduct. And he hasn't managed to get a job anywhere since. The breeder has friends in a lot of high places and he wasn't content with just getting Marcus the sack. He did what he threatened. He bad-mouthed Marcus all across the industry and made it known that if Marcus was given a job at another practice he'd bad-mouth them too. No one wants to invite that kind of bad publicity.'

'No,' Phoebe said. 'I don't suppose they do.'

There was a pause and she could hear him breathing. 'Having said all that, I have to say that I'd give Marcus Peterson a great reference. Both personally and professionally. He's honest, authentic and he cares about animals. I'd have employed him myself if we'd had any need for another receptionist. Which we haven't since he's been looking. I wouldn't blame you one bit for not employing him – in the circumstances.' He cleared his throat. 'But I think he deserves a second chance.'

'Thank you very much,' Phoebe said. 'I'll let you know what I decide.'

She'd already decided. She agreed with Luke completely. Marcus deserved a second chance and no way was she going to be intimidated by someone who sounded like a very nasty piece of work. She despised bullies, especially ones who mistreated animals.

* * *

Maggie and Jenna both agreed. Phoebe wasn't surprised. Maggie had been fighting injustice on behalf of animals for the last thirteen years. Although this applied more to animals than people usually.

'I can't stand bullies,' Maggie said, sniffing. 'The client sounds like another candidate for a bag.'

'A bag?' Jenna queried.

'Over his head,' Maggie told her. 'Shame it's illegal.'

Jenna snorted.

Phoebe phoned Marcus to offer him the job and he went up even more in her estimation when he said that before he could take it, there was something she needed to know. Then he told her what she'd already heard.

'If you need to retract the offer, I understand,' Marcus added quietly.

'I don't,' she said. 'I already know about the past. If you're free, you can start in July. I think the first Monday is the fourth. Independence Day. How does that sound?'

'That sounds brilliant.' Marcus paused and added in a voice that was decidedly husky, 'Thank you.'

26

Phoebe wasn't the only one on a mission in June. Sam had been on a mission too. He was determined that Brook Riding School would come home with a few rosettes from the New Forest Show and do the school proud. His pupils were in a cross-section of classes, which ranged from show classes to show-jumping and he was working hard to make sure they did well. Preparation was key and Sam was hugely encouraging and supportive of his brood, even though some of them were easier to deal with than others.

Abi was taking Dotty in the young handler class. Archie Holt was taking Molly in the best turned out pony class. Henrietta Blackstone was riding her pony Benji in the junior showjumping. And there were a couple more in the working hunter classes. There would be quite a turnout from Brook School. Marjorie Taylor, who owned the school, was coming along to help as were several of the Saturday girls and of course their parents. Sam's hopes were pinned on Archie because he was by far his favourite pupil. Archie was surprisingly unspoiled, considering who his father was. Whereas Henrietta was a pain in the butt.

Sam was also hoping that he and Ninja didn't do too badly in their class. Especially as Jo and Abi were coming along to watch. At least he hoped they were. He hadn't seen much of Jo for the last couple of weeks. He saw her during Abi's Saturday afternoon lessons, but the focus was all on Abi then and she'd had to change her slot to earlier in the afternoon, so he couldn't stop and chat to her afterwards because he had another lesson.

Jo had also been massively busy lately. She'd told him she had two Italian students at the moment and Tesco had also given her some extra shifts. He knew she was in no position to turn down work, so he'd accepted – they both had – that their relationship was taking a back seat at the moment.

They were seeing each other tonight, though, and Sam was looking forward to it. He'd wanted to take her to a new French restaurant in Bridgeford, but she'd said she'd prefer somewhere less formal, so they were going to The Brace for a pie and a pint instead. Jo had said she'd meet him there after she'd dropped Abi at her mum's, who was babysitting.

Sam arrived early. He was looking forward to tonight. His whole life had felt rushed lately. He seemed to go from one place to the next with barely a break to catch his breath. If he wasn't working at the Post Office with his ma, he was working at Brook Stables. The longer days meant he had lessons scheduled for the evenings as well as the weekends, and if he wasn't teaching, he was riding Ninja.

Taking his own horse to the show had probably been a step too far. On some days, he wondered what on earth had possessed him to think competing again was a good idea. It didn't leave much time for a social life. Thank goodness Jo was on the same wavelength as he was. It was a blessing that she was busy too.

She was already at The Brace when he arrived. He saw her at their usual table and she'd got the drinks in, bless her. She was tapping away on her phone, but she glanced up as he arrived and put it away.

'I'm not late, am I?' he said, bending to peck her cheek.

'No, Sam. I was early.' She sounded a bit tense, and she didn't look her usual smiley self either.

'Is everything OK?' he asked, concerned, as he sat opposite her. 'Thanks for the drink.'

'You're welcome.' She paused. 'And – yes and no.'

'Would it help to share?' He took a sip of his half-pint.

Jo took a sip of hers too. 'I won't beat around the bush, Sam. I'm worried about us.'

'About us?' He looked at her and suddenly he knew why she hadn't wanted to go to the French restaurant. Why he hadn't seen much of her lately. And very possibly why she'd changed Abi's lesson to a time when there was no chance to socialise after it. He knew that look. He was about to get dumped. And, alarmingly, because he was usually pretty switched on about such things, he hadn't seen it coming.

He waited. Jo looked uncomfortable. Maybe she'd met someone else. Maybe that's why she'd made so many excuses lately.

'I like you a lot, Sam, but I don't think we're really going anywhere, are we?'

'And you think that because...?'

'For one thing, you're really too busy for a girlfriend, and for another...' She paused, took another sip of her drink, fiddled with a beer mat and then looked up straight into his eyes. 'For another thing, I don't like playing second fiddle.'

'Second fiddle? What are you talking about? Do you mean second fiddle to my work? I know it's been mad busy lately, but I thought you were busy too. You are not second fiddle, I promise.'

'Not to your work.' She sighed. 'To Phoebe Dashwood.'

He was stunned into silence. 'Phoebe Dashwood. What has she got to do with it?'

'You're in love with her, Sam. I could see it in your face when we bumped into her the last time we came in here. I know you said she was just a friend and you'd never had a relationship with her. But that doesn't mean you don't want one.'

'Hang on a minute.'

She put up a hand to stop him. 'Just hear me out.'

He shut up.

'It was obvious from the way you were behaving around her. And, to be honest, it's happened to me before. I recognised the look on your face. It was exactly the same as the look on Abi's dad's face when he left us. He went off with my best friend.'

'You've never told me that.'

'No. It's something I'd rather forget.' She sighed. 'I'm prepared to accept that I might be overreacting because of what's happened in the past. But I don't think I am. Last time we were here you told me there had never been anything between you and Phoebe. But you want there to be, don't you? Please be honest with me, Sam.'

She waited. Her face was still now, her eyes anxious.

He sighed. He knew it was pointless to lie. He didn't want to lie to her.

'OK. You're right. I did once want a relationship with Phoebe. We grew up together. We've always been close friends, but my feelings started to change when she came back from London last year.' It was his turn to feel uncomfortable, but he had to get this out. 'So I told her how I felt and she told me she didn't feel the same. End of. That's the whole story. Nothing more to it than that.'

'I see. Thank you for being honest.' She picked up her bag and put it on the table in front of her. It felt like a shield. Blocking him out. And he knew she was going to leave if he didn't say something to stop her.

'I've moved on, Jo. I'm over Phoebe.'

'But that's the trouble, Sam. You're not.' Suddenly her eyes were glittery with tears. 'And if you think you are, then you're lying to yourself. I'm sorry. But I just can't risk it happening again. There's Abi to consider. It's not just me any more. She really likes you.'

'And I really like her... I really like you too,' he added, but he could see it was pointless.

Jo was already standing up. She had made up her mind. She had probably made up her mind before she even got here and that was his own stupid fault. They should have talked before. He should have reassured her. The last few weeks had slipped by with this great shadow of an elephant hanging between them, waving its bloody enormous trunk. And he'd let it because he'd been so damn busy. But if he'd really cared, he would have insisted they see each other, hammer it out before time had made it bigger and bigger until it was too big to cope with.

'Goodbye, Sam.'

Jo walked away and Sam stayed where he was at the table, a lump in his throat, their half-finished drinks in front of him. If he'd really loved her, he'd have run after her. He'd have begged her to come back. Told her it wasn't true. That her fears were unfounded. But the trouble was, it was true. He did still have strong feelings for Phoebe. Even if he did nothing about them. Even if he hadn't even bloody acknowledged them. They were still there. Unfinished business. At least for him. He was pretty sure that Phoebe was completely unaware of how he felt.

He downed his drink, then went to the bar and ordered another – a pint this time. He couldn't bear the thought of going home to his empty flat. Even Snowball hadn't been in much lately. He suspected his cat had a lady friend a couple of doors down. Lucky old Snowball. It would be much better to stay here and drown his sorrows. He could leave his car here and get a taxi home.

* * *

An hour and a half later after two more pints of real ale, Sam was feeling decidedly squiffy. He wasn't used to drinking. He got up, deciding it was time to go – via the gents' – he could call a taxi in the car park. The signal was better out there.

He'd just reached the old oak door of the pub when it swung open and a couple of blokes came in. Both in the heavy jeans and Barbour jacket attire of the forest. Sam recognised one of them immediately – Rufus Holt – the father of his star pupil and, in Sam's opinion, the nob of the year. Not that he'd seen the man lately. He wasn't the supportive father type – he'd only come to one of Archie's riding lessons way back when he'd first started. He'd sent Archie's Swiss-German nanny to the rest.

Sam waited politely for them to pass. It was obvious that Rufus hadn't recognised him – why would he? Besides which, he was distracted, listening to something his friend was saying, and then Sam heard a name that halted him in his tracks.

'Phoebe's a vet though – it's hardly the same...'

Rufus was nodding. 'I know.' He broke off and thanked Sam for holding the door open.

Sam couldn't move. The two men passed through and went to the bar.

He heard the man that wasn't Rufus laugh. 'You're over-thinking it, mate. Isn't it time you had a bit of fun? Especially if she's a looker. Fill your boots. It doesn't have to be serious...'

But whatever else was said, Sam didn't catch it because they'd moved too far away.

He went outside into the car park, the cold air hitting him and making his head spin. He badly wanted to know why they were talking about Phoebe. He was also acutely aware that it wouldn't do him any good to find out.

For a few moments, he stood in the car park swaying. Going back into the pub and demanding to know why they were talking about Phoebe was not going to end well. Of that he was a hundred per cent certain. The sensible thing to do would be to call a cab right now and go home and forget the whole thing.

Bloody hell. He was sick and tired of being sensible. Being the good guy – being patient and reasonable and nice. Telling the truth. Having integrity. Look where that had got him tonight.

He spun round and went back into the pub. Rufus and his sidekick were standing at the bar. Sam marched across and tapped Rufus on the shoulder. 'Excuse me, mate.'

* * *

Rufus turned and found himself face to face with a solidly built, clearly totally drunk and not very happy man. He looked vaguely familiar.

'Do I know you?' Rufus asked, instinctively recoiling from the alcohol fumes on the man's breath.

'You know my girlfriend,' Sam said. 'Phoebe Dashwood. Stay away from her.' He was swaying unsteadily, which detracted somewhat from the threat, but Rufus stepped back anyway, more shocked by the guy's words than his actions.

'Your girlfriend?'

''S'right.' The man was so drunk he could barely stand. But he was managing to jab a pointing finger at Rufus. 'Keep your grubby hands to yourself. Or you'll have me to answer to.'

At his side, Rufus heard Harrison's hissed voice. 'Come on. Let's leave. We don't need this. There are other pubs. Cancel that, barman.'

Rufus stepped away before the drunk could make contact. They were outside again a few moments later, heading for the Land Rover.

'That was bloody weird,' Harrison said as they got back in the Land Rover. 'Did you know that bloke?'

'I can't place him, but he did look familiar.' Rufus snapped on his seat belt.

'I'm guessing he's helped you make a decision, though.' Harrison shot him a sly glance as he started up the engine. 'However good a kisser she was.'

Rufus nodded. Tonight was the first time he'd spoken to anyone about what had happened. For the last few weeks, he'd done his best to get Phoebe out of his head and he'd failed. She was there when he closed his eyes and she was there when he woke up. It had been driving him crazy. He'd finally decided to share his thoughts with Harrison, who'd just got back from holiday with his girlfriend and was in a very good mood.

'But how the hell did he know?' he asked Harrison now. 'How did he even know who I was?'

'Lots of people know who you are,' Harrison said with irony, 'despite your reclusive tendencies. But I'm guessing your Phoebe kissed and told. She must have felt guilty.'

'Yeah.' Rufus shut his eyes. Harrison was right. It was best to steer clear. His instincts to try to forget what had happened had also been right. If he'd known Phoebe was spoken for, he'd have kept his distance. He did not need a deranged boyfriend picking a fight with him in a pub. He definitely did not need a scandal. And if he'd known Phoebe was the sort of woman who'd kiss another man behind her boyfriend's back he wouldn't even have been considering seeing her again.

27

Sam woke up the next day with a throbbing head and the strong feeling that something bad had happened. He reached for his phone. Crap, he'd overslept. It was nearly half seven – he'd usually have been at the stables by now. He sat up, felt sick and reached for the pint of water he must have put on his bedside table last night. He gulped back half of it and then, with a small sigh of relief, remembered that Marjorie was turning Ninja out today. Thank God for that. He'd arranged it when he'd thought Jo would be staying over.

Shit. Jo. That's what had happened. Jo had dumped him. Fragments of their conversation flicked back into his head.

'It's happened to me before.'

'He went off with my best friend.'

'I don't like playing second fiddle.'

He had listened to her fears and then he had let her walk away. Because although he'd never laid a finger on his oldest friend, a part of him had known Jo was right. He was still hung up on Phoebe. Much good may it do him because she was completely oblivious to his existence. At least she was in romantic terms.

Sam shut his eyes and rested his sore head back down again on the pillow.

Another memory was trying to break through. One he couldn't quite grasp hold of. How much had he drunk? His head was killing him.

The need for painkillers forced him out of bed and into the kitchen, where Snowball twined himself around his legs, purring.

'You look like you had a better night than I did, mate,' he told his cat, bending to stroke his black fluffy head. The cat mewed plaintively for breakfast.

Sam fed him, refreshed his water, found the painkillers and washed them down and put on some coffee. Why had he thought it was a good idea to get drunk? He was rubbish at getting drunk and real ale was lethal. He hadn't had such a humdinger of a hangover for years.

Still, at least the walk back to The Brace should help to clear his head. That was a good half an hour or so.

After a hot shower and two mugs of coffee, Sam was feeling slightly more human. Picking up his car keys, he set off for the pub. He wondered if he should call Jo. Was there a chance of putting things right between them? It seemed so totally pointless for them to break up over a romance that had never happened and never would. Maybe she would be thinking the same thing. Maybe she was having second thoughts about them splitting up.

He dialled her number, which rang and rang until eventually the voicemail kicked in. 'Jo, it's me. I hope you're OK. If you're feeling as sad as I am, mayb—' The voicemail beeped, cutting him off and inviting him to delete his message and record another if he wished.

He didn't wish. Bloody voicemails. He'd try her again later.

At least his headache was starting to go. He'd reached the forest road now and as he crossed over the first cattle grid he passed a couple of donkeys, amongst them a grey jenny and her foal, who were holding up traffic. Partly because they were on the road but partly because the youngster was unbearably cute. Some of the drivers had stopped to take photos. Sam smiled as he went past.

He was struggling to recall the end of last night. Thank God he'd had the sense to leave his car behind. He had a vague memory of calling a taxi. So he couldn't have been that drunk.

Then, just as he reached The Brace of Pheasants' swinging sign with its flying bird, he remembered the part of the jigsaw puzzle that had been eluding him. He'd bumped into Rufus Holt. The man hadn't been alone. He'd come in with a mate. They'd been chatting about something important. Sam had a vague memory of standing in the car park trying to decide whether to go back into the pub or whether to go home. Why? What had all that been about? He couldn't imagine he'd developed a sudden desire to spend time with that nob. However drunk he'd been.

Phoebe... It had been something to do with Phoebe. Sam groaned. Oh good God, what had he said? He'd said something – he knew that. He'd gone back in and he'd squared up to Rufus. The memory crashed back in, the jigsaw finally complete. And Sam groaned as he replayed the humiliating scene at the bar, over and over in his head.

* * *

Phoebe was at Tori's flat. She'd called round for a Sunday catch-up. She wanted to hear about Tori's Venice trip – her friend had just got back. But she also wanted to update her on the rabbit situation. They'd spoken a lot, but they hadn't seen each other face to face since the visit to Burley Bunnies.

They were now sitting at Tori's kitchen table sipping coffee and eating a selection of Italian snacks Tori had brought back, including Pannarello, a soft cheese from Venice, with cracked black pepper biscuits. The room smelled of olives and sun-dried tomatoes.

'Venice was blissful,' Tori said. 'We were proper tourists. We ate pizza and lots of ice cream. Italian ice cream is to die for. We went to Doge's Palace. We went to the Leonardo da Vinci Museum. We didn't go near a gondola.' She grinned. 'And we made love a lot. Harrison is definitely the one.' Her green eyes were dreamy. 'After all this time, I can't believe he was right under my nose all along. Being your neighbour, I mean. Working right next door to Puddleduck. It's amazing, isn't it?'

'Yes it is.' Phoebe thought fleetingly of Rufus. And then banished him again. She had got good at that lately. It helped that she hadn't seen him professionally either. All must be well with Archie's small menagerie – Emilia had phoned and registered a second straight-eared rabbit and another guinea pig.

'Enough of me,' Tori said. 'What's happening with you? How's Maggie? How's it all going with work? Have you employed a new receptionist yet? But, most importantly, how's your love life? Are you going to New Forest Diners again?'

'Maggie is fine. Work's fine. I'm not planning on going to New Forest Diners again,' Phoebe said. She told Tori about Marcus and the vile breeder who'd got him sacked and blacklisted and her friend agreed that taking him on was the right decision.

'I hate bullies,' Tori said. She poured them another coffee and got out some Venetian biscotti for them to nibble. 'So if you're not going to New Forest Diners again, what are you going to do about meeting men... I mean new friends.' Her eyes brightened. 'You haven't had a holiday yet. You could go on a singles holiday.'

'I can't think of anything worse,' Phoebe said. 'Anyway, I've just booked a week off work at the end of July. I've got a locum coming in. Maggie is doing back-up if Jenna and Marcus need it.'

'So where are you going?'

'Nowhere. I'm planning a staycation. I want to go to the New Forest Show. I haven't been to it for years. Apparently it's massive now. Seth is judging some of the pony classes. You could come with me. It would be fun.'

'I'll already be there. We've got a stall for the mag. Laura and I will be hard at work raising our profile. As it happens, we're doing the advertising for the show too. It's in the latest issue. I'm surprised you haven't got a stall for Puddleduck Vets.'

'There aren't enough of us to be in two places at once. We'd have to close the surgery if I got a stall.'

'Fair point.'

'But I'll visit yours,' Phoebe promised. 'I can be your ice cream buyer and coffee collector.'

'Sounds good to me.' Tori looked thoughtful. 'Talking of vile breeders – well, we aren't now, but we were just now, is there any news on the Burley rabbits woman?'

'A bit. I spoke to the RSPCA inspector last week and he told me they'd visited but that there wasn't enough evidence to prosecute. They did go into the shed where you looked, but apparently they'd cleaned up their act.'

Tori looked disappointed. 'That's all my fault. I'm so sorry I shouted my mouth off.'

'Maybe that helped. Cleaning up their act is a good thing, surely. The other good news is that she didn't have any baby rabbits for sale. There are no current adverts either. So she does seem to have scaled things back a bit. That's positive.'

'Yes, I guess it is.' Tori sighed. 'With hindsight, I should have done that completely differently. As an undercover operative, I failed spectacularly.'

'We did the best we could at the time. And Burley Bunnies won't go off my radar. I've let the RSPCA guy know that if any more come into the practice that are in trouble I'll be straight on to him and he's going to get in touch with me if they have any other complaints.'

'I did have another idea,' Tori said. 'I was talking to Harrison while we were away.'

'In between the lovemaking?' Phoebe teased.

'You've got it.' She clicked her tongue. 'Harrison suggested I play to my strengths and write up a feature. An exposé of the cruelty behind the cuteness. The truth about lop-eared rabbits. Or at least the truth when it comes to bad breeders.'

'You mean to go in *New Forest Views*? Isn't that a bit contentious for you?'

'Yes, it's very contentious, but I wasn't thinking of putting it in the magazine. Or at least not the full no-holds-barred version. I was thinking of writing it up for one of the tabloids. Harrison seems to think it would be right up their street. He has a friend who works for *The Sun*.'

Phoebe could feel her heart beating with excitement. 'Wow. That would be brilliant. But are you going to mention Burley Bunnies? Are you sure it wouldn't be libellous?'

'Not if it's true.' Tori's eyes sparkled. 'Which it would be. I've got the photos to prove it. I was showing Harrison. They're not as bad as I thought. And he thinks we might be able to tart them up a bit.'

'Digitally alter them, you mean?'

'Digitally *enhance*. Not the same thing. We'd be showing what was there. We wouldn't be lying. You could supply a quote – if you were happy to and you didn't think it would be too controversial.'

'Controversial is my new middle name,' Phoebe said, thinking of Marcus.

'Sorted. OK, I'll keep you posted on that. Hang on a minute...' She broke off and got up. 'I'm just going to check something.' Tori disappeared into the lounge and a few moments later she was back, brandishing a booklet in her hand. '*The New Forest Show Guide*,' she said, opening it and turning to the back page and running her finger down the print. 'Look – there's Burley Bunnies on the list of exhibitors. She's obviously going, touting for business for the next lot of poor little deformed baby bunnies.'

'So she is,' Phoebe said despondently.

'But that's brilliant news,' Tori said. 'It's the perfect opportunity for us to discredit her. Second thoughts, I'll stick the feature about the lop-eared rabbits in *New Forest Views* as well – a toned down version. Then I could hand out copies by her stall.'

'No, you couldn't. You'd get thrown out.'

'Yes, you might be right.' Tori's face fell. Then she brightened. 'Someone else could hand them out though. And we could organise a protest. People with placards marching up and down outside her stall. What?' she added when Phoebe rolled her eyes. 'I thought you said controversial was your middle name.'

'I don't think we'd necessarily need to hand them out,' Phoebe said. 'We just need a pile of them open at the right page on your stall. And there are other stalls who'd do that too. Some of the animal ones. There's usually a couple of vets there. And the PDSA. Jeez, Tori, I think you might be onto something.'

Tori tapped her nose. 'Not just a pretty face,' she said. 'And we definitely need people with placards. How about Maggie? That would be right up her street.'

'You're right. It would. But being in a protest might be too stressful. I'll maybe speak to Natasha instead. We'll organise something. I'm happy to march with a placard.'

'It might be better if we kept you in reserve as our expert witness. We don't want you getting thrown out either. Harrison would probably do it, though. He likes controversy.'

'When am I going to meet Harrison anyway? I thought you were arranging a time for me to meet the love of your life?'

'If you hang around for another ten minutes, you can meet him now,' Tori said. 'He just texted me. He accidentally put my charger in his suitcase and he said he'd drop it round when he was passing. He's driving Rufus to some meeting apparently.'

Phoebe jumped in her chair as violently as if she'd just spilled hot coffee in her lap. 'Rufus won't come in with him, will he?'

'Why? Would that be an issue?' Tori looked at her curiously. 'I thought you'd decided that dating the lord of the manor was definitely a no-go area.'

'I have. I definitely have.'

'Hmm, it doesn't look like it from where I'm sitting.' Tori rested her elbows on the table and leaned forward, chin in hands. 'Seriously, Pheebs, is he still living in your head rent-free?'

'He sneaks in occasionally.' Phoebe leaped up and wandered over to the first-floor window which overlooked the street below and peered out. 'Shit, a car's just pulled up. What if it's them?'

'That'll just be someone going to the off-licence.' Tori joined her. 'Don't worry. Harrison said it would be a flying visit. The chances of Rufus coming in here are remote. As far as I know, Rufus doesn't even know Harrison's dating me. Like I told you, Harrison plays his cards very close to his chest. Those two might be best mates, but they're also old-school. I'm pretty sure they don't talk to each other about anything personal. Certainly not women. Guys like that don't, do they?'

'I don't know. I guess not.' Phoebe sat down again, feeling edgy.

A few moments later, she jumped out of her skin again when the door intercom buzzed.

Tori danced across to answer it.

'Hello, lover,' she trilled.

'Hey, honey. I've got a delivery for you.'

'Come on up.' Tori buzzed him in and went to put her front door on the latch.

A few moments later, Phoebe heard men's voices outside on the landing and the significance of this only properly hit her when the front door opened and she saw Harrison, closely followed by the man she'd been trying to banish from her head for the past seven weeks. Rufus.

28

Phoebe wasn't sure who was the most shocked. Herself or Rufus. It was probably him because she'd had about thirty seconds' warning, whereas he'd had none. The look on his face was almost comical, as his gaze flicked between both women and then back towards Harrison curiously.

Harrison was oblivious. He strode towards Tori, put an arm around her shoulders and said, 'I hope you didn't mind me bringing a gatecrasher, but I thought it was high time you met my boss. Boss, allow me to introduce Victoria Williams, Tori to her friends. The woman who's been lighting up my life for the past few months. Tori, this is Rufus Holt.'

'We've met actually,' Tori said, moving towards Rufus and holding out her hand. 'You probably don't remember, but Phoebe and I called to see you one afternoon last year. And I think you were at Phoebe's launch too, weren't you?'

Rufus recovered swiftly and he took her proffered hand. 'I was indeed. It's a pleasure to see you again, Victoria.'

'Tori, please,' Tori said. 'And likewise.' She flicked a glance at Phoebe. 'No introductions needed between you two.'

'No.' Rufus looked strained, not to mention, Phoebe thought, hugely embarrassed. Which confirmed everything she'd been thinking lately. He was anxious to put as much space as possible between them. He'd clearly had no idea she would be here and wouldn't have come within a mile of the place if he'd known.

He wasn't the only one who wished the ground would open up and swallow him. She could feel heat surging into her face and neck. She met his eyes fleetingly and then dropped her gaze. The atmosphere in Tori's kitchen had gone from jovial to awkward to iceberg cold.

Harrison couldn't fail to be aware of it and Phoebe saw his gaze flip between her and Rufus and the expression on his face morphed from good-humoured to disconcerted. 'You're Phoebe Dashwood,' he said. 'Rufus's... er, vet.'

'I am.'

'And my best and oldest friend,' Tori said. 'I've been dying for you two to meet properly.'

There was an even more awkward silence. Harrison looked as though he'd been caught in a compromising situation. Rufus just looked frozen with humiliation.

Phoebe took charge. 'It's wonderful to meet you properly at last, Harrison,' she said. 'And it's good to see you again, Rufus, but I'm afraid I must dash. I'm on my way to an urgent call.' She shot a glance at an unnerved-looking Tori.

Then she swept past them all, with her nose in the air, and let herself out of Tori's door. She hurried down the stairs to the outside door as swiftly as was humanly possible.

* * *

Phoebe hadn't got as far as home – there was no urgent call – before her mobile buzzed and she saw Tori's name flash up on the console. She pressed connect.

'Are you OK?' Tori's voice was contrite. 'I'm so sorry. What the hell was all that about?'

'*That* was what I think you'd call evidence that I was right all along,' Phoebe said. She could feel anger bubbling, although she realised it was more a feeling of hurt. 'Bloody hell. Did you see his face? He was mortified. And Harrison looked like he'd seen a ghost. So much for my theory that men don't talk about their personal lives. Harrison knew exactly who I was.'

'I know. I could see that. I haven't had a chance to speak to him yet. They left very soon after you did, but I'll get to the bottom of it, Phoebe. I promise.'

'Don't bother. I honestly think I'd rather not know. Look, I'm almost home. I'll call you back when I am. Crashing the car wouldn't improve my mood any and I'm not exactly feeling in full control of myself, let alone a tonne and a bit of moving metal.'

'Sure,' Tori replied. 'Talk in a bit.'

Phoebe disconnected. As she'd said, she was almost home, but suddenly it was the last place she wanted to be, sitting in her empty cottage with a head full of buzzing thoughts and a belly full of emotion she didn't know what to do with.

She drove straight past the turn-off to Woodcutter's Cottage and kept driving. She wanted to walk. Walking was the best way she knew of clearing her head, straightening out her thoughts, not to mention releasing some of the terrible tension that was straitjacketing her body and making her feel ill.

* * *

Ten minutes later, Phoebe had parked the Lexus at Linford Bottom, which was one of the less well-known beauty spots in the heart of the New Forest. It was at the end of a long and winding road, so people only came here if they were in the know, but it was well worth the detour.

It was on the edge of the forest and a stream meandered lazily between wide sandy banks that sloped so gently you could walk right down to the softly lapping water without getting your feet wet. It was a great place for families. Kids were perfectly safe and on summer days it was full of dogs, families and picnickers. New Forest ponies, well used to humans, grazed unconcernedly on the scrubby grass. Archie would love it here, she thought, picnicking amongst the ponies. She wondered how he was doing, that sweet little boy – up in that big old house with just his guinea pigs and rabbits for company.

Phoebe dragged herself back to the present. The plantation that backed onto the stream was enclosed by sturdy wooden fencing and Forestry Commission five-bar gates, but once you were through, it was possible to walk for miles into the ancient woodland where deer and ponies and occasionally wild boar roamed. She hesitated by the nearest gate. The air, soft on her face, smelled of summer and the woods were full of birdsong and the skittering sounds of nature.

But she knew suddenly that she didn't want the forest today. She needed the peace and tranquillity of the water and of more open spaces and on this Sunday afternoon there were too many people around to get it to herself unless she walked for a while.

A woman with a dog, and a large family sprawled at the water's edge. They smiled when she went past and she nodded at them and headed on by, her hands deep in the pockets of her lightweight jacket. Only when she was completely free of people and alone again did she allow her thoughts to drift back to Rufus and linger on the memory.

His face. His almost palpable shock when he saw her – in any other circumstances it might have been funny. But it had not felt funny. It had felt terrible. Humiliating and painful and demeaning.

Now, with the benefit of hindsight, she knew categorically that up until that moment, despite what she'd told Tori, and despite what she'd been telling herself, she'd been harbouring a hope that there might be a simple explanation for why he had not been in touch. That his silence had nothing to do with an ancient poker game. Nothing to do with the fact that they came from different social classes. Nothing to do with the fact that there might be a wonderful chemistry between them but that there could never be anything else because of who they were.

All of those hopes had been smashed when she'd seen the shock in his eyes. Harrison's reaction hadn't helped. Knowing that she'd been the subject of at least one conversation between them had been the last painful nail in the coffin.

Phoebe had thought that if she stayed away from involvements she'd be immune to heartbreak. She'd been kidding herself.

A small stone skittered away from her boot across the ground and she realised she'd been stomping, not strolling. Her neck was still tight with tension. Her hands clenched into fists. She longed to scream out her frustration and tension into the still air, but that might bring rescuers running and the last thing she needed was a bloody rescuer.

She kept walking, on and on, following the stream, occasionally diverting around a coconut-scented gorse bush or patch of brambles, until, at last, the tension began to leave her body. The rhythm of her steps, the fresh air and the peace of her surroundings began to work its magic. Once or twice, she felt her phone vibrate in her pocket and she remembered she'd promised to call Tori when she got home. But she didn't want to talk. Not to Tori, not even to Maggie. She didn't look at her phone. She kept walking until she was finally feeling at peace with herself.

An hour after she'd left the car, Phoebe realised she was lost. Which shouldn't have been possible. Because surely it was just a matter of turning round and following the stream back again. Except for the fact that she hadn't seen it for a while. She paused, looked around her and realised she didn't recognise anything and she had no idea which direction she should be going in. She was no longer even on a proper path.

She wasn't usually so lax about walking in the forest. It was surprisingly easy to get lost even if you knew the area well, partly because it changed so much – every season brought a new level of growth and change. The forest's summer and winter clothes were as different as a debutante's summer and winter ball gowns.

Phoebe sighed. That would teach her not to pay more attention. Thank goodness for the person who'd invented map apps. She hooked out her phone, saw there were two missed calls from Tori, plus a voicemail notification and another missed call from a mobile she didn't recognise. She also saw she didn't have much battery life left. Better not waste it then on listening to messages. She pulled up the map app and punched in the address of the car park and waited for it to load.

* * *

Rufus had been feeling rattled ever since he'd walked into Victoria Williams' flat with Harrison and had come face to face with Phoebe. Rattled was an understatement. Seeing her had knocked him sideways and he hadn't yet managed to rein his thoughts in.

Why, oh why, hadn't he put two and two together? But then how could he have done? He'd known for a while that Harrison was seeing someone, but he hadn't realised it was Phoebe's best friend. He hadn't realised that until today, when they'd gone into the flat and he'd run slap bang into the woman who'd been haunting his nights. He'd managed to work enough to blot her out during the day, but the nights, when his mind was quiet, were different.

Seeing Phoebe again had jolted him straight back to that Friday in May. The events of that Friday were burned on his brain: the drive up to the copse; the barrels of toxic waste; the tree house; the kiss. And, more recently, the conversation with Harrison when he'd finally dropped his guard and mentioned her name. Then that lunatic in the pub, who'd said he was her boyfriend.

Rufus was jolted from his churning thoughts by someone tapping him on the shoulder. He was at a networking meeting of the Tenants/Landlord Association at Rhinefield House. His father, who was on the board, usually did these meetings, but today he was playing golf, so Rufus had inherited the job. Normally, Rufus wouldn't have minded. Sundays weren't his favourite days, but right now he'd have given anything to be at home.

'I do apologise,' he said, turning towards the woman who'd tapped him on the shoulder. 'Could you please repeat that?'

The woman, who was broad and wearing a flowery dress with a clipboard clutched to her heavy bosom, smiled at him. 'I was just saying that I think we're going into the meeting room now, Rufus. If you'd care to come through.'

'Of course.' He glanced at her name badge. *Diana Harding, Chair.* 'Thank you, Ms Harding.'

'Diana is fine. And it's Miss.' She beamed and her cheeks flushed. Then she fluttered her eyelashes and he thought, *is she flirting with me?*

This was one of the reasons he preferred to do all his meetings online. He found it so much easier to hide behind the safety of a screen than he did struggling to pick up non-verbal cues and then working out a way to politely deflect them. His father was much better at that sort of thing than he was.

Rufus glanced nervously about for Harrison and spotted him seated at the bar, knocking back an orange juice. He didn't need his friend and second in command to drive him to functions, but it gave him a good excuse to leave early.

'I can't keep my driver waiting. Not on a Sunday. You know how it is.'

That was a great line for making a swift exit and one he'd have no hesitation in using as soon as this meeting was over.

29

When Phoebe finally got back to the car park three hours after she'd left it, her Lexus had been joined by some other cars. The evening dog walk brigade had taken the place of the afternoon families.

She got in, relieved that she'd found her way back while her phone still had enough signal and plugged it in to the charger she kept in the car. Then she sent Tori a message, saying she'd been walking but had an almost flat battery and would phone her when she got in. The response came back instantly.

No rush. But thanks. I was starting to worry

When they did finally speak later that evening, the phone call was almost an anticlimax. Tori told her she hadn't heard from Harrison, who she assumed must still be tied up with Rufus. And Phoebe, emotionally exhausted from her thoughts, and physically tired from her extended walk, was keen to move on from the whole embarrassing debacle as quickly as possible.

'Seriously, Tori,' she told her friend. 'I'm tired of thinking about this. You were right about Rufus living rent-free in my head. But he won't be any more. If today has taught me anything at all, it's this. If it looks like a duck, quacks like a duck, waddles like a duck, then it probably is a duck.'

'A duck?' Tori echoed. 'What are you talking about?'

'Reality,' Phoebe said. 'I've spent long enough avoiding it. But it's time I did. I'm done with fantasising about unobtainable men. Men who think I'm OK for a quick fumble in the woods but who wouldn't be seen dead with me in polite company.'

'But, Pheebs, do you really think that's true. What if—'

'What if nothing.' Phoebe could feel her anger rising again. 'It was obvious that Rufus had the shock of his life when he realised I was his mate's girlfriend's friend. You saw him. He was horrified.'

There was a pause and Phoebe knew that Tori was struggling to find the words to deny this. Words that would help. When they both knew there were no words that would help.

'Really,' she went on. 'I want to forget all about Rufus bloody Holt. With a bit of luck, our paths won't cross again. From now on, I'm focusing on what's right in front of my nose. And I'm going to take things at face value.'

Another pause. But Tori recovered her voice swiftly. 'Does that mean you'll go to another New Forest Diners event?'

'Maybe,' Phoebe said. 'After all, it wasn't a complete waste of time. I did meet Luke Harding there and he led to me getting Marcus.'

'Tell me again when he's starting.'

'The fourth of July. We're all looking forward to it.'

'Brilliant.' Tori hesitated. 'Don't be put off dating by what's happened. There are loads of nice guys out there.'

'Hmmm. I might start online dating,' Phoebe added, knowing that was the biggest lie she'd told lately. 'That could be fun.' She crossed her fingers behind her back. 'Although I think I'll get the next couple of weeks over first. It'll be busy at work, getting Marcus up to speed and then it's my staycation. Maybe I'll research some online dating sites then.'

'But you're still going to do the New Forest Show and be around for our protest?' Tori asked anxiously.

'Yes, of course I am. I want to discredit Burley Bunnies just as much as you do.'

And it would be handy to have a cause to direct her unvented anger, she thought darkly.

* * *

It wasn't until much later that night that Phoebe realised the voicemail notification wasn't from Tori, it was from Sam. He must have changed his number.

In fact, that's what he started off by saying. She listened to his familiar voice while she was lying in bed that night, unable to sleep despite herself.

'Hi, Phoebe. I have a couple of apologies. The first one is that I haven't let you know my new number. This is it. As in, I'm calling from it now.' Then he repeated the number in case it wasn't clear what he was talking about.

Phoebe smiled. Sam wasn't a technophobe, but sometimes she did wonder if he knew the simplest things about phones. Like they had a digital display and showed numbers that had called, which was fortunate because Sam's voice was drowned out at the end of the number so she wouldn't have heard it all anyway.

'The second apology is...' Again, his voice disappeared in a whirr of stuttering and static so that Phoebe could only catch every other word. *Pub, it, drunker, wouldn't, obviously.* He finished with a line she could hear perfectly, 'I had a belter of a hangover this morning. I'm sure you'll agree I deserved it.' Then he disconnected.

Phoebe played the message back a couple more times but couldn't make any more sense of it than she had the first time. She decided to put it out of her head.

She'd assumed she hadn't heard much from him lately because he was tied up with his new girlfriend. But it would be good to catch up with Sam properly too. Maybe that was another thing she could do on her staycation. Sam could tell her whatever he had phoned up to say then.

It struck her that he was probably also knee-deep in preparations for the show. At least she would see him there. His message didn't sound as though it was that urgent.

* * *

Marcus's first week at Puddleduck Vets began with a solemn promise and ended with an argument. The promise was made to Phoebe as soon as he arrived, which was only just after she opened up. He was dressed in a grey suit, white shirt and a red silk tie, attire which struck Phoebe as more suitable for a smart office than a vet's reception.

'You could wear more casual clothes if you like?' she told him. 'Not that you don't look very smart.'

Marcus nodded thoughtfully. 'Thank you, Miss Dashwood. But I always wear a suit to work.'

'OK. If that's what you always wear.' She seemed to remember he'd worn a suit at his interview too. 'And it's Phoebe. You can drop the Miss Dashwood. It makes me feel old.' Marcus was only twenty-seven. A mere eight years younger than she was.

'Thanks, Phoebe.' He touched his hand to the breast pocket of his grey jacket. 'And thanks for giving me this chance. I promise I won't let you down.'

'That's good to hear,' she said, caught in the intensity of his brown eyes. It was hard to imagine him giving someone a left hook, however riled he got.

His first week passed like clockwork. He was, as Luke had promised, mild-mannered, polite and authentic. He was also an impressively quick learner who only needed to be shown something once and he had a memory that rivalled her brother's. Until today Phoebe had never met anyone but her brother with such a good memory for facts.

One morning Maggie had forgotten that a customer had asked about a flea treatment that they wanted to buy online but would need a prescription for and Marcus helpfully supplied the name of the drug, the customer and his cat, all of which he'd only heard once.

Then, one lunchtime, when Phoebe was going through her afternoon appointments, Marcus handed her a piece of paper. 'There's a call for later too. Miss Connor has a bull called Boris she'd like you to take a look at.' His brow crinkled. 'I'll just find the address.'

Phoebe took a step back in alarm. 'Did you say Miss Connor?'

'Yes.'

'And Boris the bull?'

'That's right.'

'No.'

'No?' Marcus looked startled.

'I'm not going. We'll need to ask Seth.'

There was a snort from behind her and Phoebe realised that Maggie had been lurking just out of sight. Before she could say anything else, Maggie collapsed with laughter, slapping her thighs and bent over with mirth.

Phoebe rounded on her. 'You put him up to that?'

'I did. I'm sorry.'

'There is no Boris the bull, is there?'

'No.'

'Thank God.'

'Your face. It was priceless.'

Throughout this exchange, Marcus was round-eyed. 'I take it there's history. Sorry, boss.'

'*You* are forgiven.' Phoebe shook her head. 'But *she* is old enough to know better.' Although the relief of discovering that Miss Connor had not after all bought a bull that needed her attention was so overwhelming that now she'd got over the shock she could see the funny side.

On several occasions, Phoebe overheard Marcus and Maggie laughing at something together, which was why it was such a surprise to hear him arguing with her grandmother at the end of his first week.

'Certainly not. No way. Not under any circumstance. Nope.' Marcus was standing up by the computer in reception and Maggie was sitting in the office chair with her arms folded and a mutinous look on her face.

'I don't see why not. I've been involved in more of them than you've had hot dinners. I can tell you that for nothing.'

'That's not the point—'

They both broke off when they saw her.

'What on earth are you talking about?' Phoebe asked, looking from one to the other. Maggie was red-faced and obviously pretty het up and Marcus looked grimly determined.

'The New Forest Show protest,' Marcus said, ignoring Maggie's frantic motions to keep quiet. 'The one about the brachycephalic rabbits.'

'How on earth do you know about that? Either of you?' Phoebe gasped. 'I told Natasha that was classified information.'

'Pah,' Maggie said, with a snort of derision. 'You don't think she'd keep something like that to herself, do you? Natasha works for me, not you. Besides, it wasn't Natasha who let the cat out of the bag. It was one of the other volunteers. I saw her with a placard and a blown-up copy of the feature in *New Forest Views*.'

'I see,' Phoebe said, biting her lip. She'd known her grand-mother would find out sooner or later but not this quickly. Tori had literally only just printed the feature. 'So why are you argu-ing?' she asked Marcus.

Before he could speak, Maggie answered for him. 'This young man thinks I'm not capable of marching in a protest.'

'I didn't say that. I said that Mrs Crowther should be mindful of stress levels in view of her previous stroke.'

'And how do you know about that?' It was Maggie's turn to look at Marcus in amazement.

'I noticed your tablets,' he said quietly. 'You left them on the desk earlier and I know they're blood thinners for people who are prone to having a stroke. My nan used to take the same ones,' he offered by way of an explanation.

'Oh,' Maggie deflated a little, sinking down in her chair as if all of the wind had been taken out of her sails. 'So what you're saying is that I should avoid every possible slightly stressful situa-tion in the world. Is that it?'

'No, but protests are different. They're controversial by nature and controversy is one of the most stressful life events.' Marcus sounded very firm on this and a little concerned.

But Maggie was not going to be outwitted by anyone, however well-meaning and concerned they were. 'Unnecessary arguments are very controversial and stressful,' she told him sulkily. 'Like the one you just engaged me in.'

'I apologise,' Marcus said, without a hint of apology in his voice.

Phoebe suppressed a smile. It sounded very much like Maggie had met her match in Marcus, or, if not her match, a very fine opponent.

'I agree with Marcus that it might not be the most sensible idea to go marching in a protest at the New Forest Show,' Phoebe interjected. 'Although I'm sure there are loads of other ways you can help.'

'I wasn't planning to be in the actual protest march itself,' Maggie said, waving a hand in a way that suggested the thought hadn't even entered her head. 'In view of the fact that it might cause me to burst a blood vessel. I'm just going along as a reserve protestor. I intend to sit quietly on the subs bench and observe the proceedings. In a non-controversial, un-stressful way.'

Phoebe shook her head and decided not to argue. It was pointless when her grandmother was in this kind of mood.

* * *

It wasn't until much later that it struck Phoebe that Maggie and Marcus couldn't have been having a rhetorical argument on the rights and wrongs of whether Maggie should be marching in a protest, which was what she'd assumed. Because Maggie wouldn't even be at the show. She'd already agreed to work at Puddleduck Vets and she couldn't be in two places at once.

Maggie must have been asking Marcus if he'd cover her shift for her so she could go. Phoebe didn't worry too much about this either, being as Marcus had obviously point-blank refused. She should have known better. But this was something else she didn't think through properly until it was well and truly too late.

30

Sam's July was spent in a frenzy of activity. He'd left several voicemails for Jo before she had finally called him back and said that she didn't think there was any point in them giving it another go. She had been nice but categoric and Sam's pride had prevented him from arguing with her.

Phoebe hadn't called him back either. She had never responded to the lengthy apology he had left on her voicemail. He'd surmised from her silence that she was too annoyed to speak to him and he didn't blame her. Mouthing off to Rufus Holt when he was half cut – no, let's be honest, drunk as a lord, oh the irony – had to be one of the stupidest things he'd ever done. If not *the* stupidest.

OK, so his intentions had been honourable – kind of – he'd been sure from the fragments of conversation he'd heard between Rufus and his sidekick that Rufus was about to take advantage of Phoebe. If he hadn't already done so – and for no more reason than fun.

Fragments of the two men's conversation would be forever lodged in his brain.

'Fill your boots. Especially if she's a looker. It doesn't have to be serious...'

Sam couldn't bear the thought that they were talking about Phoebe like that. He'd seen red, wanting only to protect her, the person who was so important to him. First as a childhood friend and now as a beautiful, albeit out of his reach, woman.

But he should have kept out of it. He should not have waded on in, stamping his size tens. It was Phoebe's business what she did, not his. One of the most important things Sam had ever learned was the bittersweet lesson: if you love something, let it go. Where had that life lesson been when he'd needed it most? How had he managed to do completely the wrong thing?

He also knew that the only way to make lasting amends to Phoebe was to honour her tacit request for his silence. So he didn't call her again. He focused completely on keeping himself in the present instead. Which was work, work and more work. He had the time for it now too. His pattern of working at the Post Office, followed by working at Brook Stables, followed by giving extra lessons, followed by practising for the show on his own horse no longer felt rushed. It felt like part of a smooth rhythm. A rhythm that stopped him from thinking about either Phoebe or Jo. A rhythm that helped him to work through the days of what could otherwise have felt like a very lonely summer.

* * *

Rufus threw himself into work, too. He was also having more counselling sessions than usual for his PTSD. This was essential because he was planning to confront his equine demons. He was planning to accompany Archie to the New Forest Show. His father would be going too – Lord Alfred was presenting prizes at the open showjumping. But Rufus was just going for the final day to see Archie's class. He was going to do the full supportive father role for the entire day.

He was driving him to Brook Stables at some unearthly hour on Thursday morning so that Archie could groom his pony, wash and brush out its mane and tail and get the animal looking its best – this was all part of the day, apparently, and essential – then Rufus was going to follow the horsebox to the show. He was going to sit through his son's class and watch him compete. It was a show class, so Archie would not be jumping, thank God. Rufus didn't think he'd have coped with that. But Rufus would be there on the ringside, cheering him on, inwardly if not outwardly, and he would stay there if it killed him. He was not... he could not *allow* himself to run away from this one. He owed it to his son.

Bartholomew Timms had been focusing on techniques that would allow Rufus to do all of this without making a spectacle of himself. Square breathing being one of them. Square breathing was a relaxation technique that Bartholomew had explained to him in their last session.

'Find a square,' the therapist had said. 'Or an oblong. Anything you like.' He had looked around the office where they sat. 'It can be a mouse mat, a computer screen, even a window or a door. It doesn't matter. It's simply a point of focus.'

Rufus had done as he'd said and fixed his gaze on a framed certificate on the therapist's wall. A certificate that listed the man's degree and qualifications.

'Good,' the therapist had nodded approvingly. 'Now I'm going to teach you how to breathe. I'm going to count you through it. Breathe in for four seconds, hold your breath for four seconds, breath out for four seconds, hold for four seconds. It's called square breathing or sometimes box breathing because each side of the square is four seconds. Do you understand?'

'I understand.' Still focused on the qualification certificate,

Rufus had done his best to keep the incredulity out of his voice. All those letters after his name and the man was teaching him how to breathe – or to count to four – he wasn't entirely sure. Either was totally ridiculous.

'It's natural to be sceptical,' Bartholomew had continued, looking at his face and correctly interpreting his expression. 'But it's the simple techniques that work. Box breathing is an Ayurvedic form of breath work that is practised in yoga. It originated in India. But the west has caught on to its value. It's a practice that's taught to Navy Seals to help them cope with stressful situations.'

'If it's good enough for Navy Seals…' Rufus had quipped.

'Precisely. Now breathe with me.' The man's tone was clipped and Rufus, sensing that he was losing patience, did as he said. After all, it wasn't so different from what he'd told Phoebe to do when they'd been coming down the tree house ladder. Square breathing was just a variation on that. A variation with the additional distraction of focusing on a box. Focusing on her breathing had worked for Phoebe.

The thought of Phoebe was painful. Bumping into her so unexpectedly when he'd been with Harrison had totally thrown him. It had been clear that she'd been as embarrassed to see him as he was to see her. The fact that she'd almost immediately left had hammered home to him that she was not interested. He hadn't believed that line about her having an urgent call. She'd probably felt guilty about their indiscretion in the woods and wanted to get away from him as soon as humanly possible. Unsurprisingly, in view of the fact she was dating Neanderthal man. Rufus wouldn't have put them together as a couple. Not in a million years. Until that evening in the pub that was imprinted on his brain, he hadn't known that Phoebe even had a boyfriend. She had certainly never mentioned one to him.

It didn't add up. He didn't have her down as a liar either. But he was sick and tired of thinking about it. And right now it was difficult to think about anything other than the show – the prospect of spending the day in close proximity to horses – or at least one horse – was blotting out everything else. It hung like a long dark shadow over his days. The nightmares were back too. Rufus dreamed about Rowena and her last day on earth. The terrible fall, the sound of galloping hooves, the crowds, the damp earth, the terrifying trip in the ambulance to hospital, the grim face of the doctor who came to tell him they couldn't save his wife. The images replayed over and over. Insomnia plagued him and the closer the show got, the worse it got.

Rufus went to bed on Wednesday night, knowing he would hardly sleep at all. Archie didn't sleep much either, but for totally different reasons. Once when Rufus got up to look out at the stars – stars often soothed him when he couldn't sleep – he saw that Archie's night light was on. A pencil-thin line of yellow spilled out from beneath his door. He went across the landing, opened the door very gently and peeked around it.

As he'd suspected, Archie wasn't asleep. He was sitting up in bed, reading.

'Hey, big guy,' Rufus said, stepping inside. 'What's up? You should be getting some kip. You don't want to be tired out for tomorrow.'

'I know, Dad. But I'm too excited.' Archie grinned and showed him the book he was reading. *Turning Out The Perfect Show Pony.* 'I'm just getting some last-minute tips.'

'You'll be too tired to turn out the perfect show pony if you don't go to sleep,' Rufus said, suppressing a shudder at the picture of a horse on the front cover. Bartholomew would have told him it was a good opportunity to practise square breathing, he thought ruefully, as he bent to kiss his son's forehead. 'Sleep tight,' he said.

'The quicker you go to sleep, the quicker the morning will be here.'

* * *

The New Forest Show had its roots well back in the past. It had started in 1920 as a small, one-day local event but had grown across the years into a major agricultural show that was spread across three days at the end of July. It took place on a Tuesday, Wednesday and Thursday and attracted close to a hundred thousand visitors across the days.

Phoebe knew all of this because Tori had told her. She had also told her that the best day to go was the Thursday because that was the day that stallholders would drop their prices and there were plenty of bargains to be had.

'That's if you're looking for a bargain,' Tori had added with a knowing look. 'You might be going for another reason. I have it on good authority that Thursday is also the day Sam's doing his showjumping class.'

'I'm going so I can help out with the protest,' Phoebe said. 'And answer any questions anyone has about lop-eared rabbits – with my professional hat on. But it would be fun to see Sam jumping. I'll go and cheer him on. I'm glad he's competing again.'

Louella had reminded her that Sam was competing when she'd gone over for coffee last Saturday. Her mother had also told her, in a very casual voice, that Sam had split up with his girlfriend.

'I'm very sorry to hear that, Mum,' she'd said. 'Sam deserves someone nice.'

'Yes he does...' Louella had left the sentence hanging in the air and Phoebe had known that her mother still held hopes that the two of them would end up together one day.

'That person is not me, Mum,' she had added. 'Just putting that out there.'

'I know that, love.' Louella had sounded affronted as if the thought had never entered her head. 'Although it does seem a shame. Sorry,' she had added quickly. 'I was only saying what I think. I will shut up.'

'Thanks, Mum.' Phoebe had hugged her. 'I love Sam, you know I do. But only as a friend.'

'I've never regretted marrying my best friend,' Louella said softly, obviously forgetting she'd promised to shut up. 'Sometimes friendship is the best basis for a long-term relationship that there is.' She'd held Phoebe's eyes. 'I'm not saying that you should settle for someone you don't love, Phoebe. Please don't think that. All I'm saying is that you shouldn't dismiss friendship as a basis for romance.'

Phoebe hadn't argued. She had thought about that conversation quite a lot since they'd had it. She'd only ever known mind-blowing chemistry with one person – and that had been Rufus. And look where that had got her. A few moments of pure bliss followed by angst, pain and humiliation. If that was the price of chemistry, then maybe it was best avoided.

She had decided that Tori was right, though. Thursday was the best day to go to the show. It also meant that she could keep an eye on what was going on at Puddleduck Vets for the rest of the week. Technically, she wasn't working. She had a locum, a vet she'd used before and who she totally trusted. Jenna and Marcus had repeatedly told her they could cope fine, especially with Maggie on hand too.

Phoebe hoped this meant that Maggie had decided not to get involved with the Burley Bunnies protest mission. She certainly hadn't mentioned it. On Tuesday afternoon when Phoebe had popped in to Puddleduck Farm, ostensibly to say hi to Jenna and

Marcus, but really to check that Maggie was around and not getting into mischief, her grandmother was in the house photocopying Tori's exposé feature which had been printed in *The Sun* a week earlier. 'I'm taking a back seat, don't worry,' Maggie had told her granddaughter archly. 'I'm helping out purely in an administrative capacity. Natasha's doing all the stressful stuff.'

Phoebe had been speaking to Tori daily and she had it on good authority that Natasha and a small group of her animal activist friends were handing out copies of Tori's article each day from the *New Forest Views* stall, as well as distributing them at various other points around the show. As luck would have it, the *New Forest Views* stall was quite close to the Burley Bunnies stall. They were in adjacent marquees. But it had all been very low-key so far apparently.

'I'm glad to hear you're being sensible,' Phoebe had told her grandmother. 'Marcus was right, you know.'

'Hmm,' Maggie had said. 'It's a good job Natasha is on the case. Someone has to get their hands dirty.'

'I'll be doing my bit on Thursday,' Phoebe had said, bristling. 'I want to see that woman stopped from profiting from bad breeding as much as you do.'

'Good,' Maggie's face had brightened. 'Eddie will be there to help too.'

'Your friend, Eddie? Is he going to the show?'

'He and Dusty Miller are both going on Thursday. Dusty loves a protest.'

'Deaf Dusty?'

'The very same. You youngsters may think you invented protests. But you didn't. Dusty Miller was one of the original tree huggers. He showed Swampy the ropes. He was on the Newbury Bypass protest back in the nineties.'

'Wow,' Phoebe had said, feeling a grudging respect. 'Hats off to him.'

Maggie had given a secretive smile which had made Phoebe wonder what she was up to. But she hadn't dwelled on it for too long. She was enjoying being off work. She wasn't doing much. She'd had a couple of long leisurely walks in the forest and she'd caught up with Frazier and Alexa, as well as her parents. She'd had precious little family time lately and she'd loved seeing the twins.

On Wednesday evening, Tori phoned up to tell Phoebe she'd just had an altercation with Belinda Bates. 'Someone gave her henchman son the copy of my feature,' she told Phoebe with some glee. 'And she tracked it back to me and came flying over, all guns blazing demanding that I stop trying to discredit her and put her out of business. You should have seen her face when she realised it was me,' Tori said. 'I've never seen anyone turn an actual puce colour before. I thought she was going to explode on the spot. She threatened to burn my stall down and every magazine in it if I didn't stop immediately.' Tori chuckled.

'What did you say?'

'I played back the recording I'd just made of her saying exactly that and reminded her that arson carries a long prison sentence. Honestly, Phoebe, it was priceless. I wish you'd been there.'

'Me too, but I will be there tomorrow.' Phoebe paused. 'I'm glad the message is getting through. If nothing else, we might be able to make a few more members of the general public think before they prioritise cute bunny looks before their health and welfare. How's everything else going?'

'It's going fine. I must admit I do like the buzz of being on a stall. Laura and I have upped the profile of the magazine quite a bit. We've had a couple of forest businesses approach us about advertising. So that's good news as well.'

'Brilliant. I'll see you tomorrow.'

'Before you go,' Tori said, 'have you done your online dating profile yet or do you need my help?'

Phoebe laughed. 'No, and no. I'll get round to it. It's not that high on my priority list.'

'No, I'd gathered that.' Tori sounded deflated. 'But, hey, you might get swept off your feet by a knight in shining armour tomorrow at the show.'

'Have I ever told you you're totally incorrigible,' Phoebe asked, and hung up before her friend had the chance to answer.

The faint hope Rufus was harbouring that freak weather conditions would mean the last day of the New Forest Show was cancelled came to nothing when he woke to the mistiest of warm blue skies on Thursday morning. He'd finally fallen asleep around four thirty. He hoped Archie had got some sleep too. When he went in to wake him up, he found he was already dressed.

'I'm wearing my scruffs to the stables and changing into my best gear later,' Archie informed him. 'I don't want to let Molly down, do I? I've got to look as good as she does.'

'You will, son,' Rufus said. 'You'll wow them.'

'Do you really think so?'

'I do.'

'Can I ask you something important, Dad?'

'Of course you can. You can ask me anything?'

'Do you worry about me?' Archie screwed up his face in consternation. 'I mean with horses. Because of Mum?'

Rufus felt his throat close. Partly because of the mention of horses and Rowena but also because of the look of concern on his son's face. In that moment, Rufus was sharply aware of two things. The first was that it was the kind of anxiousness that a nine-year-old shouldn't have to feel. Not about his father.

The second was that he couldn't lie.

They were still in the bedroom and Rufus sat on one end of Archie's four-foot bed and patted the space next to him. He felt a gentle dip as his son came and sat next to him.

'I do worry a bit,' he told him. 'I try not to, but it's hard sometimes.'

'Is it because you don't like to remember what happened?'

'It is, son. Yes.'

'Is that why you don't come and watch me having lessons?'

'Yes. That's right.' Rufus could feel the huskiness in his own voice. Talk about out of the mouths of babes.

'That must be horrid, Dad. I don't want you to feel horrid.' Archie took a deep breath and fixed his dark eyes on his father's. 'You don't have to come today. I won't be upset if you don't.'

Rufus swallowed. 'I am coming today.' He reached for his child's small hand and held it gently between his own. 'I wouldn't miss it for the world. And do you know why that is?'

Archie shook his head.

'It's because I love you more than anything else in the world.' He saw a flicker of understanding in Archie's eyes as he stared back at him.

'I love you too, Dad.'

* * *

Brook Stables had been a hive of activity since daybreak. Sam had groomed and plaited up Ninja before any of his show-going pupils arrived. He'd also made sure all the horses and ponies that were going were in from their fields and fed and not too grubby.

A couple of his pupils, including Archie Holt, were coming in early to get their ponies ready – it was all part of competing, after all, but Sam wanted to give them a helping hand. Henrietta Blackstone who was in the junior showjumping was meeting them at the showground. She had told her parents she just wanted to ride, not do any boring preparation, and her parents had passed that on to him. Despite the fact that this was totally against the ethos of the day and very unsporting Sam had felt quite relieved he wouldn't have to put up with the spoiled ten-year-old any longer than necessary.

Archie was taking Molly in the best turned out pony class and Sam was keeping everything crossed that the pair would go home with a rosette. With luck, Archie's father would behave as usual and be a no-show. Sam knew that he probably owed the man an apology over his drunken behaviour in The Brace of Pheasants, but he was in no mood to have to face him today. Not with so much else going on.

So, when Sam saw the Holt Land Rover draw into the yard and park up at just after 7 a.m. he didn't worry too much. No doubt Emilia would unload Archie and his kit, hang around for half an hour and then head off again. It was a shock, therefore, when Sam saw Rufus Holt emerge from the driver's door.

Shit! That was all he needed. A fault-finding father who had the added complication of having a justified personal grievance. Sam was pretty sure that Rufus hadn't recognised him in The Brace of Pheasants. After all, they'd only ever met the once at Archie's very first lesson, and that had been fleeting. But he was sure as hell going to recognise him now. This was not a good start.

Maybe the lord of the manor wouldn't hang about. Sam had

just come into Molly's stable to refill her hay net. He waited. Perhaps if he stayed there for five minutes – the problem would resolve itself.

No such luck. Both Archie and his father were heading across the yard towards Molly's stable. Oh well, best to take the bull by the horns then. Sam had never been a coward.

As the pair reached the stable door, Sam emerged from the hay-scented shadows to greet them. 'Good morning, Archie. Good morning, Mr Holt.'

'Hi, Sam.' Archie's voice was excited.

Rufus looked shocked. Sam saw the recognition in his eyes as he took him in and then a wariness as he stepped back sharply.

'I owe you an apology,' Sam said, looking Rufus straight in the eyes. 'The last time we met, I was very drunk. I shouldn't have said what I did. We were in The Brace of Pheasants,' he added, because Rufus was still looking a bit stunned. Something definitely wasn't quite right. But at least he didn't look angry.

'It really doesn't matter. Don't concern yourself about it. It's forgotten.' Rufus lifted a hand and blinked a few times as if he were trying to pull himself into the here and now. Then he continued, 'You're my son's instructor...? You're... Sam.' It was half question, half statement.

'I am. And he's a fine little horseman.' Credit where credit was due. 'He's very intuitive. I'd go as far as to say gifted.' Sam shot a glance at Archie, who wasn't listening, he was too busy slipping Molly a slice of carrot.

'That's good to hear. Thank you.' Rufus's voice was stilted and there were beads of sweat on his forehead, despite the coolness of the morning. Sam had a sudden, vivid flashback of the first time they'd met, all those months ago. He'd had the impression, back then, just for a moment, that Rufus was scared. He'd forgotten all about that moment. But he was reminded sharply of it now. In the busy yard, alive with the clattering of buckets and the clip-clop of hooves as horses stamped impatiently, it was blindingly obvious. Rufus was scared of horses.

That was a curveball. Sam hadn't expected that. No wonder the man looked so ill at ease. And suddenly Sam felt something that he'd never thought he'd feel for this man – compassion. Because despite the fact that he was an entitled nob, who had designs on the woman Sam loved, he was also a father who cared enough about his son to force himself to come somewhere that clearly terrified him. And, just now, he'd also been incredibly gracious when Sam had apologised for being a dick. He hadn't needed to be gracious.

'If you want to grab yourself a coffee,' Sam said now. 'There's a machine in the office. Escape from all this mayhem – yeah?'

'Um. Yeah. I will. Thanks.' Rufus grabbed the lifeline with the zeal of a drowning man. 'I'll see you in a while, Archie.'

'OK, Dad.' Archie didn't look up. He was too engrossed with Molly.

Rufus strode swiftly away in the direction of the office. Sam watched him thoughtfully. Well, that had certainly been a turn-up for the books. And he was glad he'd made his peace with the lord of the manor. Sam felt good about that. With a bit of luck, it was also a good omen for today.

* * *

Phoebe had a leisurely lie-in, which meant she didn't get up until eight, then she made herself coffee and scrambled eggs and procrastinated about what to wear. It had been a hot dry July with very little rain and the forecast was warm for today. She decided on jeans, T-shirt and trainers and a light fleece that she could tie around her waist for now but wear if it got cooler later.

She envisaged spending the whole day at the show. She planned to hand out copies of Tori's feature this morning and also some fact sheets she'd printed off from a vet site about the health problems in flat-faced rabbits. She was ready to put her money where her mouth was and tell anyone who'd listen that buying a lop-eared rabbit could lead to a lot of health problems. She was ready for a run-in with Belinda Bates too, despite what she'd told Tori about being there in a vet advisory capacity only.

She also wanted to watch Sam's class. The showjumping started at two. In between all this, she wanted to have a good look about. As well as the agricultural side of things – the pigs, the sheep, the prize bulls and the tractors – there were several big marquees full of craft stalls. Wood turners, artists, jewellery makers, upholstery designers and leather craftsmen – they'd all be there, selling their wares. Not to mention the cake-baking stalls, the jam makers, the fudge producers and the cheese sellers. Phoebe's mouth watered at the thought. The New Forest Show was an excellent place to buy Christmas presents, even if it was only the end of July. If there was time, Phoebe planned to do most of her Christmas shopping at the show. It was the best type of Christmas shopping in her view – a leisurely stroll around a craft fayre with time to browse certainly beat a last-minute dash around packed streets in December. Also, supporting local traders was a passion of hers. It was a win-win situation.

The queue of show traffic, jamming up surrounding roads wasn't so good, but Phoebe finally arrived and was directed into one of the enormous fields that served as car parks for the show, where she was waved into a space by one of the myriad car parking attendants.

The New Forest Show was run like a military operation. There must be literally hundreds of helpers. As Phoebe walked across the yellowing grass alongside dozens of other showgoers towards the main entrance, she saw the marquees in the distance, breathed in the smell of warm air and burger vans and felt a flicker of anticipation. She had no idea what today would bring, but the summer air was literally buzzing with excitement.

Phoebe showed her ticket, bought a show guide, found Tori's stall on the pull-out map and set off towards it. The showground was so big that you could have walked round it all day and still missed large sections, Phoebe thought as she threaded her way through avenues of people, many being hauled around by dogs of all shapes and sizes, past dozens of the larger stalls selling cars, hot tubs, barbecue huts – you name it, it was there.

As well as the specialist marquees for vegetables, flowers, crafts, birds and small animals, there were burger bars, coffee stalls, a candyfloss seller, even a Gypsy Lee caravan with bill-boards outside claiming that she was the real thing. A genuine gypsy by birth and marriage who had been telling fortunes since she was ten.

Phoebe paused, hoping to see her, and caught a glimpse of a black-haired, middle-aged woman clad in bangles and bright colours.

'Come on in, my lovely,' the woman called out to her, sensing a prospective customer. 'I'll tell you all about the man you're destined to marry.'

That was enough to send Phoebe hurrying past as quickly as she could. She was in no rush to hear about the man she was destined to marry. Although it would have been a fun thing to tell Tori about, she thought, as she finally found the marquee that housed her friend's stall.

As Tori had said, she was very close to the marquee that housed caged birds and rabbits. Which must be where Burley Bunnies were. Phoebe was just trying to decide which way to go when she saw a familiar figure marching up and down outside the nearest marquee with a placard on which there was a life-size picture of a lop-eared white rabbit beneath a large skull and crossbones and the words – *Cute or Cruel?*

She stared in amazement. The woman behind the placard was Maggie. What on earth was she doing here?

32

Phoebe's first instinct was to go stomping across to berate her grandmother for being here when she had promised faithfully that she'd be helping out on the Puddleduck reception. Or had she?

Phoebe bit her lip and resisted the temptation to storm over, acutely aware that this was not going to help. If anything, it would just make Maggie even more determined to stay. She'd wanted to be part of the protest from day one. Phoebe had been crazy to think Maggie would stay out of it just because her family and a couple of concerned colleagues were worried about the stress factor.

Staying in the shadow of the marquee, Phoebe watched her grandmother for a minute or two. She was clearly in her element. She was dressed in what looked like one of her old milking outfits of an indiscriminate colour, somewhere between olive and mud, and she was wearing a tweed deerstalker hat. She wasn't just marching either. Occasionally she'd stop to accost innocent passers-by, some of whom stopped to talk and some of whom hurried swiftly by.

The ones that did stop nodded and looked serious, Phoebe noticed, so whatever her grandmother was saying must be hitting the mark.

Gathering herself, she took a deep breath and went across to see the old lady.

'Hi, Maggie.'

'Oh hello. I was wondering what time you'd turn up. Been having a lie-in, have you?' Her grandmother didn't look in the slightest bit sheepish.

'Attack is the best form of defence,' Phoebe shot back. 'I thought you were helping out in a purely administrative capacity.'

'I got bored,' Maggie said, and her eyes flashed with a mixture of humour and defiance. 'You'll understand when you get to my age.'

'Fair comment,' Phoebe said and for a second they stared at each other, both trying to anticipate the other's next move.

'It looks like you're doing a great job,' Phoebe said, deciding flattery was her best course of action. 'Would you like me to take over for a while?'

'No need.' Maggie glanced at her watch. 'Dusty's due to take over at ten.'

As if on cue, Phoebe saw Dusty coming towards them through the crowds – a dapper figure, dressed in tweed. He looked as though he was wearing the same suit he'd worn to Puddleduck. He must be baking in it today. A few moments later, he arrived beside them, red-faced and panting slightly.

'Officer reporting for duty,' he said and saluted Maggie, before apparently registering that Phoebe was present, whereupon he turned and saluted her too.

Maggie handed her placard over to Dusty with an obvious sigh of relief and slapped him on the shoulder.

No more words were exchanged. But Dusty set off with the rabbit placard, his head held high.

Maggie turned to grin at Phoebe. 'There we are. Drama over. I've done some protesting and I don't seem to have keeled over. Happy now?'

'Very happy,' Phoebe said, shaking her head. She knew it was utterly pointless getting cross with her grandmother. She was only doing what came as naturally to her as breathing – she was acting as a voice for the animals she loved so much. And Phoebe knew that feeling so well because they had the same DNA. The same blood and the same passion ran through her own veins.

'Talking of dramas,' Maggie said, 'there was one yesterday at the bird flying display. A peregrine falcon flew off and never came back. Its handler looked more and more stupid, standing there craning his neck giving a running commentary to the crowd. Well, mostly he was saying, "She's never done this before."'

Her grandmother sounded smug and Phoebe glanced at her. 'And you think that's a good thing?'

'I'm not saying whether it's a good thing or a bad thing. But I'm sure that falcon can manage perfectly well on her own. She shouldn't have to do tricks to get food.'

'Fair point,' Phoebe admitted for the second time in five minutes.

'I know where they sell the best coffee,' Maggie said. 'If you'd like a cup. Or shall we have an argument instead?'

'I'm not looking for an argument,' Phoebe said, noticing a flicker of movement out of the corner of her eye, 'although I think I've just spotted someone who might be.' She gestured towards Dusty, who'd got as far as the corner of the rabbit marquee, where he'd just been accosted by a woman who looked like Belinda Bates and one of the official New Forest Stewards who was wearing a high-vis jacket.

She was about to set off across when Maggie put a restraining arm on hers. 'Wait a second,' she ordered. 'Dusty will handle it.'

They stayed where they were. They were too far away to hear what Mr High Vis jacket was saying to Dusty, but the body language was crystal clear. He was not allowed to be marching up and down with a placard. Protests were not permitted at the show. There was a lot of angry gesticulating from Ms Bates backing this up.

Dusty didn't seem to be paying much attention. When they'd finished talking, he leaned forward, held a cupped hand over his ear and shouted in a voice so loud the whole showground could have heard it, 'Speak up, mate. I'm deaf. Can't hear a word you're saying.' Then, with a nifty twirl of his placard, he turned his back on the pair and marched away, shouting at the top of his voice, 'Cute or Cruel? Get yer facts right before you buy your kids a bad bunny. Get yer facts right before you get ripped off. Get yer facts right before you spend a fortune at the vets.' Four paces and he started the chant again. 'Cute or Cruel? Get yer facts right before you get ripped off...'

'He's good,' Phoebe said, staring after him in admiration.

'Told you, didn't I?' Maggie looked immensely pleased with herself. 'It'll take a lot more than a steward and a deranged breeder to stop Dusty Miller when he's on a protest. Now, how about that coffee? Dusty will be fine for a bit.'

Phoebe went with her reluctantly to the barista a few stalls along, but they could hear Dusty's voice anyway, as they queued. By the time they'd got back again, five minutes later, a small crowd had gathered to watch him. Natasha had appeared and she was handing out leaflets to people. Some were reading them. She waved when she saw Phoebe.

Phoebe went across. 'It looks like it's going well? I've brought some more of the fact sheets too. They're in my rucksack. I was about to take some to Tori. I'll get some for you.' She shrugged off the light rucksack and retrieved a pile of sheets, which she handed over.

'Thanks.'

Natasha's eyes were bright. 'It is going well, I think. We've been slowly building up from leaflet distribution to protesting. Quite a few people have spoken to Tori about the whole issue of rabbit welfare. We had a woman from the Rabbit Welfare Association come by yesterday. They've been trying to raise awareness about lop-eared rabbits for years, but the feature that Tori wrote for *The Sun* has brought it back into the public eye again, big time. She said they'd had more calls in the last month than they'd had in the whole of the previous year.'

'That's brilliant,' Phoebe said. 'I haven't even seen Tori yet. I'd better go and touch base.' She looked about for Maggie and saw that she was conversing with Dusty, apparently effortlessly, by way of a series of signs and hand signals. 'I didn't know Maggie was so good at sign language,' she said to Natasha.

'Yes – I think she learned it so she and Eddie and Dusty could communicate better. It's handy, isn't it – those three have got a modified version that only they can understand. Must be pretty cool having your own private language.'

'It must,' Phoebe agreed thoughtfully. Dusty had obviously given up on trying to lip-read then. Probably just as well from what she remembered.

She grabbed her rucksack and went into the warm dry air of the marquee. Something about the diffused light and warmth of a marquee always reminded her of summer.

Tori's stall was halfway down and there were one or two people looking at magazines. Tori was chatting to a woman in a straw hat, but she broke off when she saw Phoebe.

'Hey, Pheebs. How's it going? Can I introduce you to Alison

Jones. Her brother, Max, is a vet – he's just qualified. Alison and Max have been campaigning about flat-faced dogs for years, so they're very sympathetic to a cause close to our hearts.'

'One must do what one can,' said Alison Jones. She had a sleek blonde bob and a slightly Roman nose and one of the poshest, plummiest voices that Phoebe had ever heard. But she wasn't standoffish or snobby – far from it – her whole demeanour was warmer than sunshine. It was impossible not to like her immediately.

'It's great to meet you.' Phoebe shook her hand and for a few moments the talk was all about rabbits.

Then Alison broke off. 'Just a mo, chaps.' She hooked out her mobile and glanced at it. 'Speak of the devil and he shall appear.' She smiled. 'Max has just this moment sent me an update. He's over at the caged birds and rabbits and apparently the Burley Bunnies crew have just packed up their stall.' She glanced up with triumph in her eyes before carrying on reading. 'They've been fending off angry customers this morning. It would seem that one or two of the rabbits they've sold have needed to be put to sleep because of dental issues. That's awfully sad,' her voice sobered. 'But as Max says, sometimes the tragedy of one is what it takes to raise the awareness of many.'

'That is very sad,' Phoebe agreed. 'But I'm glad they're packing up.' She glanced at Tori. 'I feel as though I've arrived too late to help.'

'Nonsense. If it wasn't for you, we wouldn't have started any of this in the first place. Besides, there's still plenty of work to be done. Sending Burley Bunnies packing is a drop in the ocean.'

'I quite agree,' Alison said. 'Onwards and upwards.'

* * *

Over on the other side of the show at the small equine arena, Rufus was practising his square breathing using a horse box as his focus. The irony of which hadn't escaped him.

So far being here hadn't been as horrendous as he'd expected. He'd thought that by now he'd be a quivering mess, but he was holding up well. The techniques that Bartholomew had taught him might sound banal and ridiculous, but they did seem to help. They didn't remove the fear completely – Rufus knew his blood pressure must have rocketed off the scale – but they did help just enough to stop him from going over the edge into a full-blown PTSD attack. Or at least they had so far.

The man, Sam, who Rufus had very mixed feelings about – on the one hand, he was grateful to him for being so brilliant with Archie, and on the other, he disliked him for being Phoebe's boyfriend, although that was hardly his fault – had helped considerably. Sam had been very kind. He had fathomed out somehow – maybe Archie had said something – that Rufus wasn't OK around horses. Humiliating as this might be, it was also a relief. Sam had felt like an unexpected, but very welcome ally. He had the knack of turning up at times when Rufus was struggling and distracting him by chatting about Archie or suggesting he might like to get a coffee. Rufus wasn't sure he'd have coped so well without Sam.

It was now about five minutes before Archie was due to go into the ring. Rufus was by his son's side. For the last few minutes, he'd been focusing on his son. Sam had told them both that the judges could be incredibly picky in 'best turned out' classes. It wasn't just the pony that had to be immaculate – the rider did too.

'Some judges will even check the sole of the rider's boots,' Sam had warned, 'so once Archie is mounted – we need to polish them.'

Rufus had been so astonished at this revelation that again

he'd been diverted from his fears. PTSD was the weirdest of disorders. There was a part of his mind that could stay perfectly detached – that knew categorically that his terror of horses wasn't rational. Focusing on details helped him to distract himself from the visceral, gut-churning fear that his body would descend into if he gave way to his instincts. PTSD was about survival instincts that had somehow got warped and attached themselves to ordinary situations. At least that was his understanding of it. Distraction helped.

Hence he was able to be close to Archie, who was now mounted on Molly, and because he was focusing on Archie's boots, it was OK.

Sam, who was holding Molly's bridle on Archie's other side, handed Rufus what looked like a shoe buffer. 'There you go, sir.'

The sir was definitely ironic, Rufus thought, as he took the buffer.

Archie, who was laughing, took his foot out of the stirrup and tilted it so his father could polish the sole of his boot.

Rufus hesitated. The smell of horse and leather filled his senses and his head spun. Just for a second he wavered, but Archie's voice forced him back to the present.

'Come on, Dad. Get polishing. You want me to win, don't you?'

33

Rufus stood at the ringside watching Archie riding around the ring with the other entrants. So far, so good. The square breathing, the distraction techniques and his sheer love of his son had got him through.

Archie was looking straight ahead, but when he came down the side of the ring where Rufus was, he winked.

Rufus winked back. Pride warming him. Archie was a grand little rider and he looked so happy. He and Molly also looked by far the best turned out, although Rufus knew he was probably pretty biased.

When the judge called the riders in for closer inspection, Rufus held his breath. They spent the same time with each entrant, checking both pony and rider. To his amazement, they did look at the soles of the young riders' shoes. Well, they wouldn't find any problems with Archie's, that was for sure. It might have been his imagination, but the judges, a young chap and a woman with a hat, did seem to spend longer questioning Archie than any of the other competitors.

Rufus held his breath when the judges returned to the middle of the ring for a confab.

* * *

After Phoebe had finished talking to Tori and Alison – she would mention Maggie later – she made a beeline for the caged rabbits and birds marquee because she wanted to see for herself that Burley Bunnies had really packed up and were going.

It was true, they had packed up. There was a space where their cages had been and straw littered the floor. A lone white baby lop-eared rabbit sat in a display cage on the ground.

Phoebe's heart ached for it and she crouched down and spoke to it softly. What would happen to it if Belinda couldn't sell it?

Belinda, herself, who still looked very cross, was arguing with a man who bore a striking resemblance to Alison Jones. He had the same fair hair and slightly Roman nose, although he wasn't wearing a hat. He suddenly noticed Phoebe and broke off abruptly and came across.

'If you were considering buying that rabbit, don't,' he said, in a similar plummy voice to Alison's. 'It'll die before it's a year old.'

Belinda followed him, gesticulating furiously. 'That's bloody slander that is. I'll sue you. That rabbit's fine.' She broke off when she saw Phoebe. 'You? Y... You?' Her face had gone very red and she was clearly now so apoplectic that she couldn't get her words out. She swore loudly and then, to Phoebe's surprise, she about-turned and stormed towards the exit of the marquee.

'I don't think she'll be coming back,' said the man. 'Hi, I'm Max. Sorry about that. But I couldn't let you buy that rabbit. I'm a vet.'

'I wasn't planning to.' Phoebe held out her hand and he took it. 'I'm a vet too. Hi, Max, I'm Phoebe Dashwood. I just met your sister.' She smiled. 'And don't worry, I'm entirely on your side. I've been trying to raise awareness of the health problems lop-eareds face for a while.'

'You're the vet who they quoted in the feature. I've just realised.' Max relaxed. He was as warm as his sister when he wasn't being cross.

They talked for a while longer and then Phoebe glanced over at the baby rabbit. 'I know somewhere that this little fellow could have a good home. And all the veterinary attention he's going to need,' she said quietly.

'That,' Max smiled, 'is what I'd call a happy ending.'

'They do occasionally happen,' Phoebe said. She looked at him. 'Your sister said you've just qualified. Where are you working?'

'I'm still looking. Why do you ask?'

Phoebe handed him a business card. 'I haven't advertised yet, but I'm looking to expand my practice. Maybe you could give me a call some time?'

He took the card and then shook her hand again. 'Thanks very much. I'll do that.'

* * *

By the time she had taken the rabbit to Tori's stall, settled it with some food, water and shade and asked Maggie if it was OK if they took it back to Puddleduck – of course it was – Phoebe realised that Sam's showjumping class was about to start.

'Are you coming to watch?' she asked Tori.

'You bet I am.' Tori glanced at Laura. 'That's OK isn't it, lovely? You can cope here for a bit. And keep an eye on the bunny.'

'Sure thing, boss.' Laura gave them the thumbs-up sign. 'It's a lot quieter than it was earlier.'

'That'll be because Dusty's finished marching,' Maggie said. 'That man can shout for England. I think Eddie was taking over. Shall I go and tell him we can ease off now the Bates woman has gone?'

'I think you might as well,' Tori said.

* * *

In the end, they all went across to the main arena. Phoebe, Tori, Dusty, Maggie and Eddie. It was interesting how close Maggie and Eddie were walking, Phoebe thought. They were practically arm in arm and it wasn't because they were leaning in to hear each other's voices or supporting each other physically. Suddenly it hit Phoebe like a bolt out of the blue. They were more than just friends. There was a budding romance going on. How on earth had she missed it? And how long had it been going on?

She thought back to the day of Eddie's visit to Puddleduck. That had been a couple of months ago. Had it started then? Had their deep friendship finally tipped over to romance? She remembered the chocolate cookies Maggie had made for him. And she remembered what her mother had said about friendship being a good basis for marriage. Her head spun.

Tori's voice brought her back to the present with a jolt. 'Hey, it looks like we got here just in time. They're walking the course now.'

Phoebe gathered her thoughts and stared at the group of riders who were tramping around the main arena. One woman was pacing out the distance between two jumps with blue and yellow poles as high as her shoulders. Sam was in the main group, looking very serious and smart in his jodhpurs and dark jacket.

'Jeez, those jumps are high,' Phoebe said, shaking her head. 'Some of them look terrifying, don't they?'

'They all look terrifying,' Tori said. 'Mad buggers.'

'That's a tricky corner between the double and the last upright,' Eddie said knowledgeably, and Dusty and Maggie nodded in agreement. 'That's the one to watch.'

Sam was clearly too focused to notice he had a fan club. He didn't glance their way as he came out of the ring. Mind you, there were a lot of spectators close to the rails that edged the arena.

Phoebe's gaze moved idly around and then she saw a familiar face at the far end of the oblong arena. She nudged Tori's arm. 'Is that Rufus over there? Just on the right of the ambulance? Or are my eyes playing tricks on me?'

Tori shielded her eyes against the sun. 'It might be. Harrison told me he was planning to come. Archie was competing earlier. I wonder how he did.'

'I hope he did well.' Phoebe shut up, half wishing she hadn't mentioned Rufus. Although the rational part of her mind had closed the door on her attraction to him, her body had other ideas. Her heartbeat had quickened. Her hands were suddenly clammy and she knew it had nothing to do with the heat of the summer's day.

The arena was now clear of people. The course walking was over, and very quickly the bell rang for the first competitor. It was a woman on a dark bay horse who went on to jump a steady clear round. It was a slick operation. The next competitor rode into the ring just as the previous one was doing the last part of the course.

Phoebe tried to focus on the riders, but she was only half aware of the thud of the horse's hooves, as they thundered past, the jingle of tack, and the voices of the spectators around her. Every so often, her gaze was drawn back to the place where she

thought she'd seen Rufus. He'd been standing near to the ambulance point where she could see three paramedics lounging
against a vibrant yellow ambulance. Hopefully that wouldn't be
needed today.

Then suddenly she saw Archie, who, because he was shorter,
had been until that moment obscured by the height of the white
fencing that separated the spectators from the main arena. Rufus
had just lifted him up so he could see better.

Phoebe realised that this was because it was Sam's turn. He
had just trotted into the arena as the previous rider had left with
another clear round. The competition was certainly tough
today.

Sam looked confident, totally at ease in the saddle, even
though Ninja was snatching at the reins, jingling his bit, excited to
be somewhere new. Phoebe felt herself tensing with nerves too.
She knew this meant everything to Sam and she hoped fervently
that her childhood friend would do well today. But it wasn't until
he was halfway around the course that Phoebe realised she was
digging her nails into the palm of her hand.

'Go, Sam,' she whispered under her breath.

* * *

It had been a dream round, Sam thought, as he approached the
final double. Ninja was on top form, and he felt perfectly in tune
with his horse as they flew over the second part of the double and
turned into the tricky corner. This was the only part of the course
he'd been concerned about, but Ninja came back into his stride
perfectly and they were around the corner and in line for the last
jump. Ninja cleared it like the pro he was and they were through
the finish.

He heard the smattering of applause and the commentator's

voice. 'Another lovely clear round there from Sam Hendrie on Ninja Boy.'

Sam bent low to pat his horse's neck. 'Good lad, great work. Good lad,' and Ninja tossed his head in acknowledgement.

There was nothing like this feeling, Sam thought as he rode out of the ring. It made all the hard work, the early mornings, the late nights and the sore muscles worthwhile. It was better than champagne, better than oysters, better than the best lovemaking in the world. No, maybe not that last one!

In the collecting ring, he could see Marjorie Brooks and a couple of others from the stables, all smiling and giving him the thumbs up. Rufus and Archie had appeared too and then he saw Phoebe, Tori and Maggie. Good God, where had they all sprung from? He hadn't realised they were even here. Let alone watching him. That was probably just as well. He'd have been a lot more nervous if he had known, he thought, dismounting from Ninja and grinning broadly as everyone spoke at once.

'Nice one, Sam. Well done.'

'Beautiful round.'

'You romped it. That horse is a champion.' That was from Marjorie Brooks.

Even Henrietta was congratulating him, and Sam heard Archie's clear bright voice rising above the rest. 'Isn't that great, Dad. Now we can stay and watch Sam in the jump-off.'

Sam felt as if he was soaring high on the wave of their congratulations. Everyone was smiling. Then, almost as if by some synchronicity, he met Phoebe's eyes across the little crowd. She was standing slightly further away than the others.

'Well done, Sam,' she mouthed and she clapped her hands together a couple of times – a symbolic little gesture that they'd used when they were children to congratulate each other if there wasn't the space for privacy.

'Thank you,' he mouthed back.

He saw her glance at Rufus and Rufus glance back and for a moment it was as though the two of them were locked in each other's gaze. Sam looked away. He didn't want to be a witness to whatever was going on there. It still hurt.

Besides, Marjorie was tapping him on the shoulder. 'Come on, Sam. You were the last competitor. The jump-off won't be too long. We need to get ready.'

Sam was relieved that he had the perfect excuse to ride away.

* * *

Rufus glanced at Archie, who was even more excited about Sam doing a clear round than he had been about winning second place in the best turned out class. The blue rosette was safely in Archie's kitbag and as soon as they got home, would be displayed in some prominent position.

Archie had been over the moon to get second place, particularly as the girl who'd won was a regular showgoer. Sam had called her a 'pot hunter' and had explained to Archie that this was a term used for people who should really have moved up a level but didn't because they preferred being a big fish in a small pond than risking being a small fish in a big pond and not winning a prize.

Archie had been amazingly gracious about being in second place. He had ridden up to the pot hunter after the show and held out his hand to congratulate her. And that had been one of Rufus's proudest moments. It had made all of the intense stress of today worthwhile. More than worthwhile. He'd had to blink back tears.

'We can stay and watch the jump-off, can't we, Dad?' Archie

said, his voice pleading as if he'd suddenly realised that his father might be keen to go home.

Rufus, who'd have liked nothing better than to have called it a day, nodded. 'Of course we can, son. I wouldn't miss it for the world.'

34

'And now let's welcome back Sam Hendrie on Ninja Boy, the next competitor in today's jump-off.'

Sam was only vaguely aware of the commentator's voice as he trotted towards the start. He still felt high on adrenaline and the success of getting through the first round, but he was definitely more nervous this time.

Ninja was more nervous too. As always, they fed off each other. Aware that he was transmitting his apprehension to his horse, Sam made a conscious effort to relax as they rode towards the first fence, an upright. It wasn't the easiest jump-off course he'd ever done, but it wasn't the hardest either. Sam knew it was well within their capabilities. He sat deep in the saddle, feeling his horse respond, collecting himself, in answer to the almost invisible commands. This was the bit Sam loved. Feeling at one with his horse. That subtle two-way conversation. The perfect synchronicity of horse and man. This was one of the things that made him feel most alive.

They were over the first fence. Sam began to relax a little more. They could do this. He urged Ninja to lengthen his stride as they cantered down the long stretch towards the oxer. They were jumping off against the clock. Speed was of the essence.

* * *

Rufus and Archie were watching the jump-off from the same place they'd watched the first round. There were more people there now and they weren't quite as close to the fence. Archie was lit up with excitement and even though Rufus was finding it tougher than he had earlier, he knew that staying for the jump-off had been a good call. Archie would never have forgiven him if he'd been dragged away at the eleventh hour. He glanced at his son and found himself praying that Archie didn't want to follow in his mother's footsteps and take up showjumping. By the look on Archie's rapt face, that ship had probably already sailed, Rufus thought.

He could feel his breath quickening again and his heart pumping as the tense expectation built all around him. In the ring, horse and rider were halfway through what Archie had told him was a much shorter course.

'The jumps might be a bit higher though, Dad,' he'd said gleefully. 'This round is all about speed.'

Rufus focused hard on breathing. The box shape of the ambulance was a few feet away from him. Four seconds in, four seconds hold, four seconds out, four seconds hold. He estimated he had about thirty seconds to go. Half a minute more and they could go home. Half a minute more and he could legitimately haul Archie away from the show ground and drive back to Beechbrook House, where he would be able to pat himself on the back on a job well done. He had managed what he had never believed was possible. He had been at close proximity to horses without flipping into a major PTSD attack.

* * *

Phoebe was also watching from the same place she'd watched before, this time accompanied by just Maggie and Eddie. Tori had gone back to help Laura – they'd soon be packing up the stall for the day. Dusty had headed for home.

Phoebe realised she was holding her breath as Sam came round towards the double that was followed by the tricky corner. She glanced at the clock that was displayed on the opposite side of the arena. Sam's time was faster than the previous competitor. He was doing amazingly well. If they jumped clear, he'd be in the running for a rosette. He might even win this, which would be amazing. Sam was in many ways the rank outsider. He didn't have money to throw at the sport, like many of the other competitors. He was here through sheer hard work, grit and determination.

She was so proud of him. She was also terrified for him. Those jumps were enormous. She hadn't even realised that Sam was capable of competing at this level.

She hadn't seen Rufus or Archie again. Maybe they'd already gone home. That was a relief. She focused her attention back on Sam. He was over the double.

* * *

Sam was holding his breath. They'd taken the double just right, and were going fast into the tricky corner. Too fast. He felt Ninja skid slightly beneath him, then right himself, but they were set wrong now for the final jump. They could still do it.

He pushed his horse on, knowing even as he did so that their rhythm was out. They'd either have to put in a very short last-minute stride or take off too soon. Sam didn't interfere, letting his horse make the decision. Ninja opted to take off early, gathering himself for the huge leap. But Sam was aware in those last few seconds that it was way too early. They weren't going to clear the last jump.

Even as he thought it, in that splinter of a moment, Ninja came down too soon and then they were crashing through the centre of the bright poles in an explosion of sound and panic.

Sam was aware of time freezing, standing still. It was as though the whole of the arena was frozen in a snapshot. And in that click of a camera, that blink of an eye, he was aware of blue and yellow poles flying; of the crowd gasping; of the world turning upside down; and then the ground coming very fast to meet him. Then just blackness.

* * *

Phoebe was conscious that someone close by her had screamed. Maybe it was her. She had always believed that only happened in books. That you couldn't really scream without being fully aware that you had.

In the arena, Sam's horse was struggling to its feet. She couldn't even see Sam. He'd been thrown off and there was too much in the way, bits of broken jump and poles, obscuring her view.

Two paramedics were running across the field, carrying a stretcher. Oh my God, what if Sam was badly injured. He must be badly injured. She still couldn't see him. Which meant he hadn't got up.

Unable to wait a second longer, Phoebe ran full pelt to the entrance of the ring and then charged across the arena.

She was so totally focused on getting to Sam that she was only half aware of everything else. A steward had caught Ninja and was leading him up and down. Some part of her mind registered that the horse wasn't lame. Someone else in a high-vis jacket was talking on a radio. The paramedics had reached Sam, who Phoebe could see now, was at least trying to sit up. He was conscious. That was something. She halted abruptly beside him and dropped to her knees.

'Sam, Sam are you OK? Oh my God, Sam. Say something.'

He was very white. But he managed a smile when he saw her.

'Stay still,' one of the paramedics told him. 'We need to check you over.'

'I'm OK. Except... for... ribs.' Sam was panting between words. He looked around. 'Ninja... Is he OK?'

'I think he's fine,' Phoebe told him. 'Really. He didn't look lame. I'll go and look properly in a minute. It's you I'm worried about.'

'Didn't know... you cared.' He managed a wink.

'Well, I do.'

'Did you black out?' a paramedic asked Sam.

'Not sure... Maybe...'

Phoebe fell quiet, aware they had a job to do. She felt slightly sick. When she'd seen him fall. When she'd realised he was hurt, she'd been jolted by the strength of her feelings. She'd felt so shocked, it had scared her. She couldn't bear it if anything happened to Sam. Now, as she knelt next to him on the sunburnt grass, she was stunned by just how much she did care.

* * *

When Rufus had seen Sam's horse hit the jump, everything had slowed down. The poles had scattered in a burst of slow motion, bright blue and yellow thrown in the air and held there, freeze-framed for a second against the blue of the sky. The crowd's gasp had resonated against his eardrums, reverberating like music in an echo chamber. There had been a dry metallic taste in his mouth and he'd been forcibly flung back into the past. Back to another summer's day, another accident, another tragedy.

In the next second, he'd been aware that he was backed up against the spectator fence, his arms outstretched flat back against the wood, shouting, 'Nooooo, noooooo,' a long drawn-out wail of a word. He had no idea how he'd got there. He was only vaguely aware of his surroundings. A fleeting image of the horrified face of a woman close by. Of the curious gaze of a man.

He was vaguely aware that someone was calling his name. It was Archie. His voice high and frightened. 'Dad, Dad, Dad.' Over and over.

Rufus put his hands over his ears to block out the sound. He couldn't breathe. He slid down the fence, until he was on the ground, his hands over his face now, feeling the racking shuddering, wanting only to curl into a ball. Every atom of him screaming for escape.

He was rocking, back and forth, back and forth. He had no idea why, but it was helping. It felt soothing. Primal, rhythmic and soothing.

Another voice he didn't know was calling through a long tunnel. 'Mate, are you all right? Do you need a medic?'

'Dad, Dad, Dad.'

Rufus bit his lip hard and tasted blood. Something Bartholomew had told him was repeating in his brain. Chew a chilli. Stay in the present. It's not real.

Chew a chilli. How were you supposed to magic a chilli out of mid-air? The humour of not having a chilli to hand when you needed to chew one caught in his throat and he swallowed hard, aware that he was a hair's breadth from total hysteria. What the hell was happening to him?

Two paramedics were carrying Sam now on a stretcher

towards the gate a few feet away from them. Rufus heard Sam's voice protesting. 'I can walk. Seriously, I can walk.'

'Dad.' Archie was crying now, his eyes wide and afraid, as he knelt down too on the grass. 'Dad. What's wrong?'

His son's voice was like a rope thrown into the abyss where he was still clinging on by his fingertips. With a supreme effort of will, Rufus forced himself back into the here and now. This was not the past. It was not Rowena on that stretcher. It was not the day of his wife's death. He was OK.

He was not OK. He was shaking from head to foot. But he could do this. He forced himself to breathe. He must do it. He must. He must. The words became a mantra.

He leaned forward and caught Archie's hand. 'I'm sorry, son. It's OK. I'm OK.' If he said it enough times, maybe he would believe it himself.

* * *

Phoebe, was walking alongside the stretcher that carried Sam, and they were almost back at the ambulance when she became aware of a second drama unfolding by the gate. A man was sitting on the grass just beyond the spectator rails. His knees were drawn up to his chest and a boy was crouching in front of him. A semi-circle of space had cleared around them. Even so, it took Phoebe a second or so to realise the boy was Archie.

Sam saw them at the same time she did. He grimaced and Phoebe looked at him.

'Oh my God, Sam, that's Rufus and Archie.'

'Yeah. Looks like it.' He was still white.

Phoebe hesitated, torn between staying with him and checking what was happening with Rufus and Archie. The boy looked distraught. Rufus didn't look much better.

'Go see,' Sam said. 'I'm fine.'

'I'm coming to hospital with you,' she argued.

'No need.' He paused, his breathing still slightly shaky, and made a huge effort to control his voice. 'I think they're more in need of your help than I am.'

The paramedics were opening the ambulance door and shifting Sam inside.

'I can't leave you,' Phoebe said.

'Yeah, you can.' Sam held her gaze. 'You really like Rufus – don't you?'

Totally off guard, she stared at him. 'I thought I did. We had a moment.' She frowned. 'It was just a kiss. He's avoided me like the plague ever since.'

Something flickered in Sam's eyes. 'I think that's my fault – I bumped into him – in the pub. He mentioned you... I was drunk... I told him to back off. I said I was your boyfriend. Did you... not listen to my voicemail?'

There were still gaps between his words. As though he was struggling to breathe.

'What voicemail?'

'Are you coming to the hospital or not?' The paramedic's voice interrupted their conversation, his question directed towards Phoebe. 'We need to get going.'

'I'm coming,' Phoebe said, even as her thoughts jumbled and spun. What voicemail? What was Sam talking about?

'She's not,' Sam said. 'We can catch up later, Phoebe. Seriously. Sort things out. Look after Archie. Tell my ma I'm OK. Make sure Ninja's OK. Let me know. I'll keep you posted.' He gave her shoulder a gentle shove. 'Go see Rufus and Archie.' His voice was husky. 'Please.'

Phoebe shut her eyes to blot out the pain in his. 'OK,' she said, stepping back as the ambulance door slammed firmly in her face.

* * *

Inside the ambulance, Sam gave up the pretence that he was fine and laid back down on the stretcher with a groan. He had a horrible feeling that this was more than his ribs. When he'd hit the ground he'd been winded. All the air had been punched out of his lungs. And that feeling hadn't gone away. It was getting harder to breathe and he felt mightily sick.

It had been very hard sending Phoebe to Rufus. But his integrity had compelled him to do it. If you love something, let it go. Deep in his heart, Sam knew that, this time, he'd done the right thing.

Phoebe was still trying to make sense of Sam's words as she went to see Rufus and Archie. What did he mean he'd told Rufus to back off? Why would he do that?

But she swept these thoughts to one side when she got closer to Rufus. He was standing up now, but she had never seen anyone look so haunted. His face was whiter even than Sam's had been and his eyes were blacker than midnight.

Archie didn't look much better. When he saw Phoebe he ran to her. 'Dad's not well and it's all my fault. I shouldn't have done it. I shouldn't have made him.' He was sobbing and gulping between sentences.

'Hey, hey. It's all right.' She hugged him and he clung to her. His small arms were tight around her chest and she could feel him trembling. For a moment, she held him, murmuring soothingly and thinking that Sam had been right to send her to Rufus and Archie. They were both in a state. She had no idea why, but something bad had happened. Was it Sam's accident? She knew Sam was Archie's instructor and had been for about a year. That was probably a close relationship. It must have been awful for the child to see him fall and get hurt. 'Sam will be OK,' she told him. 'He's fine. I've just been talking to him.'

'He won't die?' The child's voice was stricken.

'No, I'm sure he won't.'

'Do you promise? He won't die like my mum?'

She caught her breath. Oh my God... She glanced up, aware that Rufus had taken a step closer. He seemed to have gathered himself a little. He was rubbing his face and swallowing. His Adam's apple bobbing.

'I'm sorry. My wife. Rowena.' He shook his head again. 'She died in a riding accident. Archie wasn't there, thank God. But I was... I saw it.' Rufus blinked a few times. 'The scars run deep. You know.' He flicked a hand in an attempt to be casual. But it didn't come off as casual.

Phoebe's mind flew back to that afternoon in the forest. The way he'd dealt with her panic attacks. How he'd confided he'd had them himself after his wife had died. That was how he'd known how to help her.

But he'd had more than panic attacks she realised suddenly, as the jigsaw pieces fell into place. 'You have PTSD?' she said to him softly. 'Because of what happened.'

'Yeah.' His face closed down as if he were deeply ashamed and Phoebe felt a huge surge of compassion. He didn't need to tell her it was triggered by horses. Shit, it must have been hell for him, coming here today, and then to see what he'd just seen.

'It was brave of you to come,' she said quietly, aware that Archie had quietened too now. Apart from the odd sniff, he'd stopped sobbing, but he was still hugging her and she was still hugging him.

Rufus dismissed this with a shrug. 'Is your boyfriend OK?'

'Sam isn't my boyfriend,' she told him. 'We're just friends. We've only ever been just friends.'

She saw surprise flash in his eyes. 'But I thought...'

'No. If I'd been with Sam, I would never have... well, you know...' She shrugged, conscious of Archie's presence and knowing anyway that she didn't need to finish the sentence. Rufus was well aware of what she was talking about. 'Are *you* OK?' She turned the focus back onto him. 'Is the attack over?'

'Yep.' He looked embarrassed.

And she knew this must be so hard for him. This proud man, having to admit that there were times when he didn't have control over his emotions – or his actions. She had never known anyone who suffered with PTSD, but she was well aware of what it was. It had come up in her training, the current thinking being that it wasn't a disorder that was exclusive to humans. Animals could suffer from it too.

'I'm OK,' he added, his voice more measured this time. 'Thank you.' His gaze was fixed on Archie now. 'I'm sorry, son,' he said. 'I'm so sorry that I... that I overreacted.'

'Was it my fault?' Archie sounded terribly vulnerable.

'Absolutely not, buddy. It's just one of those things.'

'Because of Mum,' he said earnestly.

'Because of Mum.'

'Will Ninja be OK?' They both looked at Phoebe.

'I'm going to check him over now,' she said. 'But I'm sure he will be. Yes.' It was a good moment to leave them to it anyway, she thought, feeling a huge well of emotions swirling about in her as she forced a smile. 'I'll keep you posted. OK?'

'And about Sam?' Archie asked anxiously.

'And about Sam,' she said. 'I promise.'

* * *

By the end of that day Phoebe had established that Ninja was in a lot better shape than Sam was. The horse was shaken but perfectly sound. He'd got away with a small cut and a slightly swollen tendon on the near fore, where he'd hit the jump. A hose-down of the tendon for a few days was all that would be needed, and he'd be as right as rain.

Sam had come off a lot worse, with two fractured ribs and a ruptured spleen, which had been diagnosed when he'd got to hospital. His spleen was then removed in an emergency operation from which he was recovering.

When Phoebe went in to see him the following day, with grapes and a get well soon card, she found him sitting up in bed wearing burgundy striped pyjamas.

'Hello, Pheebs. Thanks for coming in. And thank you for checking over Ninja.' She had sent him a WhatsApp reassuring him that his horse was fine, which he'd obviously read as soon as he'd been able to. 'What do I owe you for your professional services?'

'Don't be daft.' She pulled up a chair to the bed. 'I'm your best friend. There is no charge.'

'Best friends, even after what I told you yesterday about doing my best to wreck your chances with the lord of the manor.'

'Even after that,' she said, smiling. She might have been cross with him if the circumstances had been different, but she couldn't be cross with him here.

'Maybe things aren't wrecked?' he hedged. 'Did you manage to have a chat? Was he all right?'

She told him about the PTSD and its cause and Sam's face sobered. 'That explains an awful lot. I never thought I'd be genuinely concerned about our lord of the manor, but...' He wrinkled his nose. 'That can't be easy.'

'No. It can't. And as for your other – not very subtle – enquiry,' she said, 'we did touch on the fact that you and I weren't an item. But he didn't rush in and ask me out.'

'Oh,' Sam said, in a way that made it impossible to tell how he felt about this.

'Mum said you'd split up with your lady?' Phoebe murmured. 'I hope that wasn't acrimonious.'

'Not really, no.'

He looked so sad that Phoebe changed the subject. She told him about the rabbit protest march, and how Belinda Bates had finally left the show in a rage, saying they'd ruined her business.

'I'd love to think she'd decided to call it a day and close down her business and never breed another rabbit, but I don't suppose that will happen. Maybe the best we can hope for is that she'll think about what she's doing.'

'Yeah.' Sam looked thoughtful. 'I suppose it's a case of supply and demand.'

'Yes. A matter of continually bringing it into the public eye and raising awareness.' Phoebe sighed. 'Little by little.' She stood up. 'I'd better let you get some rest. Everyone else sends their love by the way – Maggie, my mum, Tori, and everyone else at Puddleduck.'

'Send my love back.' Sam gave her the thumbs up. 'And I hope that you and Rufus get it together – if that's what you really want?'

'Thanks, Sam.'

* * *

As she walked out of the ward and along the hospital corridor, Phoebe asked herself the same question. What did she really want? What would she do if Rufus turned up at her door and asked her out to dinner? It was such an unlikely scenario that she almost laughed out loud.

She had managed to get Rufus out of her head. Or at least she thought she had until yesterday. Several emotions had been stirred up yesterday and none of them had truly settled.

She was still mulling over how shocked and scared she'd been when she'd thought Sam was badly injured. Would she really have reacted like that if she'd just seen him as a very good friend? One thing she was sure about was that she didn't want to lose Sam's friendship. If they moved into a romantic relationship and it didn't work out, then she would lose him as a friend. There was a niggling suspicion in her heart, too, that was telling her that settling for someone just because the man you truly wanted wasn't available was a bad idea.

* * *

Phoebe was relieved to get back to work on Monday. It had been an unsettling weekend. She'd visited Sam in hospital again and he'd told her that with luck they'd let him out on Monday or Tuesday. She'd also called by to check on Ninja, who was fine, and reported this back to Sam.

She'd phoned Rufus to let him know about Sam, because she'd promised Archie that she would, and Rufus had thanked her and had then apologised because he'd had to go – apparently he was urgently needed. Phoebe had wondered if this was true or whether he still felt embarrassed that she'd seen him in the throes of a PTSD attack.

She'd talked to Tori a lot about her contradictory feelings and a little bit about them to Maggie. Funnily enough, they'd both said the same thing, albeit with slightly different words.

Tori had said, 'Don't beat yourself up about it – just let the dust settle and see how it pans out.'

Maggie had said, 'There's no rush, is there. Sometimes "wait and see" is the answer.'

Phoebe had decided this was good advice. There was a part of her that wanted to phone Rufus again to check that he and Archie were OK. But she didn't do this. She had kept them updated about Sam, as she'd promised she would. Rufus knew where she was if he wanted to get in touch with her. Which he clearly didn't. Because he hadn't.

She decided to focus on work. It was now Monday evening and she, Marcus and Jenna were at Puddleduck Vets, having just seen out the final patient. They were getting ready to close down for the day. Maggie was there too; she'd just come in to pick up some medication for Buster's arthritis.

Maggie, Marcus and Jenna were talking about the success of the Burley Bunnies protest marches.

'I've had a Google alert on the adverts,' Marcus told them all. 'I've been checking them regularly. And I saw this morning that they've all been removed. That's got to be good news.'

Maggie punched the air with glee. 'Here's to direct action,' she said. 'It never fails.'

The others nodded approvingly. Phoebe joined in now she'd finally forgiven Maggie for going behind her back. It turned out that Maggie had been over at the New Forest Show every day it had been on. She had been chief protest organiser. Even Tori hadn't mentioned that!

'Never mind direct action,' Phoebe said, ten minutes later when Marcus and Jenna had gone and she and her grandmother were alone, 'can I ask you a direct question?'

'Of course you can. But I reserve the right not to answer it.'

'Are you and Eddie more than just friends?'

'Do you mean are we stepping out?' Maggie said with a small sniff and an indisputable sparkle in her eye.

'Yes. Are you stepping out?' Phoebe could no longer contain her curiosity. 'And if you are when did that start? And why didn't you tell me?'

'We may have been out to dinner a few times.' Maggie smiled self-consciously. 'And as to why I haven't told you. I don't tell you all my secrets, as you know.' She blinked and to Phoebe's surprise, looked a little guilty.

'I know you don't,' Phoebe said. 'I should never have tried to stop you doing the protests. I was only looking out for you.'

'I know you were, darling.'

'And I don't mean to be nosy about Eddie. I'm really pleased you're "stepping out". Eddie's nice.'

'Yes he is. He's a good man. We've always rubbed along nicely.' A reflective look stole into her grandmother's eyes. 'When he left Puddleduck to go and live with his son, I missed him a lot. It sometimes takes a change in circumstances to make you realise how you feel about someone. But I didn't do anything about it. I suppose I just thought, well, that ship had sailed. And I told myself to stop being such a stupid old woman.'

'You've never been that.'

'Thank you.' Maggie smiled. 'Then when Eddie came back regularly for visits, because we weren't working, we started talking a lot more. His deafness was a problem, but then we learned British Sign Language, well, we learned a slightly adapted version, and having our own secret language was incredibly romantic. They say that communication is the key to relationships, don't they.'

'Yes,' Phoebe said, feeling warmed. She didn't think she'd ever heard Maggie say so much about relationships before, but the expression on her face was very soft. 'Does this mean he'll come back and live at Puddleduck again? Is that on the cards too?'

'Funnily enough,' Maggie said. 'We were talking about exactly that at the New Forest Show.'

'In between protest marches?' Phoebe asked.

'Yes.'

They both smiled. Then they both jumped as the door of Puddleduck Vets opened and Phoebe realised she must have forgotten to turn the sign to closed.

'I'm sorry, but we're closed,' Phoebe began and then stopped because it wasn't a client, or at least it wasn't a client they didn't know. It was Rufus.

'I... was hoping to catch Phoebe,' Rufus said. 'It's not to do with an animal...'

His hair looked damp and his shoulders were misted with rain. A summer shower.

'She's all yours. I was just going,' Maggie said, leaping out of the swivel chair where she'd been sitting and making for the rain-spattered door surprisingly swiftly for a seventy-three-year-old.

Rufus held the door open for her. Then he shut it gently and took a couple of steps towards the reception desk.

Phoebe waited. She was tempted to say something flippant, like, 'You couldn't keep away then?' or 'To what do I owe this honour?' but neither of these things seemed appropriate. Rufus looked pretty serious.

Even so, she was unprepared for what he did actually say when he got to the desk.

He cleared his throat. 'Over the weekend, we caught some fly-tippers on camera. They were dumping toxic barrels in the same place they dumped the last lot, which made me think they were the same fly-tippers.'

'Wow. Did you manage to stop them?'

'We did.' He looked pleased with himself. 'There was – shall we say – an altercation and words were exchanged. More than words. Harrison was not happy. But, suffice to say, they're unlikely to be dumping waste or anything else for some time.'

'Good,' Phoebe said. 'It was worth fitting a camera then.'

'Yes. We also passed on the CCTV footage to the authorities. So in due course there should be a prosecution too.'

'Great news.'

He was standing a few feet away from her now. He clearly wasn't in any hurry to go.

Phoebe flipped open the hatch of the reception desk and went through it to meet him. 'Thank you for keeping me informed. It's good of you.'

He nodded. His eyes were very dark. But not from fear this time. It was attraction that widened his pupils. She knew it as surely as if he'd told her in some secret language that existed only between the two of them. The chemistry sparking between them was so powerful it could have lit up the national grid.

'Was that all you came by to tell me?'

Phoebe waited. She was not taking one step more towards him. He must be the one to make the first move this time.

'No...' Rufus shut his eyes. 'I did not come round to tell you about bloody fly-tipping. Oh God. I can't believe how hard this is. I haven't done it for years.'

'Told a woman about fly-tipping?' she teased.

'Asked a woman out to dinner,' Rufus stammered. 'Asked... Asked you. Phoebe, please would you like to have dinner with me?' The last few words came out in a rush and she smiled at him.

'I'd love to.'

'I haven't been able to get you out of my head,' Rufus said.

'However hard I've tried. You've haunted my days and my nights. Even when I thought you were with someone else, I couldn't forget about you. And I know I'm damaged goods and I'm probably the last person on earth you're interested in, but I thought maybe we could just have dinner and talk and see... That's if you wanted to do that.'

'There is nothing I'd like more,' Phoebe said. 'Funnily enough, I haven't been able to get you out of my head either.'

'Really?' He looked stunned and amazed and delighted, somehow all at the same time. He had such an expressive face. And now he did step towards her and in the next second they were in each other's arms. He was taller than her but not much and for a few seconds they stayed quite still, their gazes locked.

'Really,' she said, struggling for composure, because all she really wanted to do right now was to kiss him. To see if it was as perfect as their first kiss had been.

But they weren't in some romantic forest now that smelled of pine needles and sunshine, they were in her workplace which smelled of dogs and disinfectant. Anyone could walk in and interrupt. It was broad daylight on a rainy Monday afternoon – there was nothing at all romantic about rainy Mondays – and they'd just been having a conversation about fly-tipping toxic waste. How could any of this possibly be making her feel so starry-eyed?

Her heart urged her to kiss him. Her common sense told her to wait. There was no rush. Her common sense didn't stand a chance. Her heart took it away.

She tilted her head. He bent his and their lips met. His were very gentle and then urgent. And it *was* as perfect. It was *more* perfect. And it *was* as romantic. *More* romantic. It was a kiss that didn't need sunsets and pine-scented forests. It was a kiss that only needed the two of them. It was a kiss that lifted Phoebe into the stratosphere, and then some.

She knew now that she had been right to wait. To see what unfolded. She had her answer now. It was as crystal clear as daylight and as vibrant and glittering as the rain that now spattered the plate-glass windows behind them. It had to be Rufus. It had always been Rufus. And she knew in that moment that the whole of their future lay ahead of them in a bright and sparkling journey, of which this moment – this kiss – was only the very first step.

When they finally drew apart, she saw that Rufus was looking as dazed as she felt and that, behind him, high in the sky, as vibrant and as dazzling as new romance, arched a glitteringly beautiful double rainbow.

ACKNOWLEDGMENTS

Thank you so much to Team Boldwood – you are amazing. Thank you to every single one of you who works so hard to bring my books to my readers in paperback, audio and digital.

As always, my special thanks go to Caroline Ridding, Judith Murdoch and Jade Craddock, Shirley Khan and to Alice Moore for the gorgeous cover.

A big thank you to Rhian Rochford for her help with all things VET in the Puddleduck Farm series and a huge personal thank you to Rhian for working out my dog Ella had a rare autoimmune disorder last year and saving her life. Words don't cover it. Thank you also to Beth Yeatman. I could not write these stories without your help, ladies. Thank you also to Sheila Parkhurst for animal behaviour high jinks.

Thank you to Tony for his fabulous geographical knowledge and the recce trips.

Thank you to Gordon Rawsthorne for his enduring support. He still endures a lot!

Thank you, perhaps most of all, for the huge support of my readers. I love reading your emails, tweets and Facebook comments. Please keep them coming.

MORE FROM DELLA GALTON

We hope you enjoyed reading *Rainbows Over Puddleduck Farm*. If you did, please leave a review.

If you'd like to gift a copy, this book is also available as an ebook, large print, hardback, digital audio download and audiobook CD.

Sign up to Della Galton's mailing list for news, competitions and updates on future books:

http://bit.ly/DellaGaltonNewsletter

Coming Home to Puddleduck Farm, the first instalment in Della Galton's heartwarming Puddleduck Farm series, is available to buy now.

ABOUT THE AUTHOR

Della Galton is the author of more than 15 books, including *Ice and a Slice*. She writes short stories, teaches writing groups and is Agony Aunt for *Writers Forum* Magazine. She lives in Dorset.

Visit Della's website: www.dellagalton.co.uk

Follow Della on social media:

facebook.com/DailyDella

twitter.com/DellaGalton

instagram.com/Dellagalton

bookbub.com/authors/della-galton

Boldwd

Boldwood Books is an award-winning fiction publishing company seeking out the best stories from around the world.

Find out more at www.boldwoodbooks.com

Join our reader community for brilliant books, competitions and offers!

Follow us
@BoldwoodBooks
@BookandTonic

Sign up to our weekly deals newsletter

https://bit.ly/BoldwoodBNewsletter

Lightning Source UK Ltd.
Milton Keynes UK
UKHW041020210223
417380UK00004B/221